HEADLOCKS AND HEARTBREAK

TITAN WRESTLING

VAL SIMONS

To Rebecca, whose willingness to be my friend on Slack changed the trajectory of my life.

AUTHOR NOTE

I'm excited that you're taking a chance on this book, and maybe you're doing that because you're like me and saddened by the lack of professional wrestling romance novels. I think we should all write ten more, then exchange them with each other.

I do want to be honest and say I've taken quite a few liberties with the realities of professional wrestling, both the business side and the sport side. What you're about to read may not be an accurate representation of any current professional wrestling promotions, nor is an attempt to, but the spirit is there! This is a romance novel, and these people are fake, so it's okay if it's not quite there.

Thank you, and I hope you enjoy the book!

CHAPTER 1

FOR THE FIRST TIME IN TWO YEARS, WADE DONOVAN WAS LEADING THE newest cohort of contracts around the arena, begrudgingly pointing out areas of interest as if a single one of them would give a shit about anything besides the ring, the hallway of accolades, and how well their noses could fit up Mike Palazzo's asshole.

Wade's fall from grace was a topic of hushed conversations amongst the rookies, which was expected, but still humiliating in a way he hadn't anticipated. Every glance in his direction felt like an unspoken judgment, a reminder of the heights he had once reached and the sudden crash that followed. He didn't blame them for discussing it; they didn't know each other. The rookies owed him nothing. All they knew was that "Viper" Donovan was leading them around the grounds, shielding his own eyes from the reminders of his past.

Wade wasn't a grouch. It was just hard to smile after he sat on the top rope of the ring, one leg casually draped over the turnbuckle to present a facade of the confidence he'd lost years ago, only to smell the acrid, pungent scent of burning hair. When it happened, he'd jumped off the ropes onto the canvas, cursing Mike under his breath.

"Mike! I thought you got the lights fixed. Why are they so low?" he shouted over his shoulder.

"I thought I did! Sorry, looks like they dropped. Are you done in there? I can turn them off." Mike replied, his voice carrying across the open, high-ceilinged space of the arena. The aging championship banners did little to muffle the sound.

"Yeah, please." He hissed as he rubbed at his tender scalp, hoping most of his thinning hair was still there. An uncomfortable warmth spread up his cheeks, and he was thankful his tawny skin hid the physical evidence of his embarrassment. He heard a few snickers coming from the small group of new, young athletes who served as annual reminders of his youth slipping through his hands. "Um, anyway, like I was saying, this is our main practice ring. We also practice outside the ring on the mats, but it's good to get a feel for the height and flexibility of the canvas when you're working through your choreography."

The most tenured wrestler signed to Titan Wrestling, a small but well-respected and popular professional wrestling promotion based in Portland, Oregon, Wade had been with the organization for ten years. He'd been there four years longer than anyone else, and in many professions that would indicate a level of importance, skill, or even income. At Titan, it simply meant Wade hadn't been good enough to move up the country's largest promotions.

Most days, Wade liked that he was a spry thirty-two and made a living as a professional wrestler. He earned enough to keep a small but charming apartment in a fun part of town, and he liked that the other guys could look up to him for coaching and support. Titan's owner, Mike, was even training him to take over some day. But sometimes on bad days, he felt pathetic. He felt old at thirty-two. His apartment was small and spartan, and the neighborhood he normally liked felt dirty and loud. He assumed the other guys wondered what he still had to offer Titan, and that Mike was just training him to take over because Wade had nothing else going for him.

But, despite the lingering embarrassment he felt from burning his head, it wasn't a bad day. The new group of wrestlers were eclectic, passionate, and eager for Wade to show them the ropes. And he was interested to hear about their backgrounds, and how they decided on this nightmare of a career.

For Wade, it was all he ever considered. His parents couldn't have cared less about his initial interest in wrestling, and their disinterest turned to dismay when they realized he had plans to make it a career.

He had been six the first time he watched a wrestling match at home in his family's living room, dazzled by both the moves and the tight, shiny pants. He begged his older cousin to throw him in a suplex, and the first time he hit the couch, bounced into the air, and landed on the ground with a breath-stealing thud, his fate was sealed.

As a kid, he wrestled in his backyard with neighbors in a ring he made of firewood logs. He created a persona for himself under the name Viper, a nod to his signature move, the Serpent's Embrace. It was an immobilizing maneuver where he wrapped himself around the legs of his opponents, tripping them. He learned in middle school biology class that vipers kill their prey using venom, not strangulation, but he was twelve and didn't care, so Viper and the Serpent's Embrace endured.

Eager to continue the tour after the lighting dramatics, Wade squeezed himself through the ropes of the ring. He hopped down to the worn and tired mats, each of the new wrestlers following. One by one, they left the ring with increasing flamboyance. It reminded him of his early years when his lack of confidence drove him to one-up his fellow wrestlers at every opportunity. Their bravado was unnecessary, and honestly a little dorky, but he would be lying if he said it wasn't also endearing.

Wade watched as one of the new guys got tangled in the ropes on his way out. He was a cute powerhouse named Monty, whose face had been etched into Wade's memory the second he saw the guy's audition tape. Monty's arms scrambled to reach the curtain below the ring, but his flailing only tightened the ropes' grip, forcing him to give up and look towards the group for help.

Wade was honestly a little confused by the physics behind it. If he hadn't witnessed it himself, he wouldn't have believed it was possible for someone to get so elaborately tangled after just a few seconds. He looked down at the poor guy dangling just inches from the floor, then bit his lips between his teeth to stifle a smile. The other rookies were doubled over laughing at Monty's misfortune, so Wade stepped over to untangle his foot. As he gently lowered Monty's shoulders to the mat, his other foot tumbled down, causing his entire body to flatten against the mats. He grimaced, but then smiled up at Wade before rising to his feet.

"Thanks. Wow. Okay. It's so nice to meet you. I'm honored, and now humiliated, to be here. I'm Monty Hill," he said, brushing his pants off and holding his hand out to shake Wade's. Monty's long blond hair was cascading down to his shoulders, and Wade was close enough that he could smell the sweet scent of coconut wafting from his head. He tilted his head and looked up at Wade, which caused several loose curls to spill from his shoulder, and all Wade could think about were the dozens of wrestlers he'd been half in love with during his childhood. Monty was smiling, and his slightly too-big eyes were shining like he was excited, but his cheeks were flushed and his hand was clammy. "I mean, maybe you know me by Romeo? But that's not my real name, obviously. It's like a play on words, you know? Monty, Montague, Romeo… Well, my real name is Montgomery, not Montague, but literally nobody calls me that. You can just call me Monty."

"Yes, I am familiar. My real name isn't actually Viper," he said, trying to earn a smile from the equally nervous and adorable newcomer. "I read all your bios and watched your tapes before you arrived. It's nice to officially meet you, Romeo."

He didn't mention that he'd specifically remembered Romeo, or why, because that was… unprofessional. And definitely not why they were there. So he collected his thoughts, cleared his throat, and lifted his hand to guide the group down a long hallway. It was Titan's hall of fame, festooned with belts and medals on one side, framed photos showcasing moments of Titan history on the other. He pointed out photos of Titan's owner, Mike, posing with some of the biggest names in wrestling, and smiled at the excitement bubbling up on the faces of his four new colleagues.

"I haven't met a lot of these people, obviously, but Mike was a big name back in his day. Um, I guess you're all well aware of that," Wade said, feeling stupid. Mike, the owner in the photos, was a retired wrestling superstar, and the biggest reason people wanted to work for Titan. "I've been with the organization for ten years now and we've seen lots of guys move to CWA. Our most recent departure was my long-term tag team partner, Limpet."

Limpet, whose real name was Larry, now had a full contract with Central Wrestling Authority, the country's largest and most well-known wrestling promotion. Titan was the biggest West Coast farm promotion for CWA, offering developmental contracts for up-and-coming wrestlers. Those contracts could turn into larger ones for some of the most promising wrestlers. But it was difficult to get there - unattainable for most - and Wade knew that all too well.

Wade stopped in front of a framed photo of himself and Limpet at their last tag-team championship match. Whenever he lingered too long looking at photos of the two of them, his mind flooded with regret that weighed on him. He thought about the night of the match and how life-changing he'd expected that moment to be. And it was life-changing, but not in the way he'd hoped. Wade sobered quickly when he remembered he was being watched by four men whose lives at Titan were just beginning. He owed it to them to set aside his own baggage and play up the possibilities that lay before them.

Ignoring his churning gut, he pointed at the photo and told the story of the match to the group and even managed a weak smile at the memory.

He shared what a high it had been to be the title champions two years in a row and how much fun their rise to fame had been. But he didn't let them know he'd been so convinced his path to CWA was a sure thing that he'd been blindsided when only Larry received the buyout offer. He also didn't share that Larry had kept it a secret from him for weeks until Wade saw the paperwork on Mike's desk, or that the resulting confrontation between them had been one of the worst moments of his life.

After the initial blow-up with Larry, Wade had left the arena in a rage. The other wrestlers at Titan saw the whole thing go down, effectively ruining any chance Larry had to tell them his news the way he'd wanted. It had created a wedge between them that never resolved, despite Wade's efforts. Larry moved to Boston without a second glance. Even now, two years later, Wade felt like he was floundering. His popularity had plummeted after Larry left, and because of that, Mike gave him less ring time. Limited ring time kept his ratings and online engagement low. It was a vicious cycle he wanted to escape, but he didn't know how to do well on his own anymore.

"Well, that's kind of it for the tour. We can end here," Wade said, shuffling the rookies through the door into the empty locker room. He pressed his hand to Monty's back, closing in behind him as he shut the door. He moved his hand when he noticed Monty turn around, smiling.

The locker room was at the end of the arena's Hall of Fame, and it was the same uninspired yellow color as it was when Wade started. It always smelled like stale sweat, no matter how clean it was. Years of discarded knee pads shoved in laundry baskets and sweaty wrist and ankle braces hung on hooks had made their olfactory mark, permanently. The laundry baskets squeaked when they moved around and the storage room door was rusted shut. But the room also offered each wrestler a locker with an engraved plaque, endless clean towels, and despite its flaws, Wade knew it was where the best storyline ideas were born. Wade felt at home there.

"You each have your own locker and cubby," he said, rubbing his hand over his own locker displaying the name Viper. "There are showers back there, obviously. And if you need anything, I'm around a lot. I'll post my number on my locker. Feel free to text me. I think Mike said Sunday night is the first time we're gonna meet up and do some skills tests, so get some sleep this weekend and I'll see you guys on Sunday, if not before. I work out here most days." He impulsively glanced at Monty when he said the last part.

The guys fanned out in the locker room, the rookies now joined by the more seasoned wrestlers. Everyone started chatting and joking around, so Wade watched them, mentally matching each wrestler with a potential rival or tag teammate.

He could see himself working with Monty. They were about the same size and their styles complemented each other, and the flexibility Monty showcased in his audition video would just… help with some new moves Wade wanted to try out, or something. If he wanted to excel, he needed a partner who could meet him at his level, and Monty Hill happened to match that description.

He looked around to make sure he was mostly alone, took a small notebook out of his pocket, and wrote himself a note to run his ideas by Mike. Then he looked at Monty, and while his eyes hungrily worked the lines of his body, he wondered how obvious his attraction to Monty would be if he paired them together.

CHAPTER 2

MONTY'S ANKLE WAS SORE AFTER BEING TWISTED UP IN THE ROPES, WHICH was absolutely not planned and exactly as embarrassing as one would think. Only maybe it was even more embarrassing, because he'd been tangled up not only in front of three men he'd just met but also Wade Donovan, whose wrestling career had been inspirational to Monty since he was a teenager.

Well, inspirational was a misnomer. A more honest way to describe it would be that Wade Donovan was Monty's personal highlight of his years-long obsession with all things wrestling. He knew everything there was to know about Wade's career. His highlights and struggles, his childhood, his shoe size. Monty's move to Portland wouldn't have happened if he'd never spent hours of his teen years reading about Wade.

Compared to most of the guys at Titan, Monty discovered wrestling late. He was in high school, and his blooming sexuality had zeroed in on one specific aesthetic—side swept bangs, thick-framed glasses, and visible tattoos. Mustaches were optional, but encouraged. He discovered a streamer who fit the bill and spent weeks watching him play WWE2K14. The game itself seemed fine, but he had to do research to understand what was going on. What became more interesting to Monty were the athletes and writers behind it all. He read industry autobiographies, watched interviews and documentaries, and attended every live wrestling event he could find for years. Then, surprising even himself, he joined a wrestling school and amateur promotion outside Boise, Idaho when he was eighteen.

He limped slightly as he walked home. He'd hoped the short walk would help him feel better, but it was hot and the air was stagnant and stuffy. The difference in humidity continued to be a struggle, Boise offering a slightly more arid climate, and while he'd never mention that to anyone because he knew he was being a baby, he hated it. Fortunately, his apartment was nearby, chosen because he was committed to an ambitious and totally unrealistic goal of moving to CWA within two years. That meant practicing as much as possible, as often as possible, and with anyone who would have him. He was giddy thinking that anyone could someday include Wade.

A vibration in his pocket reminded him he hadn't reached out to his mom more than a couple of times since he'd arrived in Portland a few weeks earlier. He'd left his whole family back in the Boise suburbs and was on his own for the first time in his life, despite being twenty-four. He called his mom every Sunday because that seemed like a reasonable routine. But every once in a while, she called him just to chat, which was great because he secretly wanted to call her every day.

Moving to a new city alone had been harder than he'd expected. It was lonely and a little scary. Coming from the small town where he grew up, the hustle and bustle of even a small city like Portland felt overwhelming at times. His apartment was small and musty, which was a stark contrast to the airy, open house he grew up in. He didn't have any friends yet, which meant he was alone with his thoughts too much. And worst of all, he didn't know how to cook, which left him endlessly hungry for a home cooked meal.

His phone continued to ring, so he brought the phone to his ear and smiled.

"Hi mom," he said.

"Monty? How are you?" His mom's voice came through the phone, sweet and gentle.

"I'm good, I guess! I had a weird day. How are you? How's everything going at home?"

"Things are just fine here. Dad and I miss you. Becky misses you too. Don't you, girl? Say hi to your brother!"

"No, it's okay, I don't need to talk to—"

The sound of heavy breathing interrupted Monty and he sighed, then waited for his mom to take the phone away from the dog's ear.

"Mom," he said flatly.

Becky panted harder.

Monty groaned and looked up towards the sky, waiting for the walk sign to change. When the signal turned white, he rubbed his eye and stepped into the street with one foot, still waiting for his mom to take the phone back from the dog. His frustration grew, taking his attention away from his surroundings. He charged ahead, wishing he was home, out of the sun and away from the arena. Neither he nor the driver of a black sedan was paying enough attention, and the driver slammed on their brakes moments before they hit him.

"Holy shit," he said. He jumped back on the curb, the car stopped in front of him, other cars pulling around them aggressively.

"Monty? Why are you cussing at Becky?" His mom's tinny voice cut through the fog in his head.

"Oh, no, um. Sorry mom. I wasn't cussing at Becky," Monty said, trying to catch his breath. "I just had a close call in a crosswalk. Jackass!"

A surge of adrenaline gave him confidence to kick the car's tire, but he regretted it immediately. It hurt even more than his clumsy departure from the ring. He grabbed his foot and groaned.

"Ugh, God!"

The car's window rolled down slowly and a familiar pair of dark brown eyes peeked over the lightly tinted glass.

"Monty?!" his mom's voice echoed. His phone had slipped from his ear and his shoulder had it pinned closer to his cheek.

"Wade?" Monty gasped.

"Monty, I am so sorry. I didn't see you."

"Oh, that's okay, I'm okay!" He put his foot down when he noticed Wade, hoping he wouldn't mention the kick. "Um, I'm sorry I _"

He heard his mom's quiet voice again.

"Monty? Who is that? Who's Wade? Wait, Wade Donovan?"

He clenched his jaw from embarrassment, as if Wade could somehow hear his mom through the phone. The chaos of the moment and his proximity to Wade made his heart race and his face sweat, and his phone slipped even further. But even then, with the phone halfway down his face, he could hear Becky barking and his mom continuing to ask him what happened. His limbs felt shaky, seeing Wade reminded him of his embarrassing blunder at the arena, and the heat was suffocating him. He wanted to escape, but there was nowhere to go.

"I gotta go, mom. I'll call you soon. Give Becky a kiss for me." Monty hung up on his mom and gave Wade a small smile and a shrug. He attempted a chuckle and said, "Moms, huh?"

"Monty, jeez. I feel terrible. You look like you're having a rough time. Can I drive you home at least?"

"Oh, I actually live right there," Monty said, pointing towards his apartment across the street. "I'm still getting used to the walk and was distracted when I was crossing the street. My mom put Becky on the phone, and I love Becky but like, she doesn't talk. And I miss my mom and everything, but every time I talk to her when I'm out of town she makes me talk to Becky first and I'm just not really sure how to get through to her that Becky isn't great on the phone? But at least I can't smell her breath through the phone, I guess," he chuckled awkwardly.

Wade looked up at him, his face blank and unmoving. Monty twisted his lips.

"Becky is a dog…" he said, quietly. "Um. A big fluffy one. I probably have a picture of her." Monty unlocked his phone with his still shaking hands and started scrolling through his photos. He looked up to see Wade smiling sweetly at him. It made his stomach feel tight. He found a good picture of Becky and he held up his phone, but he noticed Wade looking in the rearview mirror looking at a car behind him that was inching closer.

"Oh, maybe you can show me at the arena on Sunday? I'm sort of blocking traffic here." The motorist's horn conveniently punctuated Wade's comment and the driver screamed out his window for Monty to get his big, dumb ass out of the crosswalk and that he clearly had more muscles than brains. Monty slumped and watched Wade grimace. Another thing to add to his embarrassing list.

"See you soon, Romeo. I'm sorry again!"

Wade waved and rolled up his window, continuing his drive through the crosswalk and away from the arena. Monty raised his hand in a wave, a pointless gesture because Wade was already driving away, then he hit the button for the crosswalk again. This time, he paid attention. He passed by Sacky's, his new favorite bar, and made his way to the back staircase that led to his apartment.

He opened the door and was immediately disgruntled by the chaos. With no one around to provide Monty with a healthy dose of internal shame, his apartment was a disaster. He made a mental note to get a grip and finish unpacking, because if he ever wanted to date, or God, just have friends over, he would need to get his apartment under control. But that was future-Monty's problem.

He flopped onto the shitty couch that came with his apartment and opened up his laptop, which was still open to Titan Wrestling's talent page. He was reading about *all* the current wrestlers, thank you very much. It was nothing more than a coincidence that the friendly face greeting him when his screen turned on was that of Wade Donovan. But when he looked back at Wade's photo, he groaned, reliving his embarrassment for the thirty-fifth time since he left the arena. He cut over to Titan's YouTube channel to watch clips of various matches on mute, trying to learn as much as he could about his new coworkers. He called his mom at the same time.

"Hi again," Monty's mom said when he answered, cheerful as ever.

"Sorry about that earlier. Wade Donovan almost ran me over in a crosswalk!"

"Are you okay? I knew you moving to the big city was a bad idea. There are crazies out there, you know. I once read that ninety-two percent of men who leave their parents' homes will get into a car accident at some point," she said.

Monty could imagine her with a hand clutched against her chest and rolled his eyes. She was a wonderful, sweet mother, but so dramatic.

"All I'm saying is, the house is open to you if you want to come home."

"Mom. I'm fine. Portland doesn't even have a million people,"

Monty reassured her. "And I don't think that's a real statistic at all. I'm just calling back to let you know I'm fine."

"Okay. You'd tell me if you weren't, right?"

"Yes, mom. I promise. But hey - guess what? I went on a tour of Titan's arena today and met all the other new guys, plus a few of the old ones. I mean, not old, but like, accomplished. Experienced. Seasoned. You know what I mean."

"I do. Did that include Wade? I was hoping you'd see him soon. Was he just as cute in person?"

"Mom!" Monty choked out. She laughed on the other end of the phone. "Stop it. But yes, he was there. And yes, he was very cute. Obviously." He glanced at his laptop where Wade and another Titan wrestler called King Garto were in the middle of a cage match. Wade was climbing the cage, all his brawn and skin on display. He pulled his eyes away so he could focus on his mom's chittering.

"Actually, I do have something to talk to you about," his mom said tentatively. "Uncle Dan got an ice fishing cabin booked up in the Northwest Territories for a week over Thanksgiving. Do you want to come with us?"

"Do I want to go with you, dad, and Uncle Dan to sit in a tiny cabin in the Northwest Territories, in November, for several days? No, I do not."

"Okay. Well, if you change your mind you let me know, alright? I can get you a ticket. You just say the word."

"Thanks mom. I'm actually pretty tired. It was a long day. I have the next couple of days off, but I'm heading to the gym to work out with some guys and I think I'll go to IKEA. Sunday I'll be at the arena doing skills tests. So I'm staying busy, mom, I promise. Love you."

"Goodnight, sweetie. I love you."

CHAPTER 3

ONCE A WEEK, WADE MADE THE DRIVE ACROSS TOWN TO VOLUNTEER HIS time at the vet clinic owned by Mike's wife, Linda.

Having grown up in a small university town in northern Minnesota, he loved being outdoors and loved being around wildlife. His personal, non-career related goal of becoming a certified wildlife rehabilitator in Oregon required maintaining a relationship with a veterinarian who would oversee his care, and Linda was happy to do it.

It was an uncomfortably warm day when he was driving to Linda's clinic, so when he spotted an opossum laying on the side of the road, he slowed his car to check on it. Last winter, he'd helped Linda care for an opossum while it recovered from a skin and tail injury. That opossum, whom Wade had named Grubs, had been released after a few weeks, and it had been rewarding enough that he'd worked closely with Linda ever since.

She once told him it wasn't uncommon for baby opossums to remain alive inside their mother's pouch for several hours or even up to a day past her death. He guessed the opossum laying on the ground now was seriously injured or dead because of the heat, so when he reached the opossum, he rolled it over to check for babies. He found a pouch and tried to check for joeys when the opossum's leg moved slowly but purposefully to stop his intrusion. When he realized she was alive, he let out a small gasp.

"I'm sorry," he said. "I have to see if you have any babies in here. This will be quick, and then we'll get you some help."

He checked inside her pouch and found nothing, but was delighted to find one tiny joey hiding behind her. She was a little bigger than his palm, with big beady eyes and a mouth full of pointy teeth. He looked around for a bit, but didn't see any other babies. He gathered up the mother and baby gently and put them in the cat carrier he kept in his car.

"We'll be there soon, guys, hold on."

"HEY WADE," the front desk employee said when he walked in. "Who do you have there?"

"Hi Camila. I found an opossum and a joey. Is Dr. Palazzo busy?"

"No, she's available. Go on back."

Wade pushed the swinging door open with his shoulder and carried the carrier to the surgical table in the middle of the back room. Linda walked over with a curious look on her face.

"Who's this?" she asked.

"I found an opossum. She has a baby. They're both alive, but she was on the pavement and I don't know how long she was there."

"Oh, no," Linda said. "Poor girl. Thanks for bringing her in. Let's take a look."

Linda took the opossum out gently and laid her on a towel. She started a basic exam to check on the mother before she looked at the baby. Linda explained she was going to run some tests and get some scans done, but Wade was welcome to tag along to watch the process. He agreed, of course.

While she poked and prodded at the two opossums, she looked up at Wade and smiled.

"So, Mike tells me you had a new cohort start today," she said.

"Yep. Four new guys."

"How are they? Any stand-outs?"

"You know Mike. They wouldn't be there if they weren't stand-outs," Wade said.

Linda paused to check on the joey. "This little one is big enough now that if her mom doesn't make it, she'll probably be okay."

Wade frowned. "Is the mom going to die?"

"I don't know. I hope not, but I don't know what's going on with her. My primary concern is her milk supply being rancid if she's sick or badly injured. It's hard to tell if anything has bitten her, but when she's more stable, we'll take a closer look."

"Okay."

"Mike told me you were setting up the teams again this year. Is that for the entire season?"

"Yeah. Well, maybe. Obviously there will be other matches around the region, but rivalries and tag teams will be for the full season."

"Got it. Who will you be working with?"

"Oh, I'm marrying one of the new kids. His name is Monty."

Linda gave him a look of confusion.

"Married. Like, wrestling married."

Linda's face stayed blank.

"We'll be working together a lot. You know, for someone who's married to *Mike Palazzo*, you remain woefully uninformed about the entire industry," he said, smiling. "I'm beginning to think you do it on purpose."

Linda rolled her eyes. "I have more important things to do than learn your lingo, Wade." She smiled, then stepped away and had a vet nurse help her with imaging of the mother opossum. He watched her start an IV for hydration, and she let him give her some prophylactic antibiotics. She placed the opossums in a warm, dark kennel and pulled up a chair next to the computer for Wade to sit on.

"See that here?" she said, pointing at the image on the screen. "That's a broken leg and tail. My guess is she was hit by a car. I don't have high hopes for the mom, Wade, I'm sorry. She seems to have some internal injuries as well. She's not stable enough to do surgery right now, if that was even an option."

Wade nodded. He wasn't surprised. He thought she was dead before he even picked her up. "What about the baby?"

"Well, we'll keep her with the mom for now. Again, she's a decent size. If something happens to the mom, we'll be able to take care of her."

Wade nodded again. "Okay." He got up and walked over to the kennel to look at the mom again, but the lights were dim in that corner of the room and she was in a box with a towel over it. With his hands in his pockets, he bent down to peek in and caught a glimpse of her little black and white foot and tiny pink toes. "Can we call her Larva? Like we named Grubs?"

"No."

"Maggot?"

"No!"

"Worm?"

"What is wrong with you?" Linda asked.

"Okay. What about Juliet?"

∼

MONTY STOOD at the edge of his living room with his hands on his hips. He scanned the room and whistled at the sight before him.

"How did I even have this much stuff to bring?" he asked aloud to his mostly unfurnished, but somehow still chaotic, studio apartment.

He Googled "how to organize an apartment" and found dozens of unhelpful blog posts written by people who were starting from an already tidy space. He read through a few of them but grew increasingly irritated at the bright, staged apartments being used to illustrate the authors' organization and decorating skills. The posts all had photos of beautiful trailing plants hanging in front of sunny windows or a friendly-looking cat perched on a specialized cat shelf that probably cost more than his monthly grocery budget.

His apartment was small and weird shaped and it had a single window in the main room. It was dark, and so little natural light came through the north-facing window that his only option for greenery was going to be a fake plant. The worst part of his apartment was the carpet, which was old and brown. He guessed that was to hide old stains, which he chose to think about as seldom as possible. Moving into an apartment sight unseen may have been a bad idea, but he couldn't afford to move to Portland and find something temporary before he put down his deposits. He scrubbed at his face and sat on a box of books.

He was feeling a little out of his depth because this was all so new to him. His parents owned a plot of land and a big farmhouse, and he never felt pressured to leave so he just... didn't. They had a hobby farm and a few animals, so he helped out when he could in between his wrestling matches, which paid him small amounts here and there, and his entry-level job. He'd never earned much money, so his mom encouraged him to live at home while he saved up for his move to Portland.

He made a list of things he might need, from an entire bed to kitchenware, and hoped he could afford everything. His mom would give him money in an emergency, but he really wanted to do it on his own. Before he could convince himself he couldn't, he hopped in his car and drove to IKEA.

OKAY, IKEA was overwhelming. Monty had never stepped foot in one and he could not believe how many people were there. The lights were bright and everything was a blinding yellow, which would have been okay if the entire population of his hometown hadn't been there. He passed by a pillar that held tiny pencils and grabbed a few, using them to keep his hands busy.

He went up an escalator and was thrust into a maze of showrooms with a ridiculous number of options. He weaved around the rooms, his mind unable to focus on anything, and ended up on another escalator that took him down to a sea of carts. But they weren't normal carts, they were weird platform things he'd never seen before. They had wheels that moved in all directions and instead of a cart basket, they just had a place to hang a bright yellow bag. He frowned and regretted his choice to attempt this outing alone, but he pushed forward, following the arrows on the floor.

He eventually made his way to the bedroom area where he stood in front of the bed linens, trying to decide which color bedding would match his swirly brown carpet. Eventually, he picked up a set he thought looked nice. It was white and had lots of small, colorful flowers that could brighten up the space. He shoved it under his arm and went to the area across the aisle with throw pillows, and felt overwhelmed all over again. He sighed so dramatically it attracted the attention of a very handsome IKEA employee.

"You okay over there? I wasn't sure you remembered where you were, you'd been looking at those bed sets for so long," he said, smiling at Monty.

Monty looked up from his task. He picked up a blue throw pillow and held it up to the bedding set. "Does this match?"

"I think so," the IKEA worker said. He stepped closer to Monty. He smelled nice. "I think a green one would look nice too, because of the stem color on the duvet."

"Stem color," Monty said under his breath. "Got it. And that's better than trying to match a petal color?"

The IKEA employee laughed. "I don't think it matters. It was just a suggestion."

"Okay. Sorry, this is my first time decorating. I just don't want it to look bad. I hope to have people to impress someday," Monty said.

"Aw. You're doing great. A lot of people wouldn't even consider throw pillows! I'm Aaron, by the way. Do you want help? I can walk around with you for a while."

"I'm Monty. Are you allowed to do that?"

"I think it'll be okay," Aaron smiled.

Aaron led Monty through IKEA, replacing his furniture cart with a shopping cart, tossing things in as he passed them. Monty could feel his blood pressure dropping and his hands relaxing.

"Do you entertain much, or do you think one set of glasses will be enough?"

"I don't entertain much, but I would like to be able to have people over. It's just a studio, so not much room. It's also shaped weird and has a little alcove I have to figure out what to do with. I could put a fake plant in there, I guess? Does IKEA sell fake plants? Or maybe a big pot with some sticks? Maybe I'll do a little housewarming thing if the guys at my new job want to."

"Ooh, new job, huh?"

"I just moved here from Idaho to work for Titan Wrestling."

Aaron stopped walking abruptly, and Monty ran into his back. He spun around, his face lit up with a wide, beaming smile. "Shut. Up. You're a wrestler?!"

Monty grinned. "Yeah. I just started with Titan this week. It's been a big change."

"This is incredible. My partner, Ronnie, and I are the biggest wrestling dorks. We watch matches over at Titan Arena all the time!"

Monty deflated a bit at Aaron's mention of a boyfriend. Not that he thought Aaron was interested in him. They were at his job, for Pete's sake, and Aaron was just being helpful. But they'd been getting along and Aaron was pretty good looking, and Monty wasn't used to being on his own so much, so he'd thought maybe…

"Well, you should definitely come this season. I can get you tickets. Perks of knowing the talent," Monty said. He flipped his long hair and pretended to wave to invisible fans.

"I would love that. Ronnie's birthday is soon. Can we exchange info? I hope that's not weird. Don't feel pressured. I just think you seem cool and also you're a wrestler, so I'll get major brownie points if we become friends."

"Sure! Hey, did you ever wonder if brownie points were called that because at some point there was some sort of program where you could trade points for a brownie? I did, but then I read it had something to do with wartime food rations, which was depressing. Unlike brownies."

Aaron narrowed his eyes and smiled. "You're a fun guy, Monty."

They explored together a bit longer, but eventually left to get back to work. Even if Aaron wasn't a romantic connection, Monty was excited to have made a potential friend. He continued through to the furniture bays and picked up the bed and TV stand he'd picked out. The mattress had to be delivered, but he was okay sleeping on his air mattress another few nights if he had to. He drove home and hauled everything up to his apartment, alone, thankful for his strength. By the time he got everything upstairs, he was tired enough for a nap.

With nobody there to tell him not to, he sprawled out on the terrible, lumpy sofa he couldn't afford to replace and drifted off.

CHAPTER 4

AFTER WORKING OUT WITH SOME OF THE GUYS AT TITAN, WADE WENT straight to the bar closest to his friend Madeline's house. Working out meant he'd been in close proximity to Monty, so he asked Madeline if she could go out for a drink with a goal of getting him off his mind. They hadn't even spent any time together alone, and each of their encounters had been brief, but neither of those facts seemed to stop him from developing inconvenient… feelings. He tried to convince himself that the excessive time he spent thinking about Monty was because of his renewed excitement around wrestling, but it wasn't really working.

When he'd called Madeline, she'd asked if everything was okay, perhaps a sign that he'd become more asocial than he realized. He said yes, everything was fine, and apparently that told her there was something interesting happening in his life. So she said she had a lot of questions, mostly about the new guys, and she'd meet him at the bar as soon as he could get there.

He walked into the bar fifteen minutes after they got off the phone. When he got there, Madeline was already waiting for him across the bar, so he pointed to a table and sat down, signaling that he'd wait for her there. He prepared for the inevitable barrage of questions, and took a deep breath as he watched her approach.

"So, tell me more about Monty," she said, putting a round of drinks on their table.

"Uh, hello to you, too. Thank you." He grabbed the drink she brought and took a big sip, trying to buy time before her interrogation began. "What do you want to know? I mean, I don't really know him that well. I've only met him a few times, and we were in a group every time. Working out mostly. I only met him the day I gave the tour of the arena to the new people. I think we might be paired together as rivals. It's nothing big."

"Hmm." Madeline's eyes sparkled.

Wade groaned. He knew she wasn't buying his indifference, but he was exhausted after a long week. He just wanted to hang out with his oldest and dearest friend without thinking about Monty and all the very ill-timed feelings he had bubbling up.

"I mostly want to know why you always mention him by name and keep calling the other guys 'the other guys.'" Madeline said, grinning against her glass. "It's just not like you! You've been so quiet on this front since Larry."

"This front? What front?"

"You know… the dude-front. Hot dudes. Partner dudes. Hot partner dudes."

"Hot partner dudes? Is that what we're reducing Larry to?" Wade laughed.

It felt good to laugh about Larry's quick departure from his life since so much of his reflection had historically involved tears. They wrestled together but were also romantically involved for years, living in Wade's apartment. So, when Wade found Larry's CWA contract and stormed out of the arena, he'd ended up at their shared home. Larry arrived shortly after and told Wade he was sorry he hadn't mentioned it before, but it was done. He would miss the sex and if Wade was ever in his neighborhood, he should reach out. When Wade asked, politely, what the fuck that meant, Larry shrugged and said he thought they both knew this was just until one of them moved on.

He remembered Larry's apathy towards his devastation and how Larry stayed emotionless while Wade made a fool of himself, begging him to reconsider the breakup. His eyes had been blurry and red from trying not to cry, visible proof of Wade's emotions that had irritated Larry throughout their relationship. He told Larry he was willing to move to Boston, he'd just need some time to save money. That they could stay together, long distance, in the meantime. He thought of the sting he felt from Larry's vicious parting words: *I've outgrown this. A relationship will hold me back, and I can't risk you weighing me down. Not with everything I have ahead of me. It's not my fault CWA didn't want you, and I can't put my dreams on hold for something that will never happen.*

A lingering part of Wade still felt he could have prevented Larry from leaving him if he'd just handled himself better, but Madeline assured him that wasn't the case. Larry was a jerk, and that was that.

Perhaps noticing Wade's slumping shoulders, Madeline diverted his focus back to her. "Well, actually, I don't know if I'd call Larry hot. He's the one who wore baggy leather pants in the ring. I hate a baggy leather pant wearing wrestler. Yuck."

"I know you do. I do too, for what it's worth. Like, it's gotta be hot in there." Wade took another long sip of his drink, hoping he'd derailed Madeline's train of thought. "I mean, I know it is. I tried them once. Awful."

"Anyway…" Madeline dragged her finger through the condensation in her glass. "Spill."

Wade glared at her. "Seriously, Mads, there's nothing to share. He is just a new wrestler at Titan along with several other new wrestlers. I'm setting up partner lists for Mike and I think we would complement each other, so I paired us together. We're about the same size and skill level, and I think we could, you know, help each other out."

Madeline waggled her eyebrows.

"Not like that," he continued. "In a totally platonic and unsexy way. He's just really talented and we could push each other. Oh, I almost hit him with my car on Wednesday."

"Excuse me?" Madeline squeaked. "You didn't think to mention that? What a meet-cute."

Wade groaned again. "First of all, that's not how we met. Also, I didn't actually hit him. But I almost didn't see him and had to slam on the brakes. He told me he was talking to his mom's dog on the phone and I got all flustered and called him Romeo, which is… ugh. Then I drove away. So what I'm saying is, even if I did have romantic, sexy feelings for him, it's never gonna happen. Which is good. It shouldn't happen, anyway."

Madeline started to say something, but Wade stopped her when he looked at his phone. He had a text - well, actually, many texts - from an unknown number. He looked up at Madeline and showed her the screen, and her face lit up.

"Could that be your platonic and unsexy coworker Romeo reaching out? See what he said!"

"It could be. It could also be someone else. Relax." Wade's heart sped up as he unlocked his phone and opened up the text messages.

> hi Wade, it's Monty
>
> or Romco
>
> whichever
>
> oh my god, sorry. you know who Monty is. I got your number from the locker room. I was just going to see what time you were going to be at the arena on Sunday for practice
>
> sorry, you do not owe me an answer
>
> wow, seriously, please ignore these

Wade grinned and showed Madeline the screen again and she burst out laughing.

"Oh, my God. That is so cute. You may think innocently of Romeo here, but I don't think the same could be said for him," she said. "Aw."

Wade rolled his eyes at her and started typing back.

> Hi, Monty. I think 3...

Madeline looked at Wade's phone and squinted her eyes to read his reply.

"That's it?! Poor guy rambles on for five messages and you say 'uh, I think three' with an ellipsis?" She put on a deep, stupid-sounding voice when she recited his message.

"Six messages. And I will see him on Sunday at three, so what's the problem? Ugh, don't you have a baby to get home to?" Wade said, scowling at her. He finished up the last of his drink and got up from his seat.

"I have the night off! You can't get rid of me that easily. And I have way more questions."

Wade grinned and kissed her cheek, then headed to the bar for another round.

A couple of hours later, Wade walked home in an attempt to clear his head. It was a quiet and uneventful walk, except for the itch in his fingers to reread the texts Monty sent him. The innocuous texts that offered nothing beyond simple curiosity about whether they'd see each other (with many other people) on Sunday. He didn't even know why he cared. He barely knew the guy. But Monty's texts were just so cute, and Wade liked the idea of working with him and seeing what they could achieve together. He let his mind drift to Monty's audition video and how it blew the others out of the water. Their styles were so similar it seemed like fate that Monty ended up at Titan, and he couldn't wait until they got in the ring together.

Madeline was right that this was the first time Wade had even a single romantic thought about a guy since Larry, but pursuing Monty romantically just wasn't an option. Monty was too young and full of promise to want to be held back by a relationship. Besides, Wade had already dated someone with a developmental contract so he knew what the end goal was - and that would never include Wade. So he was going to do his best to give his own career one last shot, and for better or worse, he couldn't think of anyone better equipped to help him get there than Monty Hill.

His phone vibrated and his traitorous heart skipped a beat. He glanced down, hoping Monty had sent more rambling texts, but instead he was met with a text from Madeline that contained a photo of her sleeping baby.

WADE APPROACHED Mike's office door on Sunday afternoon carrying two green smoothies. He knocked twice and pushed the door open with his foot, peeking his head around.

"Have a minute? I wanted to go over the new teams I was going to suggest for this evening's class," Wade said, handing over one smoothie.

"Yeah, come on in, Wade. I was just getting ready to come find you. I wanted to chat." He scrunched his nose, grabbing the drink with a pout. "Ugh. Thanks for this."

"Chat?" Wade's eyebrows shot up.

"Yeah, nothing too bad. Just wanted to discuss the upcoming year, what to expect. I know we've been relying on you a lot for administrative tasks here and it's.. I don't know, I'm a little worried it's encouraging you to put your goals on the back burner. I kind of thought once you got back on your feet after Larry, things would go back to normal. I feel like you've been struggling since he left and it's probably not helping that I'm asking you to take on so much responsibility around here."

"I enjoy learning this stuff. I don't mind. But I don't know, Mike. I'm thirty-two and haven't made any great strides in years. CWA may just not be in the cards for me. I'm working on accepting that."

It wasn't Mike's fault, not entirely. Wade knew he'd been slipping since Larry left. At first, it was because of heartbreak. Mike knew the two of them were together, but it wasn't the kind of thing they talked about openly. Larry always said the secrecy he demanded was because he wanted to be taken seriously as a tag team. He said if people around Titan knew they were together, it would make them seem cutesy and unserious. Wade didn't fully agree or even understand, but he went along with it to keep Larry happy. It meant Wade was isolated from any potential support group he had at Titan and the downstream effects had been worse than he'd expected.

When Mike witnessed Wade's world crumble down around him without understanding exactly what was happening, his solution was to shield Wade from everything at Titan. It resulted in Wade being buried, a methodical relegation from his prior status in the wrestling world. It lasted for an entire year after Larry left. And while Wade had since healed from the surprise heartbreak, Larry's professional absence continued to leave Wade feeling unmoored. The one thing that had anchored him to wrestling for five years was gone, and he didn't know how to get back on track.

He had been working to regain fan favor over the last year, but it was slow going and he was old news.

Mike looked at Wade over the top of his glasses.

"I don't know if I'd say it's not in the cards. I think you show a lot of promise, you always have. I wouldn't keep you around if you didn't believe in you. And thirty-two in professional wrestling isn't thirty-two in basketball," he said, flashing a sympathetic smile. Or a pity smile. "You're just lost right now. But maybe it's time to change things up? Whether that's your own personal goals, your angles, or your… reputation."

Wade grimaced.

"I think it's time for you to turn heel. It's probably *been* time. Niall suggested it, actually. I think this could really work for you."

Wade swallowed. He knew, in reality, this wasn't a bad thing. It was another angle to work, a way to refresh his image and give the fans a new version of Viper they didn't have before. And he hadn't been a "good guy" face in a long time, not in any tangible sense. The fans didn't care about him at all, so being a "bad guy" heel wouldn't be any worse.

They both sat in silence for a few seconds until Wade was sufficiently uncomfortable. He cleared his throat.

"Um, well, here's the list I put together," Wade said. He handed it over and Mike read through the names.

"Will and Dicky, sure, that makes sense. But why Amit and Niall?"

"I think Amit's style will throw Niall for a loop. I watched Amit's tape again last night and he's so creative with the high flying moves. Niall is set in his ways, and I don't see that changing unless we do something to throw him off his game. He needs to unclench, and what better way to encourage that than pairing him with an annoying rookie?" Wade said. He sipped his gross smoothie and thought for a minute before he continued. "To be totally honest, it also just seems like it will be really fun to watch. They're like oil and water."

Mike snorted a laugh and tapped a pen against his lip. "Yeah, okay. Got it." He went through more of the names and nodded slightly. He looked up at Wade with a small smile. "You and Romeo, huh?"

Wade looked at the desk and nodded, knowing if he looked at Mike in the eye he'd give something away. He didn't even know *what* he'd give away, but Mike would figure something out and he wasn't ready to deal with any of that.

"I mean, like I've said, we would complement each other. We're, you know, similar sizes. Similar styles. If anyone can help me get out of my slump, I think it's him. New blood, and all that." Wade traced the wood grain on the table with his finger to avoid Mike's scrutiny.

"Yeah. I get it. Sounds good, Wade." Mike smiled and handed the papers back. "Are you good to lead tonight or do you want me involved? I have an electrician coming by, but I can make time."

"I got it. Tonight I was thinking we could start having everyone plan a match with whoever they're paired with. Then we can set the season's schedule, start angle promos. I can keep up on the social media stuff. One you've heard from the scouts, we can adjust as necessary."

"Sounds like you have it all figured out. Take a breath. Focus on yourself. Oh, by the way, are you joining us for Thanksgiving this year? Linda is in planning mode and I told her I'd get a headcount. I know, I know. It's early, but I can't change her."

Wade got up and pushed his chair in. He rubbed his hand over his short hair and looked at Mike. "Yeah, of course. I'll be there. And, um, I'll figure it out, I promise. I won't let you down."

"You never let me down, Wade. I just worry about you. I want you to be happy."

Wade gave a short nod and turned around. He left the office as quickly as he could, blowing out a breath as he closed the door, his stomach in a stew.

Mike was the closest thing he had to family at this point besides Madeline. He didn't have Larry anymore. His parents had given him an ultimatum: go to college or say goodbye to their financial support. He chose wrestling, and the animosity his parents harbored around his decision had led him to have limited contact with them starting around the time he turned twenty.

He'd met Mike shortly after his retirement from CWA. He founded Titan and took Wade under his wing immediately. *You're the next big thing,* he remembered Mike saying. After some time, Mike introduced

Wade to his wife Linda, and the two had given him somewhere to go for the holidays every year since.

Regardless of what Mike claimed now, Wade knew he was a flop. Whatever he did with Monty this year needed to be spectacular, because he didn't deserve another shot. Forcing it would be insulting to Mike. So he needed to succeed, and needed to remind Mike why he'd taken a chance on him all those years ago. He rolled his shoulders back and made his way to the gym to warm up.

CHAPTER 5

Monty looked at the mirror in front of the squat rack and saw Wade come in wearing a tank top and sweatpants, probably looking to warm up before the evening's events. He had headphones in, which was disappointing, because Monty wanted to pop over and say hi.

But maybe it was for the best. The last interaction between the two of them was Monty spamming Wade's phone with too many texts, all of which went unanswered until Wade replied, once, that he'd see him at the gym around three. In the history of embarrassing text messages, they weren't the end of the world, but that didn't stop him from reliving the exchange over and over, preventing him from getting much sleep. Monty's face curled in on itself as he relived the exchange again.

With the bar placed back on the rack, Monty wiped down the equipment, took a drink of water, and scrubbed his hands down his face. He cringed internally and thought about the germs he'd rubbed into his mucous membranes. Curious how much longer he had before he could justify ending his workout, he glanced at the clock on the wall, which happened to be directly above the treadmill Wade was using.

Monty did his best to look quickly, but he couldn't help giving Wade a once-over. Or maybe a twice-over. He was just so… hot. Monty was used to being around attractive, athletic people, but there was something about Wade that caught his eye the first time he saw him being interviewed on a wrestling channel on YouTube over eight years ago.

He'd been sixteen the first time he saw the tiny, pixelated image of Wade in an interview. It was a life-changing moment that resulted in two goals. One, he was going to wrestle professionally, even though the chances of becoming successful were slim; and two, he was going to meet and become friends with Wade Donovan. Monty also made a secret third decision to become more than friends with Wade - a lofty goal with a lot more late-night fantasy than he was comfortable sharing with anyone.

Wade's warm up had turned into a full on run. Sweat was pouring off of him. Monty kept stealing glances, attempting subtlety but failing. But Wade was all broad shoulders and muscles and powerful thighs and it was impossible to look away. He had short black hair and a colorful tattoo of an Oregon Grape - half blooming, half flowering - on his taut, muscular forearm. It surprised Monty because Wade didn't seem like a flowers-and-fruit kind of guy, but he really liked it. He smiled in Wade's direction and could swear he was looking at him out of the corner of his eye, but he reminded himself that Wade probably wanted to keep his eye on Monty because of his texting behavior earlier in the week. Monty focused on his own workout for the rest of their session.

After hopping off the treadmill, Wade made his way to the showers. Monty cursed internally since he, too, was heading to the showers.

It was fine. They were both professionals and there was an unspoken rule about not ogling other people anywhere clothing was being removed. Monty was really good at following the rules since he was openly bisexual and, unsurprisingly, the wrestlers he worked with were often less than enthusiastic about his attraction to men. The last thing he wanted was to be labeled a pervert, so he took a deep breath and followed Wade towards the showers at a safe, non-creepy distance.

Fortunately, the shower was uneventful. He kept to himself and faced away from Wade. He gave himself a mental pat on the back and got changed as quickly as he could, because it was time to head to the arena to get paired with his new partner. Not a tag-team partner, which was fine, but the person with whom Monty would spend the next couple of months, filming promos and developing angles before the season's schedule was released.

He really had to impress Mike with whatever routine he came up with if he wanted a chance to get more ring time. More ring time meant more fan engagement, a key metric that indicated to CWA he had money potential. Every year at about halfway through the season, CWA scouts came to Titan to observe matches and report back on where the developmental contract wrestlers ranked. It was rare, but not unheard of, for wrestler contracts to be bought out after one year with Titan, and Monty wanted that more than anything. But regardless of the likelihood, Monty was ready for the opportunity to show off.

He'd been brainstorming ideas for the match he and his partner could perform on scout night and he knew he needed someone strong enough to throw him. There were only a few guys big enough, Wade being one of them, of course. But Monty wasn't going to kid himself into thinking Mike would place them together. Wade's skill level probably required someone with more experience. Monty had been wrestling for years, but it hadn't been under the guidance of someone like Mike. Truthfully, he wasn't sure where he measured up, but was pretty sure they'd all find out this evening.

Monty's stomach twisted with nerves as he thought about all the ways the evening could pan out. His brain created unhelpful images of him walking up to the ring only to be told he was fired, or the worst wrestler any of them had ever met. He imagined Mike asking him to show off various moves, only to be mocked by the group. He reminded himself he'd had to try out for an opportunity to be here, and so far he'd done well. He finished zipping his boots and slammed his locker shut before jogging down to the main ring.

The guys were gathered near the ring when Monty finally arrived. He noticed a clipboard hung up on the outside of one corner and he watched as wrestlers found their names and then, subsequently, their assigned partner. It felt a bit like high school, finding out if you'd been picked for the role you really wanted in whatever play the drama club was putting on, or if you'd be assigned the role of Tree #4. Not that he was speaking from experience.

Before he reached the chart, he heard raised voices and stopped to turn around. He looked off to the right and saw Amit and Niall standing in front of Wade, arms flailing, spittle flying.

"Are you kidding me, Wade? Amit? I watched his tape with you and I *told* you it would be a nightmare to work with him because he doesn't respect the time-honored classics. Why would you pair me with him, you asshole?" Niall was turning a pretty, tomato shade of red and his forearms flexed from the clenching of his fists. Monty was pretty sure a vein couldn't burst out of a forearm, but if it *was* possible, he was also pretty sure he was moments from witnessing it.

"What is that supposed to mean? You think I want to work with you, you narrow minded has-been? At least I'm trying new things, making the sport more exciting and not copying what's been done for literally decades, Niall. Grow up."

"Grow up? You fucking grow up, Amit. Stop acting like the work that's been 'done for literally decades' is beneath you. You don't respect the elders of this industry," Niall said, gesturing to Mike.

"The *elders*? Mike is, like, fifty years old! He has a seven-year-old. I'm pretty sure his wife is younger than you."

"Oh my god, you are insufferable." Niall turned to Wade, pointing a finger in his face. "Wade, I swear to God, I will twist your balls until you scream. Right here, right now. I want to be paired with someone else."

"Oh, great, threatening Wade Donovan's balls? Great idea, idiot. He's like twice your size and four times as strong," Amit said. "If your way is so superior, then show me how to be better. Don't be such a little bitch."

"What did you just call me?" Niall said as he approached Amit. Niall's jaw clenched and Monty honestly thought he might have heard a tooth crack.

"I called you a little bitch."

Monty looked over to Wade, and for the first time since he'd joined Titan, he saw a big, open-mouthed smile on Wade's normally stoic face. His eyes were wide and bright with amusement. Monty wasn't sure if anyone, anywhere, had ever looked happier about an argument than Wade did at that moment.

Then, a surprising laugh erupted out of Wade. Amit and Niall paused their argument and looked at him in disbelief. He laughed so hard Monty was a little worried he was going to hurt himself. Monty couldn't help but giggle. Not at Amit and Niall, they were honestly a little scary, but at Wade. Of course Amit and Niall didn't realize that. They both turned to Monty and narrowed their eyes, then started walking towards him. Monty's mouth opened, ready to plead for his life, when Wade interrupted them.

"Okay, okay. Stop, guys. Take a walk," Wade said, wiping an actual tear from his eye. "Oh, my God. That was so good. I am so happy."

Niall and Amit scoffed and walked towards the doors, a hushed argument reigniting between them, all four of their arms in a controlled flail.

The rest of the guys had paired off and were busy practicing and discussing their matches. Monty remembered he needed to go check out who he was partnered with and made his way to the clipboard hanging off the ring. He didn't actually see any other individuals around, and if he hadn't talked himself down just moments before, he might have been a little worried he had been cut from the roster.

"You're with me, Romeo," Wade called from the corner where he'd been standing with Niall and Amit.

Monty looked around, forgetting for a moment that *he* was Romeo. His heart skipped a beat with the realization that he'd be working with Wade. Then he smiled and jogged over to him, hoping he would remember how to breathe when he got there.

"THAT WAS WILD," Monty said.

Wade laughed again, and Monty's smile grew. God, it really had been a while since he'd felt like this about someone.

"It was. It was totally what I was hoping would happen. Niall needs to get knocked down a peg and this makes it easier for the rest of us," he said. "I do feel kind of bad for Amit, though. He seems like a nice guy. I hope Niall doesn't corrupt him."

Wade bent down to re-lace his boot and out of the corner of his eye he noticed Monty was twisting his hands together. He looked nervous.

"So, um. We haven't really had a chance to talk yet, just the two of us. I'm excited to be paired with you. I've followed your career for a while. You're like, a big reason I wanted to go into wrestling. I saw you on a WrestleTalk interview when I was in high school and I was like, 'wow, I would kill to do him.' I mean, do that. Wrestling. Not you. I just meant… Oh, God." Monty's hands flew to his face and his finger poked his eye. "Oh, God! Ow!"

Wade pressed his lips together with his teeth and stared at Monty. He tried not to laugh. "Um. Are you okay? I mean, your eye?"

"Yeah, yeah," Monty said, blinking rapidly. "Boy, this is really not how I envisioned getting to know you."

"I'm having a great time so far," Wade joked.

"I bet. Who wouldn't love to watch an idiot poke his actual eyeball five seconds after meeting someone they've looked up to for years? I'm so embarrassed. I'm sorry."

Wade was confused by Monty's confession, but before he could ask for clarification, he noticed Monty's eyes looked wet. It wasn't clear if the tears in Monty's eyes were from the finger poke or embarrassment, but he didn't like the idea of Monty being upset. And that was something he didn't want to unpack at the moment, so he ignored it. He reached his hand out and placed it on Monty's shoulder. The warmth of it seeped into his palm.

"Take a deep breath, Monty. Or maybe like four deep breaths. Relax. I'm excited to be working with you, too. I put us together because I saw a lot of myself in your audition tape. So let's just sit and chat, talk about our goals, and see how the evening goes."

"Okay. Sorry. Thanks. I'll just…" Monty gestured towards a table and chair set on the side of the arena.

"After you. I'll go grab us a couple of waters and some paper in case we want to brainstorm. Wait—" Wade leaned in close to Monty's face and inspected his eye. He tried his best to breathe normally, but it was hard. They were so close. He breathed in Monty's scent—soapy and clean, with a hint of coconut.

Right, because they'd just been in the showers. At the same time. With rivulets of water finding their way down the lines of Monty's back. He wondered if they had done the same thing on his chest and abs. Or maybe the water found its way down to his hips and Adonis belt, or maybe even lower…

He jerked up, putting some much needed space between them. "Ah, yep, your eye seems okay. I thought I saw something earlier, but it all looks good. Do you need ice or anything?"

"No. I think I'm okay. My eye is a little tender, but it's fine. The rest sounds good. I'll be waiting over there, then," Monty said, hurrying towards the table.

Wade watched Monty walk away for a few seconds longer than necessary. He was wearing sweats that hugged his muscular thighs and showcased his ass. It was tight and round, and when Wade realized he was ogling it, he took off towards the mini kitchen. Niall was there, leaning against the wall, with his eyebrow raised in Wade's direction and a stupid-looking grin on his face.

"Um. Hey?"

"Just to be clear, I still hate you. I *will* get you back for the Amit situation, and it may still be in the form of twisting your balls. But don't think I don't see what's happening here," Niall said, pointing back and forth between Wade and Monty.

Wade pulled Niall's hand down. "Can you please not point so obviously? I don't want him to think I'm talking about him."

"And why not?"

"Because it's rude? And also he seems nervous to be working with me and I really think it could go well if we try, so I don't want him to complain to Mike that I'm being a dick and gossiping about him or whatever."

"Uh huh."

"What?" Wade said, glaring at a still-smiling Niall. "Oh, shut up. Whatever you think you saw, you didn't."

Niall mimed zipping his mouth shut before turning around. He sighed and his face went blank as he headed over to where Amit was sitting, pushing soft black curls off his forehead.

. . .

Two hours later, most of the guys had moved to watching practice fights in the ring.

The sound of shouts and cheers drew Wade's eyes to the ring. It currently held rookie Dicky Birk, whose stage name was The Assassin, and Will "Chainsaw" Ganymedes, a Titan veteran of a couple years. He was well loved and respected by both casual watchers and more rabid fans, and Wade appreciated his presence around the arena.

Wade didn't know Dicky very well, but thought the two might be a good fit. Dicky was like a juiced-up honey badger and needed someone who could neutralize his temper. Will was friendly and innocent, never assuming ill intent from anyone, and he tended to bring out the best in people.

"Where did Amit and Niall go?" Monty asked, breaking Wade's concentration on the ring.

"Oh, huh. I don't know," Wade replied, looking around. "Suspicious."

Monty looked at Wade and raised his eyebrows. Wade huffed a quick laugh and looked back towards the ring, worry growing in his gut. The fight was really heating up. He started walking over, hoping Monty would follow.

Neither Dicky nor Will were talking through what they were doing. They appeared to be in an actual fight. The guys around the ring didn't seem to notice – some of them were cheering and laughing, probably because the less experienced Dicky was dominating Will by the time Wade got to the ring. Will raised his hands in a boxing stance with fists clenched, but his posture was defensive. Dicky's face was the angry - tight, with narrow eyes and a creepy grin. His huge muscles were almost trembling with some sort of... excitement, or maybe rage.

Dicky charged at Will, grabbing one of his arms and twisting it behind his back in an immobilizing chicken wing maneuver. Dicky's other arm went around Will's neck, bending Will's head to his shoulder before he clasped his hands and squeezed.

"Wade, get this jackass off of me!" Will yelled, kicking at Dicky fruitlessly. "Fuck off, Dicky! What the fuck is your problem?"

Dicky's face relaxed but his unsettling grin stayed put. He leaned down to whisper in Will's ear while he looked down at Wade. Wade couldn't make out what he said, but he was already on his way through the ropes and into the ring when Dicky released the hold and Will dropped to his knees.

"Jesus, Dicky!" Will said as he rubbed his neck.

Wade watched Dicky stalk towards him.

"Wade Donovan," he said, proffering his hand. "I've wanted to meet you up close and personal, but I haven't seen you around much. I suppose that's not unusual these days, huh?"

"Ah, yeah. I've been busy working on some stuff for Mike, but I'm here now, working with Monty," he said, pointing his thumb over his shoulder.

"Monty Hill? Why the fuck is he stuck with Titan's own Jeremy Blaze? Did he pull the short straw?" Dicky said.

He was looking for a fight, Wade told himself. He didn't have to engage. Dicky didn't even know Wade. He turned to look at Monty to see if he'd heard Dicky's jabs, and thankfully he was mid-conversation with Amit, who had reappeared. The rest of the guys, though, were watching the ring attentively. Wade's face drooped, and he looked down at his feet.

He hated knowing everyone thought of him as the leftovers. The half left behind. And Dicky's insults confirmed it—people thought he was washed up and irrelevant. But worse was that Dicky's insults weren't even unfounded. He *was* the Jeremy Blaze to Larry's Eric Wingman.

Where Eric Wingman famously threw Jeremy Blaze through a barbershop window, ending their tag-team partnership, Larry simply dumped Wade and left the city, never looking back. He supposed the physical pain of flying through a glass panel and the emotional pain of being dumped were different, but both were pretty terrible.

Wade was lucky to still have a job with Titan at this point, and the guys all knew it. He felt a swell of embarrassment when he thought about how he believed Monty was actually excited about working with him.

"Just… take it easy, okay? Tonight was supposed to be fun. You don't have to get so rough. Get to know each other's styles before you fuck up and break his neck," Wade warned.

"Sure thing, coach," Dicky said. He smirked at Wade and clapped his shoulders. "Wouldn't want to upset Dad's favorite. Still haven't figured out why he keeps you around. See you later."

Wade shrugged Dicky's hands off of him and watched him hop out of the ring and head towards the showers. Wade jumped to the mats and Monty rushed over and put his hand on Wade's arm. He flinched involuntarily and Monty pulled his hand back, offering an apologetic smile.

"Is everything okay? That was crazy. I've heard about Dicky. I used to train with a guy who trained with him, and from what I hear, he's totally unhinged. He's a great wrestler, though, so I guess I can see the appeal. Sort of a diabolical genius type, but instead of taking over the world he just, like, wrestles people smaller than him."

"Yeah, it's all good."

"Well, it's about time to wrap up here, right? I overheard Mike saying the electrician was going to have to shut off the power and stuff. I was thinking about stopping by Sacky's for a beer, if you're interested. We can trade Dicky Birk secrets. Well, okay, I don't have that many, but I could make some up. I'm a decent storyteller. I DMed my high school's D&D club for two years." Monty said, and then visibly cringed. "God, okay, anyway… Sacky's?"

His smile looked so hopeful it actually hurt Wade's heart. He did not want to go get a beer and discuss Dicky Birk. In fact, he didn't really want to get a beer at all. But it didn't matter, because he was going to go to Sacky's, and he was going to drink a beer, because all he really wanted at that moment was to make Monty happy.

"Sure, Monty."

CHAPTER 6

Sacky's was busier than it usually was mid-week. Monty tried not to go out drinking too often, partly because he was broke, but mostly because wrestling after drinking was just as bad as it sounds. But he had the day off tomorrow. He had tentative plans to clean his apartment and maybe create an account on a dating app just to meet people. And even if he didn't invite anyone over, he should probably make some friends other than Aaron.

Wade looked overwhelmed when they walked in and that was the exact opposite of the good vibe Monty was hoping to bring when he invited Wade out. Maybe Wade wasn't super social, or maybe he didn't drink. He didn't think to ask if bars made him uncomfortable or if there was somewhere else he'd rather go. In an effort to prevent an anxiety spiral, Monty headed straight for the bar and ordered the cheapest beer they had on tap.

"Also, whatever he's having. Put it on my tab?" Monty said.

"I'll have the same," Wade told the bartender and turned to Monty. "Thanks. I'll get it next time."

Monty's chest warmed at the indication there would be a next time. Then he remembered people just say things sometimes, and reminded himself to take tonight one step at a time.

There weren't any tables open, so they each took a stool at the bar, which was a tight fit for Monty even when he wasn't sitting next to someone of a similar size. Their arms brushed against each other as they settled into their seats and then their thighs pressed together. Wade was warm and firm. Monty took a deep breath.

"Cozy," he said, eyes crinkling. "So… Dicky sucks, huh?"

Wade barked out a laugh and it made Monty feel a little dizzy. Making him laugh felt like an achievement, and he wanted to do it again.

"I'm just kidding. I'm sure he's a great wrestler. Well, I mean, I know he is. But yikes, right? Poor Will. I hope his neck is okay."

"Will is fine. He's used to being flung around the ring. I actually thought they'd work well together because Dicky needs someone to help him chill out. I guess that didn't work out too well…" Wade said, picking at a damp coaster.

"Ha! Yeah, I guess not."

Wade was quiet, but he surprised Monty when he picked up his beer and extended his glass towards him in a silent request for a cheers.

"To new beginnings?" Monty said, and Wade tapped his glass against Monty's.

They talked for a while about Mike and Titan and what it was like in the beginning. Wade seemed happy to share his stories from when he was still green and Titan was just getting off the ground. He told Monty about how the first time he met Mike he tried throwing him with a snap down, but Mike saw it coming a mile away and pinned him so quickly he wasn't even sure what happened. Monty laughed so much at Wade's version of the story he got beer up his nose.

"Maybe you guys can reenact it for the group," Monty said.

"That would give Dicky too much ammo for my taste."

"Ah, forget Dicky." Monty waved his hand. "Like I said, that dude sucks."

"That's true," Wade said, the corners of his mouth curling into a hint of a smile. Monty made a mental tally—two smiles in one fifteen-minute conversation.

"So, you really did choose all the teams this year? I dunno why I kind of thought you were kidding before."

"Yeah, I've been doing it for a couple of years now. I think Mike gave me that job after Larry left so I felt a little more useful. When he left I kind of… I don't know, lost my way a little bit."

"Oh, yeah. That makes sense," Monty said, kicking himself. He was trying to set up an opening to discuss their new, blossoming professional relationship, and instead, he reminded Wade of his old, ruined professional relationship. "But you seem to be doing okay now, right? Mike seems to think you're the bee's knees."

Wade nodded. "I guess so, yeah. We're pretty close. I go to his house for Thanksgiving every year. It used to be Larry and me, but you know."

"Larry isn't invited anymore?" Monty asked. "Why?"

"Larry isn't invited anymore." Wade laughed awkwardly. Monty did not count that one on his Wade Smiling tally stick. "Mike kind of decided the way Larry handled the breakup wasn't worthy of an ongoing invite. Well, at least after I finally told Mike the truth behind the breakup, which took me a while."

"The breakup? Like when he left Titan?"

"That, yeah. But Larry was also my boyfriend for five years. It's not a secret or anything. It just wasn't something we shared much at the time. He broke up with me when he left Titan."

Monty's eyes widened. "I'm sorry, you and Larry were together for *five years*? Wait, you're *gay*?"

"Well, last I checked." Wade smiled. "I mean, I guess Viper isn't gay, so maybe that's why you didn't know. But it's not really a secret that I date men."

"Oh. That makes sense. Yeah, I remember that match with you and Limpet years back, the one where you brought your girlfriends to the locker room and had to fight Giant Jim and what's-his-name because they touched your 'women.'" Monty laughed. "Man, this is a funny job, huh?"

Wade chuckled. "I suppose it is."

"Was that weird? Working with Larry when you were dating, and putting on an act with other people? Like, character girlfriends and stuff?"

"That part was okay. The part where he left me in real life was harder," Wade said.

Monty wasn't sure if he should laugh, so he didn't.

"Sorry, bad joke. We were together for a long time. We broke up when he moved away. He didn't ask me to come with him and made some comments that made it pretty clear he wasn't planning on asking me to, so…"

"Oh. I'm sorry," Monty said, taking a sip of his beer to buy time until he thought of something to say. "I'm sorry to hear that. I followed you guys for years and never knew. I don't think anybody knew, and I don't think he's said anything since he got to CWA."

That seemed to be the wrong thing to say because their conversation hit a lull. And that was disappointing, because Wade being gay opened up a whole world of possibilities – ones he hadn't let himself consider beyond his own fantasies, but that he really wanted to explore. But Wade didn't look at Monty again. Instead, he took a sip of his beer and took his phone out, swiping to a waiting text message. It was a photo of a cute baby. Wade tapped back a quick note and put his phone back in his pocket.

"Cute baby," Monty said, and then flushed. "Sorry for peeking."

"Ah, thanks. That's Gavin, he's my best friend's baby."

Monty raised his hand to order another beer. When the bartender looked at Wade, Wade shook his head. An awkward length of time passed and neither of them spoke.

"I'm sorry," Monty finally said.

"Hmm?"

"I made things awkward by bringing up Larry, right? Or whatever I said, who even knows at this point. I won't mention Larry again, though. I'm sorry."

"You don't need to apologize for any of that, Monty. You're great. This has been great. I'm just in a bad mood tonight." Wade pressed his thigh against Monty's assuringly. "You know, if it's okay with you, I think I'm going to head out. Thank you for the beer. I'll get yours next time."

"Okay."

Wade started to turn in his stool, but stopped himself and said, "Hey, do you want to meet at the arena this week to practice one-on-one? I can reserve the ring so we can take our time."

"Yeah! I—Yes. I would like to do that." Monty was surprised and excited, but was pretty sure he played it cool. "Let me know when. You can text me. Or call. Or let me know at the arena or whatever. I'm not picky."

"Okay," Wade said, smiling again.

That made *four* smiles. He was calling it a success.

"Goodnight, Monty."

"Bye!"

Wade leaned into Monty to get off of his stool. Monty steadied him with his hands, enjoying the feel of Wade's brawny arms. They held each other's gazes for a moment until Wade turned around. Monty watched Wade leave, already missing the feel of his warm body pressed against his own.

After another beer and chat with the bartender, Monty closed out his tab and headed out. The night was surprisingly cool, so he buttoned up his flannel that now smelled like Wade, and headed upstairs to his apartment.

He had a pleasant buzz going and let his mind drift to things he liked about the evening they'd shared, like Wade's willingness to join him for a beer after a long day. And his openness about his relationships with Larry and Mike. His reassurance when Monty felt like he had embarrassed himself. His heavy thigh pressed against his own. Those strong hands picking at a coaster.

Then he thought of the same strong hands picking him up and maneuvering him at practice. That led to thoughts of those strong hands being used gently on his face and body, touching his bare skin. Unbuttoning his shirt and feeling his chest and stomach. Maybe those hands would make their way lower, tentatively brushing the top of his jeans. A few fingers might slip inside the waistband, feeling Monty's skin. He could use those fingers to pull Monty's hips closer, and then he might feel Wade's lips on his jaw and neck.

Monty shook his head of the thoughts, grinning, and tried to conjure up more innocent fantasies. It didn't work, but Monty had arrived home, so he headed to the bathroom and turned on the shower. Once the water was warm, he stripped down and stepped into the shower, closed his eyes, and felt his way down his body to get Wade out of his system.

CHAPTER 7

Wade and Niall had just finished a tag team match in Salem against two local wrestlers. Their presence was supposed to drum up hype for the local indie promotion. It was also intended to introduce Wade's heel character to a wider audience. It did both successfully.

The small arena had sold out, and Wade even signed a couple autographs for the first time in a while. The night was fun, but Wade was exhausted and needed a coffee for the road, so he and Niall stopped by a gas station. He sat in the car after making his purchase and watched Niall through the window. He appeared to have been roped into a conversation with a few guys inside, so he FaceTimed Madeline.

"I need help," Wade said into the phone, happy that she was around and willing to talk.

"Of course. What's up? Oh my god, hold on." Madeline's face disappeared from the screen. Wade heard rustling and screaming— she had three kids now, which seemed absurd to Wade. A kid or two, sure, but *three?*

He loved her kids, though. He knew he wanted to be a dad someday. He didn't have a great relationship with his parents anymore. They spoke rarely and hadn't seen each other in months, and Wade was positive he could be a better parent than that.

Larry had always put off the kid conversation, and whenever they hung out with Madeline and her husband, Kenny, he was grumpy and seemed put out by their kids' presence. But he didn't want to think about Larry right now, so he held the phone up to get a look at what was going on and buckled his seatbelt.

"I swear to God, Wade, I am going to pull my hair out. Your niece and nephew took all my makeup out and gave each other makeovers —and by the way, they were supposed to be in bed two hours ago. I hope Gavin takes after you," she said, hoisting her newest addition up so his face was visible on the screen, too. He was so cute and so round.

"Not your husband?" Wade grinned at the phone.

"God, no. I mean, Kenny is great. But what if little Gavin took after his uncle Wade? Strong, kind, quiet… not currently at work, leaving me to fend for myself…"

"Should I call back?"

"No! I want to help. Help with what? Help with your Romeo?" Madeline ribbed.

"I guess… although, to be clear, it is still platonic, and should still stay that way."

"Why?"

"Well, I don't know. A few reasons. At the arena earlier this week, we practiced together and things went really well. He's the perfect competitor. But we went to watch a couple of the other guys fight and I had to break it up a bit. You know how it goes."

"I do. Very sexy. Continue," she said, smiling.

"This guy Dicky got aggressive, and when I jumped into the ring, he sort of laid into me about being pathetic. He called me a 'Jeremy Blaze' and said I only have a job because Mike and I are close. Monty has asked twice now if I'm the one that paired us together and asked about my relationship with Mike, and… I don't know. I'm feeling a little insecure, like maybe Monty is using me to get closer to Mike?"

"Why would he do that? He already got hired there."

"Well, I know, but—"

"How much of this has to do with Monty and how much of it is your own insecurity? I know you and Mike talked the other day. Did he give you any indication that your job wasn't safe?"

"No. In fact, he's turning me heel to give me a fresh angle. And you know he's sort of training me to take over some day, if I don't make it any further."

Madeline hummed quietly, her eyebrows knitted together. Wade had to look away. He hated feeling like Madeline pitied him.

"Okay, well, that's good. And would you be this concerned about being used if you were working with someone other than Monty?"

"I guess not? I don't know. I haven't cared this much about anything in a while, really, and the only change has been Monty. So, take that as you will."

"Uh huh."

"I'm excited about our upcoming matches. We decided on key moves to showcase for the scouts and it all looks pretty sick. I'm ending with a new finisher. I think if I land it right, it'll be awesome."

Madeline smiled at the phone again. "Hear that, Gavvy? Uncle Wade is excited about something! Or someone…" She poked Gavin's cheek, getting him to give a big, gummy smile at the phone. Wade smiled back.

"I just want Monty, well, I mean, all the guys, to see me for me, not as Larry's aging ex-partner or Mike's charity case who can help them schmooze. I have so much baggage. It just seems impossible to be taken seriously."

"Okay, Drama King. So the new guy got under your skin. He sucks. He's probably trying to take down the toughest guy at Titan so everyone is afraid of him. Like prison, you know? Isn't that what they say?"

"Um, sure."

"Listen. Monty seems nice based on everything you've said about him. It doesn't seem like he's the type of guy who would pick fights to get ahead, or employ some convoluted plan to get into Mike's good graces. Especially if hurting you would make Mike angry."

"He said Gavin was cute."

"Of course he did. Did you show him lots of photos?"

"No. He saw the one you sent when he and I were having a beer and said he was cute. I said he was my best friend's kid and then that was it."

"That was it?"

"Yeah, then he apologized for being weird. I told him I had to go. And that was about it."

"Good God, Wade." Madeline rubbed her free hand down her face. "You let him think it was weird for him to call a baby cute? When are you seeing him next?"

"He wasn't weird, and it wasn't about Gavin. I told him I was gay and that Larry and I were together for a while. He asked me about it and felt bad, I think. I will see him next week sometime. Probably Tuesday."

"Okay. Text him and tell him you had fun with him and that you look forward to seeing him on Tuesday."

"Wouldn't that be weird if I sent it like, days later?"

"I don't think so. Poor guy is probably at home thinking he fucked up with you."

"Fucked up *with me?* I don't think so."

Madeline groaned. "Just… text him, Wade. I really have to go now. Things are suspiciously quiet. Let me know how it goes."

"I will. Say goodnight to the kids for me."

Wade hung up and read through the messages Monty sent when they first met. He smiled at the message string and typed out a note.

> Hi Monty.Thank you again for the beer. I'm sorry I wasn't better company. See you Tuesday?

> of course!! It was really nice to see you outside of the arena.

> always nice to relax after work.

> this is to say, yes, see you at 2pm Tuesday. omg. sorry for being weird - again.

Wade decided to be brave by responding again. He sent off his reply right as Niall slid into his seat.

> I like weird. ☺

"Damn, those guys would not shut up. They claim they used to fight with Mike, but I'm pretty sure they're lying." Niall put the key in the ignition and started the car. "I'm gonna ask Mike, though. Otherwise that's just like, stolen valor. Some of us really do have to get beat up by Mike."

Wade laughed at Niall, but made the mistake of laughing while looking at his phone.

"Who are you texting over there? Why do you look happy?"

"Don't worry about it." He turned his screen off and put the phone screen down on his lap so he wouldn't be tempted to look for a reply on his drive home.

CHAPTER 8

MONTY WAS CURLED UP BENEATH THE RING AT TITAN ARENA CLUTCHING a garbage bag of stale popcorn. His hiding spot was dark and weirdly damp, and it smelled so rank his nostrils burned. He wasn't sure if it had ever been cleaned, based on the layers of dust and cobwebs. He made a mental note to talk to Mike about it if he survived.

After weeks of training and watching small matches, Mike was finally debuting Romeo in his first official match with Titan. It was a low-stakes charity event where kids voted for which four wrestlers would compete in the headlining match. He was chosen, along with Wade, Dicky, and another long-time Titan wrestler named Anthony. The match was a combination "over-the-ropes" and submission match, which meant the only ways to win would be to get their opponents over the ropes or force them to submit. The winner would be awarded a special belt designed by the kids who spent time at a local children's nonprofit.

His nerves were shot with the anticipation of debuting with Titan. He'd wrestled long enough that he knew what he was doing, but his promotion in Boise was so small. He made thirty dollars a match and performed in front of a few dozen people. Titan was a lot bigger. The arena held thousands of people, and according to Mike, the charity event was one of their biggest nights of the year.

He'd been underneath the ring for over an hour. He ate popcorn nervously, which was a terrible idea both because it was stale, and he was about to wrestle three men, but he couldn't stop himself. He tried to focus on other things, and when his attention wasn't broken up by the violence above him, he imagined various outcomes of his imminent debut.

His latest daydream, a fun one where he and Wade went out after the match, was interrupted when he saw the lights go dim through the fabric of the ring curtain. His heart picked up and the lights flashed, and the sour smell of the floor was replaced with a suffocating cloud of pyrotechnic smoke. Finally, he heard the sound of the music signaling the start of the match. The crowd cheered when the other three wrestlers came in from various parts of the arena.

The ring shook and he felt the weight of the other men rattle the springs directly above his head. He knew the plan was for Viper to get taken down by Anthony and Dicky immediately to allow them to wrestle each other, and he listened to the footsteps and body slams, trying to figure out where they each were. He closed his eyes and breathed deeply while he waited to start.

"I don't know, Junior! Mr. Palazzo said we were supposed to have four wrestlers here, and I only see three! Where is Romeo? I have Romeo written down here!" Titan's announcers, Junior and Rex, yelled about how there were supposed to be four wrestlers.

That was his cue. Romeo rolled out from under the ring, dragging his popcorn bag behind him. He was wearing a feather lined cape and a masquerade mask and he ripped both off as soon as he left his hiding spot, throwing them to a hired manager who stood on the mats. Romeo jumped to the apron before launching himself through the ropes.

"There he is, Junior! Titan's newest powerhouse – Romeo! Mr. Palazzo said he's top talent – we gotta keep our eye on this one, cause when he steps into that ring, you'd better believe they're gonna get what's coming to them," Rex said.

It hyped Monty up in a way he hadn't expected. He bit back a smile and glared at Anthony and Dicky.

Romeo did a double arm clothesline against them and they both fell to the ground. Dicky flipped over, his legs ending up on the ropes, and Anthony bounced wildly, rolling all the way out of the ring, onto the ground.

Before the match, Wade told Monty whenever they did these charity matches the wrestlers would oversell their moves, flinging their bodies dramatically and acting angrier than usual. The kids loved it, but it was ridiculous to witness up close.

Dicky climbed up on the ropes and sat on the top, allowing Romeo to make quick work of him. He used Dicky's top-rope perch to dropkick him out of the ring.

Anthony was next. He'd climbed back into the ring, allowing Romeo to toss him backwards after an elaborate chokehold that involved holding him several feet above the ground for five full seconds. Romeo's arms were shaking and his hair was plastered to his face with sweat, but he managed to throw Anthony onto the mats below the ring.

The audience cheered when they realized it was down to Romeo and Viper. Monty felt effervescent, ignited by the crowd.

"I can't believe how quickly Romeo took care of those guys, Rex! What are we witnessing here?! Will Viper be next?" The ring announcers were yelling back and forth, getting the audience excited about Romeo.

"Viper looks exhausted, Junior, I'm a little worried. Will this new young talent be too much for him to handle?"

Viper had been sitting in the corner catching his breath, which was never because a wrestler needed the rest, and always so the fans and cameras could focus on another part of the match. When Anthony and Dicky were thrown from the ring, Viper jumped up from his sitting position and stalked towards Romeo. His eyes were narrow and his brows were furrowed and he honestly looked terrifying. They locked eyes and circled each other.

Viper launched himself off the ropes and flew at Romeo. He clotheslined him and Romeo ended up on the ground. Romeo crawled towards his popcorn bag, much to the delight of the kids in the audience. When he reached it, he stood up and held it above his head. Kids were screaming and he saw Mike laughing at the announcer table. He used both hands to swing the popcorn bag at

Viper's face and it connected, immediately exploding and launching popcorn all over the ring. It took everything in him not to laugh before he leapt at Viper and tackled him, flipping him onto his back.

After several more minutes of wrestling, most of which was on top of popcorn, Viper gained the upper hand for the final time. He tied Romeo up in a sharpshooter, a submission hold designed to force an opponent to tap out and forfeit the match. It was painful, too, compressing Romeo's lower back. He screamed on the canvas.

"Romeo's back is breaking! His back is breaking!" Junior yelled. He ripped his microphone off. "Viper is going to kill him if he doesn't stop!"

At that, Romeo collapsed on the canvas and tapped out in submission. The ref hopped into the ring and held Viper's hand above his head, naming him the winner of the match. The audience was cheering and Viper put his foot on Romeo's back in a tacky display of domination. Monty just stayed on the ground with his eyes closed, soaking in the experience of his first real match.

"That was unreal, Junior! I think Romeo got popcorn all the way up to the nosebleeds. A great victory by Viper, wiping that smug smile off Romeo's face. But Viper better watch out, because I don't think Romeo will take too kindly to being taken down at his own debut."

Monty squeezed the water out of his hair as he walked into the locker room, expecting to see the guys ready to congratulate him on his debut. Instead, he found it empty. It wasn't surprising, considering he'd been the last one backstage and had to chat with Mike after the match. That was plenty of time for everyone else to take off.

And he hadn't expected a party or anything. He was a grown adult being paid for his work, so he swallowed his disappointment.

He mostly just wanted to hang out with someone, because he was bored, and sick of looking at the walls of his dark, cluttered apartment. He pulled his phone out from his cubby and opened the dating app he'd downloaded on a whim. But he didn't really have time to date if he wanted to focus on work, and it seemed like a lot of work for just a hookup, so he gave up almost immediately.

He heard the door open and he stood to pull his shorts on. He turned and saw Wade, showered and dressed, carrying a small plastic box. It looked like Tupperware.

"Knock, knock," Wade said.

"Wade! Hey! I thought you'd left."

"I did, for a minute. But I'm back now," he said, lifting the box.

"Oh, well, welcome back! I think everyone else left, though, so…"

"Yeah, they're all waiting for you at Sacky's. I offered to come get you because nobody remembered to tell you. Oops." Wade smiled.

Monty didn't know what to say, and was a little afraid he was going to cry, so busied himself with packing his bag.

"Thank you for coming to get me. That was nice of you. I probably would have figured it out anyway. Maybe. But still, very nice of you."

"No problem," Wade said. He looked uncharacteristically nervous. "I, um, brought you this. My friend Madeline makes really good desserts, and…"

Monty looked at the container Wade held out. He removed the top, and inside was a dressed baked potato. It was topped with an enormous swirl of sour cream and sprinkled with chopped nuts for some reason. He glanced up at Wade, confused.

"That… is a potato."

"It's not a potato."

"Wade." He approached Wade with his hand outstretched and placed it against his forehead. "I'm a little concerned about you right now. Did you hit your head? What did Anthony do to you while I was under the ring?"

"Stop it," Wade said, laughing. "It's not a potato!"

"How many fingers am I holding up?"

"Oh, my God. It's not a potato! It's a potato cake? I looked up what desserts people eat in Idaho and this was at the top of the list. I assumed you'd know it. That's cocoa powder on the sides there, and that's whipped cream," he said, pointing to the toppings.

"I've never seen one of these in my life," Monty said. He was smiling so much his face hurt. Wade brought him a *cake!* And not only that, he asked his friend to *make it.*

"Well… Then I hope you enjoy learning about your culture. I'm sorry it's been kept from you."

Wade pulled two forks out of his pocket, which Monty thought was a little gross, but he didn't care. He removed a piece of lint and took a bite of the weird potato cake. It was unexpectedly delicious.

"Wow, okay. Idaho food culture is a lot better than I thought," Wade said.

"Well, don't get ahead of yourself."

CHAPTER 9

"I think I'd probably buy a house in, like, Scappoose," Monty said.

He and Kenji, one of Titan's other full-time wrestlers and Anthony's tag-team partner, were discussing what they'd do if they got rich working for CWA. He squatted, holding a medicine ball away from his chest. He threw it at Kenji as he stood up again.

"With land. I want some cows. I don't know much about this area yet, but my aunt lives over there. She likes it."

"Ugh. Not me. I'd buy something in Lake O."

Monty scrunched up his face.

"What?!" Kenji asked. "It's pretty. It's near a lake. What's not to like?"

Monty caught the medicine ball. "Nothing, it's fine. Just not my scene. It's also just hard to live in my stupid apartment, so if I do move, I want something sprawling. My place is so small I can't even get a cat."

"Well, that's all temporary. Once you get your new contract, you can leave your tiny apartment for a bigger one in Boston," Kenji said. He put the medicine ball down and wiped his forehead on a towel. "But you're close to the arena, right?"

"Yeah. I've been able to come here every day since we started. I've sparred with most of the guys and it's been pretty helpful. Have you spent much time in the ring with anyone else?"

They walked over to the treadmills to start their cool-down.

Monty started walking while Kenji got more water. When he returned, he hopped on the treadmill next to Monty and matched his pace.

"I haven't really spent much time with anyone. I should. I got put with Anthony. He's cool, but I don't think he really cares about the next step and it's tough because I really do."

"I get it. He's got a kid, right?" Monty asked.

"Yeah. Something like that. How is it working with Wade?"

"It's good! Yeah, really good. Different than I thought."

"Different how?"

"He's… quiet. I kind of thought he'd be this big, social superstar."

Over the years, he'd watched so many interviews with Viper that he figured he understood Wade's personality, which was stupid. He knew the difference between a wrestler's real life personality and character as much as anyone. But where Viper was loud and outgoing and always hyped up, the real Wade was quiet and phlegmatic. He was hard for Monty to read.

"Huh."

"I mean, it doesn't matter. He's a great partner in the ring. We've been sparring a lot, I think because he wants me to feel comfortable here, which is so sweet of him. Um, I mean, cool of him. He's a good coach, too, he's been helping me with my form on a few things. Oh, and we went out and had a beer last week, and we're still friendly. So, yeah! It's going well."

Kenji paused and gave Monty a knowing look and a subtle smile. "That's good, Monty. I'm glad. Maybe I should try to come more often and see who else I can work with. Anthony and I have a road trip coming up. We're heading to Bellevue for a few days. When I come back, I'll try to spend more time here."

"You should! I'm here a lot. I'd love to fight you."

Kenji left to go to his part time job. Monty couldn't remember what it was, exactly. Something to do with plants. Monty stuck around the arena, hoping to run into Wade. Not for any particular reason, just because he wanted to discuss the final run-through they had planned for the following day. If Wade happened to look hungry when Monty saw him, and he happened to agree to go get some lunch with him, then that would be okay.

He walked down the hall towards the locker room and heard Mike's voice coming from the direction of his office. His feet moved a little faster so he could see if Mike was talking to Wade. They were together a lot. When he reached the front of the arena, he saw Mike leave through the front doors and Wade standing near them, holding an envelope. Wade turned around, and when Monty made eye contact with him, he gave a nod.

"Hi!" Monty said.

"Hey, Monty."

"I was wondering if you wanted to go through the match one more time before tomorrow."

"Oh. I do, but I have to run this to the post office," Wade said, holding the envelope up. "Mike said it's something tax related and is urgent, otherwise I'd be able to."

"Oh, okay. Yeah, no problem!"

"Do you, um, want to come with me? We can discuss the match, if that would be helpful," Wade said.

Monty was sure it would *not* be helpful to discuss the match. They'd talked it to death multiple times, and even practicing it in the ring was unnecessary at this point. But Monty wasn't about to tell Wade he wasn't interested in spending time with him, so he just smiled and said, "Absolutely."

They walked together to Wade's car and climbed in.

"Hey, remember when you almost hit me with your car?"

Wade groaned. "Come on, man."

Monty laughed, and when he buckled his seatbelt, their arms bumped in to each other.

They discussed the upcoming match for a few minutes, but as expected, it was less helpful than Wade had suggested it might have been, so they moved onto other topics on their drive back. It was going well. Monty was being surprisingly cool, and Wade was smiling at his stories and anecdotes.

The story about the time he accidentally broke the ring at his first promotion outside of Boise was a big hit. Monty landed a crossbody on his opponent and when they fell, they landed on a soft spot of the ring. It was rickety even when it was new, and they landed the move just right, so their combined weight broke the ring when they hit the ground. The posts each fell individually and one almost hit Monty. He rolled out of the way before it did, and when the fourth post fell, the entire platform crashed to the ground. Wade was getting such a kick out of it that Monty found a clip of the match on YouTube.

"That's hilarious. It looks like you guys did it on purpose. Maybe you should run that by Mike," Wade said.

Monty turned in his seat to look at Wade. He looked so good in his jeans and white t-shirt, the bright fabric contrasting with his skin in a way that made Monty feel all tingly.

It was tempting to reach over and touch Wade's forearm just to see what it felt like in a more casual setting. Probably firm, he guessed. And warm. But that would have been weird, so he didn't. Instead, he tried to think of something else to say. But Monty had very little going on in his life, so he brought up his apartment, which he was realizing he did pretty often. He made a mental note to think of other things to talk about.

He told Wade about how he took so long to pick out bedding that an employee took pity on him and picked out housewares for him; how the drive home was stressful because he had to tie his trunk shut with flimsy twine, the kind that frays apart, and he just hoped the furniture stayed put; how he nearly backed into his neighbor's car because he was confused about the distance, but fortunately she honked at him before he destroyed his new furniture and her car.

"So then I had to bring everything upstairs on my own. I hadn't really thought it through when I bought a bed frame and TV stand, but fortunately I've got these guns," he said and flexed his biceps. He gave one a kiss, making Wade laugh. "But God, it was so hot that day. On the plus side, I got a friend out of it. I met a nice guy there, Aaron. I told him I could get him tickets to matches at Titan, but then when I got home, I didn't even know if that was true, so I might have to buy them myself. What was I thinking, right? But he said he wanted to come watch me wrestle, so we exchanged numbers, and…"

Wade's eyebrows raised but he looked straight ahead at the road, saying nothing. He watched as Wade's hands gripped the steering wheel a little tighter.

"Um, so anyway, do you know if we get free tickets or anything?" he asked, trying to end the awkward silence.

"You can invite people. Mike can put them on a list."

"Cool, cool. That sounds good." Monty drummed his fingers on his knee.

While it was unclear to Monty what he'd said this time to make Wade uncomfortable, he sure did seem to have a penchant for it. He hated it, but he wasn't sure how to avoid it. He just talked a lot and sometimes said stupid stuff, but usually people were willing to call him out on it. Wade seemed to shut down when he got uncomfortable, and that made Monty nervous, which made him want to talk even more.

He was about to do exactly that, then apologize for saying whatever stupid thing he'd blurted out, but Wade's phone rang and he answered it on speaker. Monty was shocked. He couldn't imagine people listening to him attempt to get through a phone call. He constantly interrupted and talked over people, which made phone conversations with anyone other than his mom difficult. His intention was never to be rude, he was just an impulsive guy who loved to talk. And maybe Wade wasn't a fan of that. If that was the case, it was unlikely Wade was a fan of Monty, and that made him wish for the car ride to be over.

"Wade?" the voice on the other line said.

"Hey. What's up?"

"Hey, I need you at the clinic. Can you swing by? It won't be long, but I have an emergency calving I have to attend."

"A calving? Like… cows?" Wade asked.

Monty was confused, but also very interested in this new information. He would like to see a cow.

"Yeah, I'm trying to get more experience with large animals."

"Wow, okay. News to me."

The voice on the other end chuckled. "I'll fill you in soon. Can you come by?"

"I'm on my way," he said. He turned to Monty. "I'm sorry to do this. Do you have like half an hour to spare? We're close to the vet clinic where I volunteer, and it sounds like they need me for something. If that's going to put you out, I can get you back first."

"No, yeah, for sure! I'm all yours," Monty said. He sighed and then blushed slightly and turned to look out the window and waved his hand towards Wade. "Sorry. You know what I mean." Monty looked over without moving his head and saw the briefest smile appear on Wade's lips.

"Sure."

∾

ON THE DRIVE to the clinic, tensions between them simmered. Wade felt stupid for clamming up when Monty mentioned his new friend. He wasn't great at handling unpleasant emotions, and he was struggling with the emotional roller coaster of his developing crush on Monty and the reality of their futures. They couldn't be together, not the way he would want to be, but it still sucked to hear Monty talk about someone who probably used "watch him wrestle" as code for "wrestle him naked."

He told Monty about studying for the wildlife rehab certification and all that went with it, like the opossums he found, and how the mother had been hit by a car but the baby was strong and healthy. He did *not* tell Monty he named the baby Juliet, something he was now deeply regretting, because every second in the car brought them closer and closer to that embarrassing truth.

"We were optimistic about the mom's health after a day or two because she really rallied. She had a broken leg so she wasn't very mobile, but we didn't realize how lethargic she was…" Wade said.

"Oh, that's so sad. Is she okay now?"

"Well, no. She passed away a few days ago. Her problems were more severe than Linda realized, so the mom was euthanized." Suddenly worried Monty would think he and Linda were monsters, Wade added, "It was kinder than letting her suffer!"

"I believe you. I've had a lot of animals in my life."

"Right," he said, relieved. "Anyway, that means the baby needs a surrogate parent."

"And that's you?"

"Well, and Linda. I've been helping, though."

They pulled into a spot near the entrance of Linda's clinic. Wade hopped out and rushed to open the front door, letting Monty walk in before him. The door chimed when they entered, prompting Camila to look up from her computer. She glanced at Monty and opened her eyes wide while looking at Wade, silently communicating she thought Monty was cute. He glared at her, silently communicating she should fuck off.

"Hey Wade," she said, smiling at him. "You can go on back. Dr. Palazzo is waiting for you."

Wade nodded and pushed his way through the door part way when he realized Monty wasn't following. He looked around and noticed him hovering by a chair with his fingers interlocked and a sweet look on his face.

"You can come back with me," he said.

"Oh! Okay, I wasn't sure. Didn't want to intrude. Or like, scare a baby opossum." Monty hurried over and walked through the swinging door Wade was holding open with his foot.

"Hey, come on back!" Linda called from behind a portable curtain. She poked her head out.

"Hi, Linda."

Monty smiled at Linda and waved before looking at Wade for an introduction.

"Monty, this is Linda, Mike's wife. She's the vet overseeing my wildlife stuff. Linda, this is Monty."

"Ohh, *you're* Monty?" she asked, emerging fully from behind the curtain with an opossum in her hands, the baby's tail wrapping around her wrist. She was using a small syringe to feed her. "I've heard–"

"She still needs to eat gruel?" Wade asked, louder than he meant to, but desperate to cut her off.

"Not for every meal. We can switch to kibble mix pretty soon, I'd say."

"Baby opossums don't suckle like other mammals so they can't drink from a bottle," Wade said to Monty as he took the baby from Linda's hands to finish the feeding. "We had to tube feed her at first, now she's eating slop. But soon she'll be on big opossum food. Their diet is hard to get right when they're super small, so Linda likes to keep them on formula for a while. Otherwise they can develop metabolic…"

He realized Monty wasn't listening to his boring speech about opossum diets when he looked over and watched Monty's face shift from curiosity to something he couldn't quite name. Monty's face went soft and dreamy and his mouth opened like he wanted to say something. He placed his hands to his mouth and made a weird squeak.

"That is the cutest thing I have ever seen in my *entire life*," Monty whispered. "Can I touch her?"

Wade nodded. Monty reached out and stroked the opossum's head gently with a single finger. She turned her head around and sniffed his thumb. She settled down then, and the combination of the warm towel, a full belly, and gentle touch eased Juliet into a deep sleep.

He heard Monty gasp quietly and looked at him, noticing his eyes were sparkly and wide. Wade swallowed hard and felt knots of dread in his stomach forming as feelings of tenderness fluttered within him. No, it was more than tenderness. He wasn't just fond of Monty anymore, he was… *infatuated* with him. His heart started beating a little faster, and his thoughts became fuzzy and jumbled. He heard Linda's voice in his periphery, but didn't register what she said.

"Wade?" she repeated.

He looked up at her and cleared his throat. "Yeah. Sorry, what's up?"

"I said I have to get going. Can you handle her?" she said, pointing at Juliet.

"Yes. We can," he said.

Monty beamed at him.

"Okay. Remember, every four hours, and keep her warm. Call me if anything happens, but you know what you're doing. Thank you, guys. Nice to meet you, Monty."

"Nice to meet you too! Thanks for letting me crash the opossum party. Sorry I got a little emotional. She is just so precious!"

Wade gritted his teeth.

Linda smiled at Monty before she grabbed her stuff and shouted her goodbyes before rushing out of the back room. Wade and Monty stood together, holding the baby opossum between them. Monty reached his finger out again at the same time Wade reached his out and they bumped fingertips on top of her.

Monty let out an honest to God giggle and whispered, "Sorry."

Wade looked around for a closet to lock himself in until these feelings passed.

He handed Juliet to Monty so he could pack up all the sterile supplies he needed, then moved Monty's hands into the best position to hold her. He used all of his emotional strength to remove his hands from Monty's.

Wade tortured himself by watching the two of them out of the corner of his eye. There was no way to deny his feelings, and he was so mad it wasn't a fluke or a fleeting panic attack that had overwhelmed him earlier. He kicked himself for letting this happen.

"We can keep her in the cat carrier I have in my car."

"Okay," Monty said, still cradling the opossum to his chest. Wade set a timer on his phone for four hours. They walked at a snail's pace to his car, Monty stepping gently, refusing to jostle Juliet.

"You won't break her," Wade said. "They travel for miles hanging onto their mom's backs, using just those tiny hands to grip the fur."

"She's just so innocent. I would never forgive myself if she got scared. This is more for me than her, I swear."

Monty placed the baby inside the cat carrier and covered her up with a towel. The only visible part of Juliet was the tip of her tail, and Wade watched as Monty stroked it gently. Juliet's toes twitched and Monty made an adorable whimpering noise that flooded Wade's body with inappropriate feelings and made his blood flow to inappropriate body parts. He bit his lip and cursed under his breath quietly enough that Monty didn't hear.

"You can put this little heating pad in there with her," Wade said, tossing it to Monty after he'd settled in his seat.

Monty set up the heating pad, then poked his finger through the door, letting it rest on Juliet's tail.

On the walk around the car to the driver's seat, Wade blew out a breath.

"You really like her, huh?" Wade said, settling into the driver's seat, trying to cut the one-sided tension. Monty seemed unaware of Wade's inner turmoil, which wasn't helped by the way Monty was interacting with Juliet. It was almost painful to be around.

"I'm not kidding when I say I have never seen something cuter than this in my entire life. And my parents have piglets sometimes! And donkeys. And other stuff, like chickens and turkeys, but those don't really like me. Not that I've ever done anything to them other than take their eggs, which I sometimes cook up for them, by the way. But yeah, this baby opossum? She surpasses all of them."

This was awful. Wade chewed the inside of his cheek to stop himself from saying something he'd regret, like, *"can I hold your hand?"* or *"do you want to move in with me and raise this opossum together for the next decade?"*

He had to figure out how to get some space.

"I have to go back to the arena for a while to do some stuff for Mike. I can drop you off if you want," he said.

There. That should work.

"Oh, yeah, that's fine. I live right next to the arena, anyway. Do you need help with anything? Oh, I can watch her while you work!" Monty rubbed his finger over Juliet's tail again, then looked over at Wade with his stupid eyes shining. "I'm being so rude to her, right? She's probably like, 'who is this clown? Stop touching me, I'm trying to sleep.'"

Wade's resolve lasted about four seconds before he said, "Help while I work sounds great, thank you."

But it was not great. Not if he wanted to create some much-needed space between them. But Monty seemed to really like Juliet and splitting them up felt… mean. And it was just one day. That wouldn't make things more intense for Wade than they already were. He could handle this.

When they got to the arena, Wade set Monty and Juliet up in Mike's office and sent Linda a text letting her know the baby was in good hands. He closed the office door to give Monty privacy, not that he requested it, or needed it, and knowing Monty, he probably didn't even want it. But Wade needed time to think by himself without being distracted by Monty's gorgeous face and heart-melting fondness for infant marsupials.

He busied himself with improvements around the arena: tightening the turnbuckles and ropes under the ring, wiping down the mats, recoiling in horror at their filth, placing an order for new ones. The entire time, he was trying to figure out how to spend less time with Monty while still being able to practice and stick to the regional trip schedules where he and Monty would be interacting. When he couldn't think of any solutions and also couldn't think of anything else to do, he pulled his phone out to send Madeline a message.

> Monty with the baby opossum is awful. He's here babysitting while I work. Please remind me occasionally that CWA contracts are the goal, not dating coworkers, otherwise I'll do something really stupid.

> Babysitting an opossum?? Send pictures

> No. Thanks for the help.

WADE JUMPED when he heard the office door close behind him. He shoved his phone in his pocket and turned around. He saw Monty walking towards him, cat carrier held to his chest, face bright and sunny for no reason other than he was just a bright and sunny guy.

"I've been thinking. I think we should name this little gal," Monty said. "I came up with a few ideas while you worked, and here are my thoughts. We've got Curly, because of her tail; Scales, because of her tail, and it kind of works on two levels, because you're Viper; Flicker, because I just think it's cute; and Opie, because I saw an opossum online named Opie and I liked it. I looked it up, and that's the most popular name for opossums. I don't know if you want something less common. Classics are classic for a reason, though."

"Those are all great," Wade said.

Monty looked proud and Wade groaned internally.

"And... I would agree with any of them if she wasn't already named."

"Oh! She already has a name? Of course she does. Duh, Monty! Sorry, I wasn't sure if you named the rehabbed animals."

"Oh, yeah, I hadn't mentioned it. We named her, um, Juliet," he said, diluting the reality.

"Juliet?! Oh, my God! This is like, meant to be," Monty said. He lifted the cat carrier to eye level and peered in. "Hello Juliet, I'm

Romeo!" She didn't acknowledge him in any way, but Monty didn't seem to mind.

"She's going to need to eat soon, so I'd rather not go home right now. But I'm done working, so you can leave. If you want."

"Oh, yeah! Okay. I can go. Unless you need help?" Monty said, his face hopeful. "No pressure, obviously."

"Oh, we'll be okay. Thank you. I'm gonna feed her and just go home and do some… stuff. I've been putting it off," Wade said. He was lying, kind of. He was just going to go home and spiral about his feelings, but he *had* been avoiding that, so it wasn't a total lie.

"Oh! Totally. Yeah, I should probably clean my apartment. I got an app that makes me keep up with chores or my virtual pet will die. Risky." He handed the cat carrier to Wade and stood there for a moment before bending at the waist to look in at Juliet. His face grew serious. "I would do so many chores to keep you alive, Juliet."

"I guess I'll see you tomorrow? We're on for practice, right?" Wade said. "I think most of the guys are out of town, so we should have the arena to ourselves."

"Yes, we're definitely on! I'll see you here at two?"

"Sounds good. Thanks for your help, Monty."

"I have never had a more enjoyable afternoon. And she slept literally the entire time," Monty sighed and the dreamy look returned to his face. "Well, anyway, goodnight! See you tomorrow."

Wade closed the office door behind Monty and locked it. He took Juliet out of the carrier and grabbed the feeding supplies he'd brought. He gave her dinner while he quietly sang the meal time song he'd made up for her:

> *'Possum in the moonlight, munching on a bean*
> *Baby Juliet, you love your trash cuisine*

Juliet closed her eyes. Wade stroked her head and thought about Monty's unnecessary offer to stay. He wished he had asked him to.

"We are so screwed, Juliet."

CHAPTER 10

THE ARENA LIGHTS WERE OFF WHEN MONTY ARRIVED, SO HE SET HIS STUFF down and flipped the switch. The room lit up easily, so whatever the electrician had done helped. He headed to the kitchen to start a pot of coffee and fill his water bottle, trying to keep his mind and hands busy while he waited for Wade.

He wasn't sure why he was so nervous about today. They had each practiced these moves thousands of times, and Monty had been in a few real matches at this point. He even got to go on a short road trip to Bend, Oregon. It was all stuff they'd done before. Professional wrestling at its core was predictable in its routines and steps, and most matches followed a basic formula, adjusted to keep fans on their toes.

The art of the sport was more fluid, and that's where he lacked some confidence. He'd never needed to perform for such a high caliber audience while being such a new face.

It's not that he expected the scout match to be the jumping point for his CWA career, but it *was* a possibility, and that was a lot of pressure. He mostly didn't want to destroy Wade's chances, because he'd heard rumblings that Wade was saying this was his last shot to make it into CWA. He supposed the nerves he was feeling were because Wade had a lot riding on this, and Monty had a lot of opportunity to fuck it all up.

That aside, he couldn't wait to spend time with Wade. They'd had a couple fun days together so far, not that it had resulted in anything. Sure, they were platonic engagements on the surface, but there was something about the tight squeeze of the barstools, the care of a homemade gift, and the domesticity of caring from a helpless baby animal that made Monty feel optimistic. He was a hopeless romantic, but even someone like Wade couldn't deny their growing connection.

Not that he would never share these thoughts with anyone, of course. Especially not Wade. He just felt like things had changed after spending more time together, and he was cautiously optimistic about the potential of their relationship. Like it could be more someday. If he played his cards right.

While he waited for the coffee to finish brewing, he flipped through the notebook he took notes on the previous day. The routine they were going to practice was deceptively simple. It didn't look too flashy, but the scouts would know the level of skill required. During the match, they'd each take the lead a time or two, attempting to mislead the audience. Monty would eventually signal the end of the match by landing a crossbody on Wade, who would then put Monty in a chokehold. He would kick out, and while he recovered, Wade would climb onto the turnbuckle and launch his finisher, a shooting star press, ending the match between them. Adding a mix of spots through the match, Monty was feeling pretty good.

The coffee was finally done, so Monty headed to the locker room, whistling and putting his stuff away. He stopped to take a look in the mirror, making sure he looked his best. His go-to uniform was black sweats, his old mid-calf wrestling boots, and a white t-shirt, but it felt wrong. He tugged on the shirt, frowning, and at the last minute, he opted for the fitted tank top and leggings he brought. At their earlier rehearsals, Wade's fingers got tangled in his sleeves, and his feet got tangled in Monty's baggy sweats.

As Monty stripped off his shirt, he heard the doors to the locker room open. He turned around to greet Wade, whose eyes darted to Monty's chest, then drifted up to his face. Wade's cheeks flushed visibly enough that Monty could see it from across the room.

"Oh. Hi."

"Like what you see?" Monty joked as he put the tank top over his head and pulled it down.

Wade laughed and shook his head, looking down at his feet. "I - sorry. I didn't mean to walk in on you."

"Wade. It's a locker room," Monty smiled. "Nude dudes are just part of the deal "

"Okay, well, you weren't *nude*."

"Maybe I just wasn't nude *yet*," he replied. "Okay, no. I wasn't going to get nude. In fact, just the opposite. I'm fully dressed and ready to go."

He noticed Wade had arrived in the locker room wearing his own leggings, boots, and tank top, and worked hard to convince himself their matching outfits were not a sign of anything. Like a telepathic connection reserved for soulmates, for example.

"Let me just put my stuff in my locker," Wade said. He walked by Monty and the smell of him lingered in the air. He smelled like cereal. Froot Loops, maybe?

"Did you have cereal for lunch?" Monty asked.

"What?"

"Cereal? You smell like Froot Loops."

"Impressive nose, Mr. Hill," Wade said, smiling. "The sugar gives me energy. Or something. I need to go wash my hands and then I'll meet you there."

"Wait! I forgot, I brought you something," Monty said. He reached into his cubby and took out a bag of food. He handed it to Wade, hoping the gesture would land.

At one point, Wade had mentioned one of his old pre-match superstitions. He and Larry would eat very specific snacks before every scout match, hoping it would bring them luck. He knew Wade had put little effort into this superstition over the last two years, for obvious reasons, but he got a kick out of learning about it anyway. Whenever Wade mentioned a new food, Monty took note. He hoped it would, on some level, show Wade he believed in him.

"Oh, my God!" Wade said, digging through the bag. "I can't believe you found all this stuff."

"It was no big deal."

Wade held up a jar of pickled herring and grinned at Monty.

"I don't know what that one is all about, but I had to go to a special German market to find it, so you'd better like that kind."

"Thank you," Wade said. "This is… really nice."

Monty smiled. "I thought it might get you back in the zone."

"It's perfect," Wade said, continuing to rummage through the bag with a smile on his face. "Perfect."

"Well. Shall we?" Monty said, gesturing towards the ring.

They left the locker room together and walked closely, their arms brushing against each other in the narrow hallway. Monty leaned into it. Wade slid into the ring under the ropes, and when he reached down to grab Monty's hand to help him up, Monty felt a jolt of frisson. They looked at each other for a moment, the air thick with tension. Monty was afraid to do anything to scare Wade off, so he gave a small, close-lipped smile.

He wanted so badly to be casual, but inside, he was like a reservoir filling with water. Wade's trepidation was a fragile dam, straining under the weight of Monty's growing feelings. If Wade let go, Monty would unleash a flood he may not recover from.

"Well, let's see what you got, Romeo!" Wade said, breaking the tension.

Monty grabbed Wade in a collar-and-elbow and Wade reached his hand around to grip his neck. Their foreheads pressed together, and they slowly spun in a circle as their grips tightened and breaths mingled. Wade broke out first, flying into the ropes in order to launch himself towards Monty. Their collision sent Monty flying before he crumpled into a heap on the canvas.

Monty jumped up and raced towards Wade before bending down and grabbing Wade behind the knees, flipping him to his back. Wade rolled over and tried to crawl away, but Monty grabbed Wade's leg and put him in an ankle lock.

"Ah, Jesus!"

Wade was laughing, so Monty twisted a little harder. Not enough to hurt him, but just enough to make him scream.

"Agh!"

He kicked out of the hold, almost hitting Monty in the face. Monty ran for the ropes, hopping up to the top. He flung his body towards Wade and his weight landed square on Wade's torso, pinning him to the floor of the ring. Monty turned his head to look at Wade. They smiled at each other for a bit. Wade's gaze was heady and potent. The intensity of Monty's feelings ramped up even further and he felt like if he didn't escape Wade's hold, he'd do something stupid, like kiss him.

He stood up slowly and put his hands on his hips. He was breathing hard, both from the physical exertion and the emotional sucker punch he was dealt from their extended eye contact. Wade rolled onto his stomach and launched into a standing position behind Monty and took him down with a single leg foot sweep, breaking his daze. Monty scrambled to sit up, but Wade got behind him and put him in a choke hold, immobilizing him again.

"God, you are way too strong. Get off of me!" Monty yelled.

"Whatever you want!" Wade said. He let go and darted towards the turnbuckle in the corner of the ring. Monty stayed on the ground and flopped backwards with his arms out. He closed his eyes for a split second and when he opened them again, he saw Wade flying over him in his finisher, a move that required a forward leap, mid-air backflip, and perfect timing to land chest to chest against his opponent. He landed it perfectly. Wade turned to Monty with a look of astonishment on his face and Monty's chest filled with pride on Wade's behalf. Both of them sprang to their feet and grabbed each other, jumping up and down in a bear hug to celebrate the flawless execution of the routine's most difficult move.

"Holy shit. That was so cool. I've never seen you land that one so perfectly!" Monty said, their faces dangerously close. Monty could feel Wade's breath on his cheek and ear. Goosebumps spread over his arms.

Wade was beaming. "I've been working on it on my own. I'm trying to hide it from Mike so I can surprise him. That's the first time I've landed it so well with an opponent. I can't believe it worked!"

"That is so going to get you your contract. I can feel it," Monty said. He stepped back so he could grab Wade by the neck with his arm. He gave him a rough kiss on the side of his head. "You are so cool, Viper."

"Thanks, Romeo." Wade patted Monty's chest.

"I'm going to go take a shower," Monty said, flipping out of the ring the same way he did the day of the tour.

"Hey, you did it!"

"Shut up," Monty said, his cheeks ruddy from hard work. And embarrassment.

He walked towards the locker room, looking at Wade over his shoulder. Wade gathered up his stuff but instead of going to the showers, he headed towards Mike's office, causing disappointment to pool in Monty's gut. He had imagined them getting changed and heading out of the arena together, creating an opening to ask Wade out again.

He decided that if he didn't see Wade again before he left, he'd send him a text when he got home, letting him know he had a good time. It would be polite and not at all creepy.

When he reached the locker room and stripped down, he shoved his boots in his locker and peeled the sweaty leggings from his body. He took off his shirt and briefs and wrapped a towel around his waist, then slipped on his shower shoes and headed towards the showers.

When he got there, he turned the handle on his favorite shower and stood under the stream of water, letting out a deep groan. He rinsed his hair, soaped up his chest and armpits, and scrubbed his face.

With his eyes closed, he faced the shower spray and let the soap run off his body. He turned to let the water hit his shoulders and stayed in that position for a while, letting the heat and pressure of the stream work his sore muscles. He hadn't worked out this hard or this often for a few months, and he was still getting used to it.

When he opened his eyes, he was surprised to meet the gaze of a very wet, very naked Wade. He looked startled. He had water dripping from his eyelashes and the tip of his nose, and Monty wanted to lick it off.

"Hi," Wade said quietly.

"Hi."

WADE TURNED AROUND and cursed under his breath. "Shit."

He poured soap onto his washcloth and started scrubbing his body, doing his best to keep his eyes to himself. But it was hard, because all he could think about was how their practice confirmed the in-ring chemistry he shared with Monty was perfect, and the out-of-ring chemistry they shared was getting there, too. The combination could allow them to reach depths of partnership beyond anything Wade had experienced, even with Larry.

But the contract was what mattered, he reminded himself. Not his desire to caress Monty's soft skin, or kiss his cute nose. Not his growing need to press his face into Monty's strong neck and surround himself with soft, coconut-scented tresses. And not the ache he felt when he imagined Monty's single dimple, the one that appeared only when he gave the most genuine smiles. The one that had inspired him to keep a list of things that made Monty laugh.

So, sure, being near Monty was electrifying. And sure, what he felt when he stopped avoiding the truth of his feelings was overwhelming in the best way, but it didn't matter. He had to stay focused.

Unfortunately, he wasn't stupid. He knew Monty had feelings for him, too, and that made it harder to hold his ground. When he'd walked into the shower, it had felt like there was a magnet pulling him to Monty's stall. But Monty was young and fresh and going places. Wade didn't have the luxury of time and he never would again. Potentially ruining the chemistry they had by dating or sleeping together just wouldn't be worth it.

Even in Wade's most pathetic dreams where they were together and maybe even loved each other, he knew Monty's time at Titan was limited. He would eventually leave to go to CWA, leaving Wade alone. Again. And he just couldn't risk that.

Wade took more time than necessary in the shower, hoping that when he got to the locker room, Monty would be gone. But It didn't work. Monty was still there, clean and sweet-smelling. He'd put his wet hair in two thick braids and he looked… precious.

"So, do you want to go get some dinner? I'm starving. I usually just go home and eat but I haven't made it to the store yet, and I read about this new place with crab legs by the pound. I love crab." Monty smiled up at Wade while he pulled his socks on.

Wade's stomach churned.

"Ah, you know, tonight isn't good for me." He turned to his locker quickly, hoping to avoid seeing whatever look he'd caused.

"Oh! Sure, yeah. Raincheck?" Monty stood and grabbed his backpack, throwing it over one shoulder. He looked disappointed, which wasn't surprising, but it still made Wade feel like an asshole. Monty turned towards him slightly, and when Wade didn't respond to his offer, he said, "I had a lot of fun today. I think this… us, together? I mean, in the ring? It could be something really special."

Wade's chest squeezed at Monty's words. *It already is special*, he wanted to say. It was more special than anything, maybe more than anyone else he'd ever worked with. But he couldn't encourage the development of anything between them beyond what it already was: a healthy, stimulating, platonic partnership.

"Totally. Well, everyone is back tomorrow. We'll show Mike the fight soon. After that, he'll start working out the scout schedule with CWA."

"Right. Sounds good. Goodnight, Wade."

Wade sat on the bench, feeling guilty and regretful as he watched Monty leave. He took his phone out and saw that Madeline had texted him a series of question marks. He sighed and called her.

"What do you want?" Wade groused when she answered.

"Don't give me that 'tude, Viper. How did it go today? Did you guys kiss?" she teased.

He could tell she was smiling, but instead of finding it charming, he was just irritated.

"That's not my name. And no, of course not. In fact, I gave myself a good pep talk while showering near him. My dick and I agreed we will not be pursuing anything sexual or romantic with Monty. Is that okay with you? You seem more invested in this than me." He cringed when he said it because it wasn't true, and she didn't deserve his wrath.

Madeline hummed.

"Is that all you need? It's been a long day. I want to get home," Wade said.

"Sure. Call me if you want to chat."

Wade hung up after saying goodnight to Madeline and then felt like dirt. But not good dirt. Old dirt that had been depleted of all its nutrients, its only purpose now to be used as fill for gaping holes from excised septic tanks. He sent her a quick apology text and promised to watch the kids soon so she and Kenny could go out. It assuaged some of his guilt, but not all of it, so he made a mental note to bring her coffee tomorrow.

When he got home, Wade tossed his shoes by the door and unpacked his gym clothes. He ate an apple while standing in front of the fridge. He fed his fish. Then he glanced at his phone. It was only eight o'clock and he didn't have to be at the arena until noon the following day.

He wished he had taken Monty up on his dinner invitation or that he'd kept Madeline on the phone. He even kind of wished Mike would call him and ask him to run errands or fix something at the arena, just so he didn't have to sit at home and think about things.

With nobody to reach out to and nothing to do, he grabbed a drink from the fridge and sat down to watch a documentary about marine life on Netflix to distract him from his thoughts. He laid his head down on a pillow and pulled a throw blanket over his torso.

His eyes opened when the sun started shining in through the blinds. He sat up and rubbed his neck, pain shooting down his back. Sleeping on the couch was never a great idea at his height, but apparently he'd needed the sleep. It was already almost eight o'clock, which meant he must slept almost eleven hours. That gave him four hours before he needed to be at the arena, so he threw on some clothes, grabbed his wallet and phone, and headed out for a run.

He ran along the waterfront, a nice perk of living downtown. It wasn't rainy, but it was cloudy, so the water looked brown and murky. He ran across the Steel bridge and turned onto the Spring-water Corridor, a path that ran for miles through parts of SE Portland. He watched the river churn, and watched floating logs bump into each other before getting sucked under the water. It matched his still sour mood – tempestuous and choppy. He left the trail and started running towards Madeline's house, swinging by the coffee shop on his way.

He stepped inside after wiping his forehead on his shirt. The barista greeted him, and as he stepped up to the counter, he saw Monty out of the corner of his eye. He was sitting with someone he didn't recognize. Someone small, soft looking, and very cute. They were sitting close together and their thighs were touching while they looked at something on Monty's phone. Their heads were so close together it made Wade impulsively flex his hands. They hadn't noticed him and Wade was hoping he could keep it that way because he really didn't want to meet Monty's… friend? Hookup? None of his business, regardless.

"Hi! What can I get you?" The barista's peppy voice pulled Wade back to the task at hand.

"Hi. Three coffees, please. Can I get cream to go? And then two of the French vanilla smoothies. Four everything bagels, cream cheese in the bag is fine." He smiled at the barista and tried his hardest to avoid looking in Monty's direction.

After he paid and shoved some cash in the tip jar, he stood to the side and took his phone out. He texted Madeline a quick note letting her know his plans. He opened his email next, desperate for anything to keep his attention while Monty and his friend were sitting so close. Why were they *so* close?

He tapped on a new email from Mike. When he scanned it, his stomach sank. The scouts from CWA were coming to a match early in the season this year, which was different than previous years. When they came closer to mid-season, the angles were rooted and the best and most popular wrestlers were already carving out their spots at the top because they'd had a few months of storytelling and matches under their belts. It gave them time to film promos and vignettes and work the fans, in person and online.

But this would throw everything off. Now it would mostly boil down to skill shown on one evening. He was good, that wasn't the issue. But he'd planned on having a few months to rebuild his online presence and get a little hype going. He groaned to himself. As things stood now, it would be a miracle if the scouts even bothered watching his match. Well, that wasn't entirely true, there was a lot of buzz around Monty… But this was just too fast. He wasn't ready for the scouts, he wasn't ready to say goodbye to Monty, and he just wasn't ready for this part of his life to be over. He pressed his nails into his palms and tried to settle the storm brewing in his gut.

"Wade?" The barista's voice rang across the shop.

Wade muttered a thanks, grabbed the drink carrier and bag of food, and turned towards the door. He walked as quickly as he could without looking weird and continued trying to avoid Monty's line of sight.

"Wade?"

Shit.

"Hey, Monty," Wade said.

"What are you doing over here? Don't you live across the river?"

"Yeah, I was out for a run and decided to grab some stuff for my friend and her family before I head to the arena. She lives nearby."

"Oh, nice! Cool." Monty nodded. "I live over by the arena, as you know, but I was over here this morning with my pal, here."

"Yeah... Nice," Wade said, unsure how to leave without being rude. He looked at Monty's friend and then back at Monty.

"Hi. I'm Aaron," the guy said. He held his hand out for Wade to shake. Wade lifted the items in his hands and gave him a flat look.

Monty's small and cute friend was Aaron, the IKEA guy who wanted to watch him wrestle. Wade tried his best to not imagine why they were together so early in the morning.

"Oh! Of course, right. Wade, this is Aaron. Aaron, this is Wade Donovan. He's the one I was telling you about! My new partner at work. He's Viper. Donovan."

"Ohh," Aaron smiled. "Nice to meet you, Viper."

"Wade is good."

"Sorry." Aaron gave an apologetic nod.

God, this was awkward.

"Well, I gotta..." Wade lifted the food and drinks again.

"Yeah, of course, okay. I'll see you this afternoon then? Oh, let me get the door for you," Monty said, walking to the door and holding it open. He leaned in close and plucked a long blond hair from Wade's t-shirt. "He's just a friend. Aaron is. He's the IKEA guy I told you about. I don't have a lot of friends here yet and he likes wrestling, so we kinda hit it off."

Wade immediately felt like an asshole. He had no right to have any thoughts whatsoever on Monty's social life, romantic or otherwise, but his behavior made Monty want to apologize anyway. Monty was new to the area and probably desperate for friends. He was just a social guy looking for companionship, and Wade was making this uncomfortable for everyone by acting like a fucking weirdo. He had to say something nice to undo the rudeness.

"None of my business," Wade said. *Seriously?* "I'll see you at the arena."

"Okay," Monty said, wincing slightly. "Bye, Wade."

Wade muttered under his breath when he got to the sidewalk. "Jesus Christ. Great work."

He walked up to Madeline's door, hitting the doorbell with his elbow. He heard screaming and heavy footfall. The door swung open, revealing two of Madeline's kids, Ramona and Jack. They were 6-year-old twins and Wade loved them.

When they were born, he'd been simultaneously horrified and besotted. They were the cutest little blobs. When they were sleeping, they were mind-meltingly sweet. But they were also so loud all the time. He didn't have a ton of experience with babies, but he had a theory they were extra loud to out-compete each other. Like it was an evolutionary trait. Cry louder than your twin so you get all the food. Admittedly, he hadn't looked it up, but it felt right.

Eventually they had calmed down and turned into bigger, friendlier blobs, but it was a year before he was comfortable being alone with them. By then, he'd loved staying at their house while Madeline and Kenny went out on date nights, with the kids using him as a climbing structure and letting him read to them. Larry would join him occasionally, but never really enjoyed it.

At the time, he didn't mind Larry's indifference to children. Becoming a dad as a gay man had some intrinsic challenges, so he didn't lose sleep over Larry's reluctance to have a talk about their future and the possibility of children. They'd had years before it would have become a pressing issue, and Wade used that as an excuse not to rock the boat. In retrospect, that probably wasn't the best way to handle a fundamental difference in life dreams, but he supposed it didn't matter anymore.

"ICE CREAM!" Ramona said, squealing. She grabbed the two

smoothies from the drink holder, almost causing Wade to lose his hold on the rest of the drinks.

"Okay, to be clear, it's not ice cream!" he said, loud enough that he hoped Madeline would hear him. "They are smoothies that contain plain frozen yogurt, honey, and vanilla bean!"

Ramona and Jack took off running towards the TV room and Wade watched them, smiling. They were such good kids. He expected nothing else from kids being raised by Madeline. Wade loved her so much, and he felt guilty all over again. When he gathered the strength he needed to face her, he looked up and saw Madeline leaning on the kitchen door frame, looking at him.

"I've come to buy your forgiveness."

Madeline grabbed the bag of bagels from Wade's hand and smirked at him. "You don't have to buy my forgiveness. But I do appreciate coffee and bagels. Come sit. Kenny is with Gavin upstairs. He had a rough night. God, I'm so tired." She stifled a yawn.

Wade sat at the table in the breakfast nook. Madeline's house was an old craftsman, typical of Portland neighborhoods. Kenny had done a lot of work on it since they had moved in a few years ago, but it retained its charm. He knew that was Madeline's doing. She was artistic and domestic and when they lived together during their attempts at college, she put herself in charge of making the house livable. They lived together until she met Kenny, and before too long, the two of them moved in together. Wade met Larry shortly after that, and then he was thrust back into a living situation where taupe was a fun color and the only things he was allowed to put on the walls were calendars and workout schedules.

"I'm sorry for being a dick last night," Wade said as he spread cream cheese on his bagel. "I just had a long, confusing day and I took it out on you."

Madeline sipped her coffee but didn't respond.

"I'm feeling a little… confused." He huffed a sad laugh. "I think Monty is throwing me off my game. You're right, I do like him. So much. And I like that I'm excited about wrestling. But I don't see how the two can coexist."

She nodded thoughtfully, but still offered nothing verbally. Wade looked at her and blinked.

"What are you, my therapist? Strategically placing silences, waiting for me to keep spewing my thoughts?" He paused to glare at Madeline. "Well, fine. The two can't coexist because I won't go through what I went through with Larry again. And Monty is fantastic, Mads. He's gonna make it. Yeah, I know, I know, I'm good too," he put his hand up to stop Madeline from interjecting, "but his engagement numbers are really good. And I just can't stay with Titan as talent anymore after this year. People are starting to talk. My options are limited, okay? I can pursue Monty and get left behind by my boyfriend for a second time, or I can just be partners with Monty until he leaves, and then next year I take over for Mike part time and find something else to do with the rest of my time."

Madeline let out a loud sigh.

"Wade, love of my life, would it kill you to just chill out for five seconds?" she said, leaning back in her chair.

"I am chill!"

"No, you are absolutely not. And it's okay. But why do you have to plan everything a year in advance?"

"I'm not planning a year in advance. I am consciously weighing the likelihood of various outcomes of this year so I can make the best decision for my future."

"Okay."

"What?"

"Well, I just think there are other possibilities. Like, maybe you both get moved to CWA. Or maybe you and Monty fall fantastically in love and he moves to CWA and you don't. But who's to say you can't go with him wherever he ends up?"

"I can't do that to Mike. He needs me."

"Mike loves and appreciates what you do for Titan, but you guys are beyond coworkers at this point. His main concern is that you're happy."

"Well, if Monty goes to CWA, he won't want to be held back by a boyfriend who couldn't hack it."

"Listen. I have no idea if you and Monty would work together because I've never met the guy, so take this with a grain of salt. But I like what I see when you talk about him, and I like that he has you excited about life again, wrestling or not. It just seems like a mistake to let that pass you by because you're afraid of one potential outcome. He's not Larry, you know? He's his own person."

Wade took a sip of his coffee, mulling over Madeline's words. Footsteps interrupted his thoughts, and he saw Kenny bounding down the stairs with Gavin wedged in the crook of his arm.

"Hey, party people!" Kenny said. When he reached the table, he handed Gavin to Wade. "Coffee and bagels? I am so glad I married Wade's best friend."

Madeline threw a wadded up tissue at her husband and handed him his coffee. Wade breathed in Gavin's scent and gave him a squeeze. Gavin beamed at Wade and reached out to grab his eyelid.

"I love this baby," Wade said. "I want one."

Madeline reached over and stroked Wade's arm gently, smiling at him.

CHAPTER 11

"I'm sorry if I made things awkward with Wade," Aaron said, stepping out of the booth where they'd been sitting. "He didn't seem too thrilled to meet me."

"Oh, you didn't make it awkward. For every one time I've been in Wade's presence and been a cool, collected person, there are two more where I've made a total idiot of myself. If he ran into me outside of the arena and I said zero stupid things, he'd probably think I was Monty's much more put together, long-lost twin."

"Hmm. Did I detect some jealousy, then? You can tell him about Ronnie if that would help."

"Oh, no, it's not… like that with us. I think he just made it very clear he's not interested in me that way."

Aaron gave Monty a sympathetic look. "I'm sorry. It's hard enough being in a new town without dealing with an awkward coworker situation."

"Oh, no, it's not bad. We get along great. I'm just really good at putting my foot in my mouth. I'm very flexible, Aaron. It comes with the wrestling," he said, patting his hip.

"Well, hey, if you ever want to come hang out with my friends and me, we have a pretty solid D&D crew," Aaron said, getting out of his seat. "We meet on Wednesday nights. I'd love to introduce you to my Warlock. He made a deal with the devil for a fast path to power, and it has come back to bite him."

Monty laughed. "I used to play in high school! I'd love that. I'll text you?"

"Sounds good. Talk to you soon, man."

At noon, Monty strolled into the arena with Wade still on his mind. He was thinking about Aaron's suggestion that Wade was jealous. He chuckled to himself because the truth was, it would make him *happy* if Wade was jealous of his friendship with Aaron. Most of his interactions with Wade seemed to confirm his suspicions that Wade thought of him as nothing more than a friend and coworker. He'd avoided spending time with Monty outside of the arena, and he'd tried to leave the coffee shop earlier without even saying hi. Neither behavior was indicative of someone whose feelings were even close to amorous.

There had been times, though, where Monty thought he might be wrong. Times Wade's gaze lingered longer than usual, or he brushed up against Monty when it was unnecessary, or he squeezed Monty in the ring when he didn't need to. But he tried not to dwell on those moments, because if he was wrong, it would be painful and embarrassing to admit.

It was emotionally draining trying to understand Wade's motivations. He just couldn't get a good read on him. His thoughts drifted and settled on what he knew to be an undeniable truth: he really liked Wade, regardless of how Wade felt.

He liked how calm and quiet he was. It was complementary to his own… boisterous personality. He liked that Wade presented himself as serious, but that he secretly loved animals and talked to them like children. He would never tell Wade he'd overheard him singing a dinner time lullaby to Juliet before he left the arena, because he'd probably move to Buenos Aires to avoid ever seeing Monty again. That didn't stop Monty from replaying it in his mind a thousand times, though. Witnessing that side of Wade had propelled his feelings from minor crush to an all-consuming fixation, and he was positive Wade would run away screaming at any hint of that.

He headed down the hall towards the locker room, passing by the photos of Wade and Larry he had now seen dozens of times. They felt different now that he knew Wade and Larry used to be a couple. In the photo Wade pointed out on the tour, Larry was on the turnbuckle holding one tag team championship belt above his head with both hands. He was yelling something, probably about being great, or whatever. Wade was on the side, looking up at Larry and he looked so happy.

When he'd previously looked at the photo, Monty assumed Wade's happiness was from winning the match. But looking at it this time, it was clear Wade's smile was deeper than that. He was proud of Larry. Proud of the person he was in love with. Thinking about what took place just months after that event made Monty hate Larry, even though they'd never met. He scowled at the photo without thinking.

Because it was just Monty's luck, Wade turned the corner to the hallway while Monty was still glaring at the photo. Wade looked up just in time to see Monty staring at it, and there was no way for him to pretend he was doing anything else.

"Oh, hey Wade. Long time no see!" Monty teased.

Wade didn't react.

"You know. Coffee shop."

"Right," he said, offering the smallest glimpse of a smile. Monty would take it. "I'm just heading to gather up the guys. I have a little announcement. Can you head to the ring as soon as you're dressed?"

"Yeah, of course. Be right there."

Wade jogged off, yelling at people to head to the ring. He didn't seem to be weirded out by Monty's interest in the photo, which was a relief. He walked to the locker room and found Kenji and Curt, who were also getting dressed.

"Hey, guys," Monty said. "Any idea what this announcement is about?"

"No, but Wade didn't look too happy, huh? When I got in, he and Mike were in the office. Wade looked like he was about to puke, poor guy," Kenji said.

"Wade did? Do you think he's okay?"

"Yeah, he seemed fine when he popped in here a minute ago. But who knows? I guess we'll find out shortly."

"It's probably nothing. Or maybe Wade is finally retiring," Curt laughed. Monty glared in Curt's direction. "Dicky said he hasn't polled well in a year but refuses to turn heel for some reason, and Mike lets him do whatever he wants. It wouldn't be so bad, right? Open up that ring time for someone who can actually do something with it."

Kenji's eyes stayed glued to his gym bag and he fiddled with a crocheted leaf keychain he'd put on it.

"What the fuck is that supposed to mean?" Monty snapped.

"What? I know you're partnered with him, but Mike won't leave you high and dry."

"I don't give a shit about that. Wade is good, Curt. He's not going anywhere unless he gets a new contract. Did you forget he used to wrestle with Limpet? Obviously, he's good."

"Hey, relax! I like the guy! I'm just saying, how long is Mike gonna keep him around if he's not making Titan any money? The flame that burns twice as bright burns half as long, and all that jazz. He *was* good. Now he's... not."

"You don't know what the fuck you're talking about," Monty said, slamming his locker shut.

"Alright, I touched a nerve. I'll leave it alone. Sorry, man."

"Yeah, do that. And don't listen to Dicky. Dude's an asshole," Monty added.

Curt grinned and nodded his head, packing the rest of his stuff in his locker.

"If *we* want to stay with Titan, we should probably head up to the ring," Kenji said.

When they made it to the ring, all the guys were standing in a half circle, Wade and Mike at the center. Monty's face was sheepish and he felt bad for being the last one to make it to the announcement. Stupid Curt.

"Thanks, everyone, for joining us. I know this was last minute and that you all have busy schedules today. Just a reminder that Lexi is stopping by to work on costumes and gear if you need help with that. She'll be in the open office near Mike's. Feel free to stop in and chat with her."

The guys nodded and Monty heard agreeable murmurs. So far, so good. He looked around to scan everyone's faces, but nobody was giving anything away. His hands were twisting with nerves, so he shoved them in his pockets.

"Thanks Wade," Mike started. "So, I know Wade mentioned an announcement and I'll just cut to the chase."

Monty's breaths were shallow.

"I wanted to share with you guys that the scouts from CWA are going to be coming to our matches starting in just a few weeks. For those of you who are newer, this may not mean anything. Normally, the scouts come halfway through the season because they like to wait to see what sort of online traction you're all getting, see what the chemistry is like in-ring and out-of-ring, that kind of stuff. Unfortunately, they had some changes in strategy, and they're coming much earlier in the season this time. It won't be as easy for you to sell yourselves holistically."

"So Dicky has a shot, you mean, since once the fans hear him talk on his promos, they'll beg him to quit wrestling all together?" Curt said.

A bunch of the guys laughed. Dicky tackled Curt, and they tumbled over one another and punched at each other playfully until Wade broke it up.

"Something like that," Mike grinned. "The point is, everything is going to come down to your skills in the ring. You still need to focus on your angles and chemistry with each other, obviously, but for the scouts, please make sure you are really wowing them with your matches. I want everyone to spend a little time thinking about whether what you have planned is good enough. They're looking for fresh and new, so make it count. As always, I'm here to work through your angles if you need me. We have writers on loan from CWA, so work with them. Post approved stuff online. You can do this. It's just going to be a little harder."

Monty blew out a breath. That was totally fine. He could do that, with Wade. He looked up to Kenji and dramatically wiped his brow.

"How are you feeling about all that, huh? I think we'll be okay. Your finisher is sick," Monty said, aiming for casual. He knew Wade was nervous based on what Kenji said, and wanted to comfort him if he could, but also had to make sure Wade didn't suspect that was his angle.

"Well, it's not ideal. But don't worry. We'll make sure you get exposure. I'm hoping I can get Mike to convince them to come a couple of times. That way, you guys all have multiple chances to showcase your skill."

"We'll all showcase our skills, you mean," Monty said. "You're included in that, too."

"Sure," Wade said.

Monty put his finger to his chin, tapping it a few times.

"What?" Wade asked.

"I'm just thinking. Like, obviously, you have a great finisher. But what if we jazz it up? The turnbuckle is fine, but you could get so much height if we pulled out a ladder."

"You want to bring in a ladder?"

"Well, yeah! It wouldn't be the first time you've used a ladder, right?" Monty said, remembering a video he'd watched in high school of Wade in a match with a since-retired wrestler named Giant Jim who worked for both CWA and Titan. It was early in Wade's career, and if Monty remembered correctly, which he most definitely did, it was the first time he'd been in a match against such a big name wrestler.

The two had introduced a ladder to their match midway through. While Wade was on the ground recovering from whatever move landed him on his ass, Jim climbed the ladder. Before he got to the top, Wade climbed the ropes and did a drop kick into Jim's knees. He fell to the floor, giving Wade time to scramble to the top of the ladder and land a frog splash on top of Jim's writhing body.

Wade hadn't won the match, but it didn't matter. All the online wrestling forums Monty frequented as a teen were on fire over Viper. He remembered being so excited that this no-name wrestler he'd been following was finally catching his big break. He almost felt smug, like he'd known Wade was gonna make it. *That's my guy*, he remembered thinking. It was after that match that Wade's popularity had skyrocketed, and shortly after that, he became tag team partners with Larry. Monty realized he probably had a dreamy look on his face and cleared his throat, looking up at Wade.

"You're thinking about Giant Jim, aren't you?" Wade said, leaning into Monty and pushing him gently with his elbow.

"Well! I mean…" Monty blushed.

"It's fine, it was a great match," he said. "Yeah, I like this. A ladder could really work here. If nothing else, it'll be a fun homage to that era. And if things go badly, the ladders will serve as gigantic, twelve foot bookends to my career."

Monty's face grew serious. "Your career isn't over after this match, Wade."

"Monty, listen. I am going to do everything I can to make this the best match of my career. I want nothing more than for you to succeed, and that means I have to do well, too."

"But…?"

"But… I think I have to be realistic about what I have to offer Titan at this point. You've heard all the guys talking. I'm not stupid. I think Dicky and Curt are going to stage a coup if Mike keeps giving me ring time over them."

Wade laughed. Monty didn't.

"Okay, don't look at me like that, please. I love wrestling and am still hopeful, but I am also a sensible guy."

"I just really believe this is going to work out, Wade. For both of us. Okay?"

Before he could convince himself it was a bad idea, Monty reached out and hooked his pinky through Wade's. Wade looked down at their hands, and then Monty felt Wade's pinky squeeze his own before he walked away. Monty rubbed his pinky with his other hand's fingers, then bit his lip as an unavoidable smile broke out across his face.

CHAPTER 12

WADE LEANED ON THE ROPES INSIDE THE RING AND WATCHED ANTHONY execute a perfect suplex on Dicky. The guys around the ring watched, smiling and laughing with each other, their voices mingling with the playful teasing coming from the women Titan had hired to act as Romeo's girlfriends.

The vibe at Titan had been different lately. It was fun and exciting, which Wade assumed was because the pressure to succeed meant teamwork was more important than ever. He called the match, designating Anthony the winner, and Dicky stormed off. Anthony shrugged at Wade, who was distracted by watching Monty and the actresses file out towards the offices. He grumbled internally before turning his attention back to Anthony.

It had been a couple of weeks since Mike's announcement, and Wade was feeling pretty good. Every day he spent with Monty moved him one step closer to reclaiming the happiness wrestling once brought him. It had been so long since he'd connected with another wrestler on this level, and he'd spent so much time being one half of Viper and Limpet, he was enjoying the motivation that came from working with a "rival" rather than a partner.

He thought if he could rebuild his brand quickly enough, he'd have a real shot at moving to CWA. Titan was already filming promos and interviews where Viper was introduced as a heel for the first time, and his new rivalry with Romeo was everywhere. They were both gaining traction.

But in the back of his mind, Wade knew this year could be his final year wrestling. He needed a plan for what he worried was the more likely outcome. He hoped that if it didn't work out, he could at least go out with a bang. It wasn't uncommon for popular wrestlers to come back for matches here and there after their initial retirement. One of Wade's favorite wrestling moments was when one of his idols, a wrestler who had retired because of injury, surprised everyone when his entrance music started playing at WrestleBonanza ten years later. He imagined himself doing that and smiled.

Because of filming, wrestling in regular matches, driving for road trips, and their own personal reasons neither of them had been honest about, Wade and Monty were spending long hours together. They talked a lot about Wade's start in wrestling and the years before and after Larry. Wade learned more about how Monty got into wrestling. He knew Monty had stumbled onto WrestleTalk's channel years ago and it was love at first sight, but at one point, Monty let it slip that it was an interview with *Wade* that sparked his initial interest. Wade beamed at the compliment and delighted in the blush that crept up Monty's chest and cheeks.

But spending more time together presented difficulties, too. As they got to know each other better, Wade's feelings for Monty grew deeper, and it made harder to keep his attraction in check. He could feel his resolve crumbling, and every day they spent together brought him one step closer to dismantling the metaphorical wall he'd erected so deliberately between them.

He did his best to channel his feelings into Viper's hatred of Romeo. When Niall had suggested to Mike earlier in the season that a Romeo-Viper rivalry should stem from Viper's jealousy of Romeo's quick rise to fame, Wade had been less than thrilled. His knee jerk reaction had been anger towards Niall and Mike. They assured him it wasn't personal, and that the idea of good vs. evil in wrestling was nuanced, as if Wade didn't know. They said fans loved both sides, and if anything, the heels had more fun. It didn't make sense for Monty's career to start as a heel, but Wade was ready, if he had to be. So he relented, accepting the terms of the rivalry.

It was easy enough, because the angle was pretty much exactly what was happening. Not that Wade was jealous of Monty, exactly. But he would be lying if he said it didn't hurt something inside of him to watch a young, handsome, marketable wrestler take off. Like it could have been him in a different lifetime where Wade had made slightly different decisions. Instead, in this lifetime, Viper would turn heel and that was the end of it. A lot of wrestlers enjoyed that role, but Wade had never wanted it.

Since Titan had officially decided on the rivalry angle, they'd been promoting it nonstop. In the past couple of weeks, they'd filmed and aired several "behind the scenes" vignettes where Viper ranted about his stupid blue-eyed, pretty boy opponent King Garto, Niall's character, did his best to calm him down.

He never succeeded, of course, because King Garto would inevitably say something about the time Romeo successfully seduced Viper's "woman," or mention the time Romeo told everyone Mike fired Viper because was too old to qualify for health benefits, or remind him of the time Romeo paid The Assassin to let the air out of Viper's tires, then filmed Viper from behind a tree, laughing when he tried to leave the parking lot.

Viper always end up punching a locker to the point of denting, using a chair to break a window, leaving rotting meat in Romeo's locker (only once, because that ended as a punishment for every employee at Titan), or in one of Wade's favorite moments, pasting one of Romeo's headshots to a dartboard.

Monty was also filming, but his storyline had a decidedly different vibe. Instead of being painted as a washed up, angry jerk on the verge of losing his career, Romeo was a playboy who gave very little thought to his rivalry with Viper beyond childish pranks, and of course, his cavalier attitude only angered Viper more.

The actresses Titan had hired to hang all over Romeo also followed him to various locations, including tour matches and the main arena. Wade had several women ask him for Monty's number after filming, and when he said he couldn't give it out, they pouted. He overheard a few of them saying he was jealous of Monty, and that the rivalry wasn't fake at all. After weeks of this, Wade's teeth had been ground to nubs.

He knew, intellectually, the stuff with Monty was an act. They were literally paid actors. But did they all have to look so happy about it? Monty was always laughing and flirting with them, and they ate it up, because who wouldn't? He knew he still had no right to form opinions on Monty's social life, not the way their relationship was. If Monty wanted to meet someone and have fun with them, that was none of his business.

Except, lately, he really wanted it to be his business. He wanted to be able to claim him, touch him, and hold him. Even if they couldn't be together long term, he was sick of fighting his attraction to Monty. Denying the feelings he'd been cursed with for so long was exhausting, and the idea of something more with Monty was becoming too tempting to ignore.

The group wrapped up their tasks for the day, the last of which was yet another promo involving Monty and a handful of women. Wade looked up when he heard loud giggles coming from the offices. He saw Monty walking towards the locker room with his stuff, bypassing the ring, and he made a snap decision he hoped he wouldn't regret. He started walking towards him, fast enough that he closed in on him quickly.

"Hey, um, Monty?" Wade said quietly. He really didn't want anyone to hear him get turned down.

"Hey! What's up?" Monty asked, hoisting his backpack a little higher on his shoulder.

"Would you like to get dinner with me? Tonight?"

Monty looked surprised, which Wade would unravel later. "Yes! I would. I would like that very much."

Wade tried to be cool. He was mostly successful, and broke into a smile with all of his bright, mostly real teeth showing.

"Great! Okay, maybe we can just go to Sacky's? Or we can go somewhere else, it's just nearby… Or do you like Thai?"

"Either of those sounds great."

"Okay. Should we meet in like an hour? I need to shower and change," he said. He considered whether he should go pick up a small gift. Was that too much? It had been so long since he'd been on a first date, he couldn't remember what to do. He smiled hopefully at Monty.

"Oh. Shoot," Monty said. "You know what? I can't. I forgot it's Wednesday. I'm going to Aaron's house tonight for D&D stuff. You know how it is. My monk came across an orc riding a giant spider and I have to try to protect the party. The problem is, someone in my party poisoned me accidentally, and that puts me at a disadvantage on my next attack roll. It's a whole thing. I begged Aaron to pause until the next time we meet, and that's today, so…"

"Oh. Okay, um, no worries," Wade said, confused. If Monty wanted to turn him down, he could come up with a less elaborate reason, surely. "See you tomorrow then?"

"No, Wade, wait. I can't tonight, but—" he reached out towards Wade, but they were interrupted.

"Monty!" One of Romeo's "women," Rosie, walked over to Monty and touched his shoulder and chest. "We're going to Sacky's tonight! Do you want to come?"

Before Monty could respond, Wade spoke up. "Okay, well, see you tomorrow, Monty. Have a good night, everyone."

Monty's brow furrowed. He put his finger up to Wade in a "hold on" gesture and turned to the woman next to him. "Uh, put me down as a maybe. I have some plans after this, but I live over here, so… maybe?"

The words were an unexpected, heavy blow to Wade's pride. He felt like an idiot.

"Well, don't be too long. Here's my number if you want to text me," she said, shoving a scrap of paper in the waistband of Monty's leggings.

Wade pinched his eyes shut and turned around. He gave a curt nod at the general area, not waiting for Monty before heading towards the locker room. He cringed at his own avoidant behavior, but he couldn't help it. He just wanted to remove himself from the situation as quickly and quietly as possible. Between Monty's noncommittal reply to the woman's invite and his weird, long-winded excuse about going to Aaron's, Wade deflated. He shouldn't have hoped for more and he definitely shouldn't have read into any of the sweet comments or soft touches he got from Monty. The only thing he should have done was stay focused on the match, the contract, and CWA.

After grabbing his gym bag, he slipped out through the emergency exit. He mentally thanked whichever smoker had propped the door open, then headed home.

CHAPTER 13

MONTY'S GAME CAME TO A NATURAL STOPPING POINT FOR THE EVENING and Aaron's D&D crew started packing up.

"Thanks for hosting, Aaron," Monty said, picking up the group's dirty dishes and carrying them to Aaron's kitchen. The rest of the guys said their goodbyes and filed out the front door, but Monty stayed behind to help tidy.

"Sure thing! I'm glad you joined our little crew. You're a great fit." Aaron cocked his head at Monty. "Are you okay? You seem… lugubrious."

"Lugubrious?" Monty choked out a laugh. "I love that word. What does it mean?"

"Lugubrious! It's like, sad or dismal looking. Gloomy. Sullen. I'm taking a creative writing course for fun. I was thinking it'd help my Dungeon Master storytelling skills."

"Has it helped?"

"No."

Monty laughed again.

"Stop changing the subject. What's going on with you?" Aaron probed.

"Just… you know. Guy troubles."

"Ah. Wade troubles?"

"Yeah," Monty said, frowning.

"What's the trouble? He's clearly smitten."

"How would you know he's smitten? You've met him exactly once. And 'meet' is generous, considering how he behaved."

"Maybe that's how I know he's smitten," Aaron shrugged. "He was clearly jealous. I can't blame him. I am very cute."

Monty laughed at that before his face fell slightly.

"Plus, you were facing the other way, but he could not stop staring at you the whole time he waited for his food. Every time I looked over, he'd look down at his feet. It was really very sweet," Aaron continued with a dreamy look on his face. "Also, I checked out Titan's Instagram page and apparently he runs it…"

Monty arched his eyebrow at Aaron.

"Stay with me! I'm not a creep. Anyone who says they don't do mild internet research about new people they meet is a dirty liar and I stand by that. Plus, I already followed Titan. Anyway, he posted about you. Well, okay, he posted about all the new wrestlers with Titan, but yours is like, extra. He listed your stats and how long you've been wrestling, but he also talked about your dog Becky and said she likes to talk on the phone. I didn't even know you had a dog. He said you are a new D&D fan, but he spelled it "D and D" so I don't think he has any idea what it is. And you're not actually a new fan. But that's why it's so cute, right? He's piecing together all these little tidbits he's learned about you."

"Well, thank you for your research, Detective. I will chew on that and let you know how everything progresses. But none of that solves my actual issue, which is that it's hard to get a feel for what he's thinking outside the ring, like, ninety percent of the time. Sometimes he seems really interested in me. Sometimes he acts like this strict business dude who couldn't possibly entertain the idea of dating a coworker. It makes it really difficult to know how to handle my own feelings. Like, do I give it a shot, or do I move on?"

"Maybe he's struggling to be open about his feelings, but there are probably signs. And maybe you don't need to wait for him to tell you how to proceed. Shoot your shot or get off the pot."

"I don't think that's how that saying goes."

"Agree to disagree."

Monty rolled his eyes. "Well, I do notice signs sometimes, which is half of why I'm so confused. But like, okay. Here's an example. He asked me out to dinner, right? I said yes. Then I remembered it was D&D night, so I let him know I couldn't make it. He seemed bummed out, which is fair. Right when this was all happening, these ladies I've been filming with asked me to go over to Sacky's with them. So I said 'put me down as a maybe,' and I think that upset him because he took off and I couldn't find him anywhere in the arena. I even asked Mike, and Mike hadn't seen him either. But why didn't he just tell me it upset him?"

"You said 'put me down as a maybe?!'" Aaron asked, incredulous.

"Okay, well, listen! I've been spending a lot of time with them and I like them. I'm not romantically interested in any of them, but why can't I go get a drink with them? If Wade is gonna be insecure about me being friends with women just because I'm bi, I'm not interested."

"You can be friends with anyone you want," Aaron said. "But maybe instead of telling them you might see them later, you could have asked Wade out for a drink instead? Or invited him to go with you? He seems insecure, but I don't think it's about you being simultaneously bisexual and friends with women. I think it's about you turning him down and then making tentative plans for the same evening with someone he's been watching get paid to flirt with you for weeks. What else could he possibly glean from that, dumbass?"

Monty finished putting the last of the glasses in the dishwasher and closed it up. He put his hands on his hips and stared at the sink. "Huh. Yeah, okay. I mean, maybe you're right."

"Yeah, I am."

"Thank you," he said, smiling. Aaron reached out and they hugged in the kitchen for a few seconds while Monty considered what to do. "Hey, is it creepy to show up at someone's house unannounced?"

"Sure, sometimes. But sometimes, it's romantic!" Aaron grabbed Monty's arms and shoved him towards the door. "Go get him, tiger!"

Monty chuckled to himself as he walked down the steps from Aaron's and took off towards his apartment. He passed a small corner store that was still open. He checked his phone and saw that it was only nine o'clock. That wasn't too late for a surprise visit, was it?

He popped into the store and grabbed a six-pack of tall boys and a small, squishy, green and black snake that was sitting in a basket by the register. The colors matched Viper's pants. After he paid, he pulled up his phone to look for an email Mike sent out when he first started. It contained contact information for himself and Wade, including addresses. Then, before he could talk himself out of it, he ordered a Lyft to Wade's apartment and sat on a bench to wait.

He looked at his phone while he waited, hoping to see a text from Wade, but he only had one notification—a missed call from his mom. He tapped the callback button and put the phone up to his ear while he waited.

"Hi, Monty!" she said when she answered the phone.

"Hi, Mom."

"Becky and I are here! We're on speaker. How are you? Are you ready for the scouts next weekend?"

"Hi Becky. Yeah, I guess so. I'm nervous, of course."

"How about Wade? Is he ready?"

"Oh, you know. He's been there, done that. I don't think he really panics about matches anymore." He didn't mention that it was partly because Wade had resigned himself to retirement after this year. He did wonder how much of that was an attempt to get ahead of disappointment and how much of it was him being "sensible," as he'd put it. It was likely that Wade still hoped to get a CWA contract and live out his dreams, but he seemed to be putting all of his energy into making sure Monty succeeded instead.

"Hmm," she said.

"Hmm what?"

"Nothing. I'm just surprised. The way you've always talked about him made it seem like he was very committed to the sport," she mused.

"He is! Did I say he wasn't committed?"

"No, but you've mentioned in the past that he is feeling the pressure, so it surprises me to hear that he's not worried about the scout visit. I wonder if he actually is stressed out about it and just doesn't want to share that with anyone. Maybe so you don't panic, since it's your first time meeting them."

"Okay, does everyone have some sort of special Wade-Donovan-Feelings machine? How could you know that?"

"I don't *know*. I'm just making an educated guess. Why? Who else knows his feelings?"

"My friend, Aaron. He thinks Wade has feelings for me."

"Wow. That would be a pretty big deal, huh?"

"Well, yeah. Obviously I'd be really happy to find that out," Monty said. His mom knew he'd had a schoolboy crush on Wade for years and he'd dropped hints to his mom about his feelings growing over the past few weeks. "He's not particularly forthcoming with his feelings, though, and I really don't want to be wrong about this, days before the scouts arrive. God, can you imagine?"

"Hmm."

"Stop saying hmm!" Monty yelled.

Monty's mom laughed through the phone. "I just wonder how well you guys would do if you cleared the air before you got back in the ring."

"Yeah… I'll think about it. I gotta go now, mom. I'll call you on Sunday. Love you. Love you, Becky."

After his mom said her goodbyes, including a few seconds for Becky to sniff the phone, he hung up and slid his phone into his pocket. His Lyft pulled up at the same time. He stood up, took a deep breath, and stepped into the car.

WADE PULLED his lasagna tray out of the oven and put it on the stove to cool for a few minutes before he cut into it. It smelled good, and Wade was hungry, but he had learned the hard way long ago that neglecting to let a lasagna sit after coming out of the oven was a fast track to a plating disaster. Not that it mattered, since he was alone, and would probably eat the whole lasagna by himself over the next two days, so who the hell cared if it looked like shit? But he deserved a pretty slice of lasagna.

"A sloppy lasagna is nobody's friend, Jojo," he said to his fish, turning off the tank's light for the evening.

It was nine o'clock and he'd arrived home an hour earlier after going to Sacky's to drown his sorrows. Clearly, he'd chosen Sacky's in a fit of madness, knowing there was a good chance he'd run into

Monty or the Romeo ladies there. He didn't, which was good, because he didn't actually want to see any of them there or have conversations with them about Monty. They'd inevitably be irritated with Wade when he refused to discuss Monty or hand out his address. He grumbled to himself, annoyed at the assumption that Wade's jealousy was because of Monty's success.

He *was* jealous, that part was true. But it wasn't about Monty's success. He was jealous of the women who were being paid to spend time with him. To hold his hands, kiss on his neck, feel his bare skin in a nonviolent setting. The idea that Titan may eventually hire one of them to be his character's girlfriend and they'd be spending tons of time together? Well, it was unpleasant to think about, to say the least. He knew how these things went. It wasn't unheard of for them to end up together in "real life."

He sat on the couch with Juliet, whom he'd picked up from Linda on the way home. Juliet had developed a temporary neurological condition that made her wobbly on her feet, so Linda had decided to keep her around a bit longer to see if it would regulate itself before release. She'd already been out foraging in Linda's yard a few times and successfully found some food, including a slug. Wade had gagged when she walked up to him eating it, but he just told her she was brilliant and gave her a pet. He sipped his beer while Juliet sat on his chest, eating from a pile of kibble and mixed vegetables. He rested his head against the back of his couch.

His eyes had shut for just a moment when he heard a light tap at the door. He turned his head, trying to figure out who would visit him this late. Or visit him at all, really. His reputation for being the life of the party the last couple of years hadn't exactly stuck around.

Madeline wouldn't drop by unannounced, which made him think it must be Mike. And there was absolutely no good reason for Mike to drop by without asking first. His stomach rolled, and he drank a big gulp of his beer before he stood up from the couch. The kibbles spilled to the floor and he groaned before putting Juliet on top of them to clean up. Another knock, slightly harder.

"I'm coming!" he snapped. "Relax!"

He unlocked the deadbolt and removed the chain before swinging the door open, expecting to see Mike's round, bearded face. But it wasn't Mike. It was Monty.

"Um… hi," Monty said. He held up a bag. "I brought beer?"

"Monty. I Ii."

"Sorry to stop by unannounced. I just… wanted to see you. And make sure you were okay. You left the arena so quickly today."

"I'm fine, Monty," Wade said gently. "Thank you for your concern. I didn't mean to worry you."

Monty bounced on the balls of his feet and looked past Wade, into his apartment.

"Oh. Sorry. Please, come in. Don't mind the mess. I don't entertain very often."

Wade scanned his eyes around the apartment. It looked okay. At least he had done his dishes earlier in the day. Monty's eyes met his and he gave him a sweet smile as he squeezed by Wade's big body.

"Looks pretty nice to me. I am a real trash heap," he said. "I mean, I'm fine as a person. I'm just kinda messy. Now that I'm on my own, my apartment has seen better days, so I don't mind a mess. Well, I guess it literally hasn't seen better days since I've always lived alone there. It's bad right now. Not that your apartment is messy. It looks really nice, a lot nicer than mine. Which isn't saying much. But again, your apartment looks really good. Tidy. Is that a fish? Is that Juliet?!"

"Yes," Wade chuckled. He loved Monty's anxious rambles. He stepped behind Monty, encouraging him to go further into the living room. "That's Jojo, my fish. And yes, that's Juliet. Can I take the beer? Do you want one?"

"Yes please," he said. He removed his shoes and started walking towards Juliet with grabby hands. "Hi, baby!"

"So, to what do I owe the pleasure? I didn't even know you knew my address. I thought you were going to be Mike. I was scared shitless."

"Oh, jeez. I know. I shouldn't have just stopped by. It sounded like a good idea in my head." Monty put Juliet on his shoulder. She curled her tail around his finger and he held on. "I used the email Mike sent us with your emergency contact information, and… Hmm. Yeah, upon reflection, this is probably not the way you intended for us to use your private information. Oh, God. I am such a creep."

"No, no, this is a great surprise. Really." Wade was smiling so much his cheeks were getting sore. He passed by the couch and walked to the kitchen to place the beer in the fridge. Monty followed. He opened two beers and passed one to Monty, who took a big gulp.

Monty seemed nervous. Wade watched his hands squeeze before picking up a tomato and feeding it to Juliet. She chewed it in his ear.

"I just took a lasagna out of the oven, if you're hungry. I'm just letting it sit."

"Oh, I'm okay. I ate at Aaron's. Thank you, though."

"Okay." Wade turned to poke at the lasagna.

"We play D&D together. He's not… I'm not interested in him, just so you know. He has a partner."

"You don't have to explain anything to me, Monty. It's not my business who you hang out with."

"I know it's not, not technically. But that doesn't mean I don't want to tell you, you know?" Monty said. He walked over by the stove to stand by Wade, who was leaning against the counter with one hip.

"Okay." Wade was suddenly unable to remember anything at all about lasagna, but he continued to stare at it intently. There was cheese on top.

Monty grabbed Juliet and placed her in the baby playpen Wade had set up. He walked back and took Wade's fingers, intertwining them.

"Wade?"

"Yeah?"

"I'm sorry. About earlier. Declining your dinner invitation and making plans with someone else in front of you. It was stupid and I would have much rather gone out to dinner with you. I was rude, but I didn't mean to be. I just really am that stupid sometimes."

"You're not stupid. And you don't owe me anything, not even an explanation."

"It's not about owing you."

"Okay," Wade said, "then what is it about?"

"It's just, um. You feel it too, right? Our connection. This chemistry between us."

Wade looked at Monty but couldn't say anything. He swallowed, trying to buy time. Monty stepped closer to him, their hands still linked.

"I think about it all the time. When we're in the ring together, I don't understand how I got so lucky. To end up working with you this closely is like my dream come true."

Wade was still quiet, but he toyed with Monty's fingers. He squeezed them and looked down at Monty's chest.

"And then," Monty continued, "when we're outside the ring, working together, hanging out together, just existing together, it's so fun. I know we just met. And please tell me if I'm reading things wrong. The last thing I want to do is make you uncomfortable, especially right before the scout match. I can leave right now, and we'll just pretend I didn't use your personal information for inappropriate reasons and didn't bring beer to your house and I didn't blurt my feelings out while you're just trying to enjoy a nice lasagna. It looks delicious, by the way. Nice browning. My mom always—"

"Monty."

"Hmm?"

He took a single step closer to Monty. Monty's breathing sped up. Wade reached out one hand and placed it on Monty's side, just below his ribs. Monty looked at Wade's hand and then up at Wade. Both of them were taking shallow breaths now, and their eyes were locked. He leaned forward and kissed Monty softly. He stepped back suddenly and dropped his hand from Monty's body.

"Sorry. Is that okay?"

"Yes," Monty said. "You can do that. You should do that."

Wade breathed out a small laugh, then lifted his hand to place it back on Monty's side, his thumb brushing back and forth over his ribs. Monty smiled, which Wade took as a good sign, so he placed his other hand on the side of Monty's neck and used his thumb to caress his jaw. The stubble felt scratchy on his thumb, the feeling of it causing an unintentional grunt to escape from Wade's throat. Monty stepped close enough that their bodies were touching.

Wade leaned forward to move his hands behind Monty's back and Monty did the same. His hands felt so good against his tired muscles. They rubbed up and down against Wade's back, finally settling above the swell of his ass. Wade tilted his chin and placed his lips against

Monty's again. Gentle at first, tentative. He continued giving Monty slow, closed mouth kisses until he felt Monty take a deep breath and let out a contented sigh. The sound of Monty's pleasure flipped a switch in his brain, opening the floodgates, destroying the wall he'd built, and Wade suddenly couldn't think of anything other than kissing him.

He turned them both around and walked Monty backwards until he hit the countertop. Monty jumped and laughed, his lips still pressed to Wade's.

"Ow," he said, smiling against Wade's lips. "Sharp."

Wade pushed his knee between Monty's legs, shoving him against the counter. He kissed Monty roughly, his tongue sliding between Monty's lips. Monty moaned again, pressing himself against Wade's knee. Wade placed more aggressive kisses against Monty's mouth, then he leaned down and nipped at Monty's neck. He bit it and sucked it gently and Monty moaned, fisting Wade's t-shirt. When he stood up straight again, pressing their bodies together, Wade could feel Monty hard inside his pants. He angled his hips to press his groin against Monty's, and they both shuddered.

Wade reached down and palmed his own aching dick, searching for relief. He let out a whimper as he went back to suck on Monty's neck and chest.

"I've wanted you since the first day I saw you get stuck in that rope," Wade said, grinding into Monty. "Your stupid foot. I'd never seen anything like that."

Monty laughed. "Shut up. I need to wipe your memory of that moment."

"No, it was perfect. It was so very you." Wade had relived that moment in his mind countless times. It was a mix of funny and tender, perfectly capturing Monty's essence. When he'd held out his hand to help Monty stand up, it felt like they were destined to be there, together, in that moment. Like they were meant to meet, even if it required Monty to make a fool of himself in front of a group of macho idiots. The feeling was clear in his mind as they mirrored it in this more frantic connection up against Wade's counters.

"I've wanted you, too. For so long. Like, an embarrassingly long time." Monty threw his head back, hitting it on the cabinet door. "Ow. Please, Wade. I need...something."

"What do you want? Tell me," Wade said. He took his hands from Monty's back and shoved them up the front of his shirt. He brushed his thumbs against each of Monty's nipples. Monty bit his lip, and his hands wandered down to Wade's pants. He was wearing joggers, which made it easy for Monty to slip his hands into the back, pulling their bodies together.

"Can I just...is this okay?" Monty asked. He pulled on the front of Wade's pants and looked up at him.

"Yes. Please," Wade said. He closed his eyes and leaned his head back as he felt Monty pull his pants and boxer briefs down to his thighs, his hard cock hitting Monty's lower stomach.

"Oh," Wade said. He opened his eyes to look at Monty briefly before he nuzzled his face into the crook of Monty's neck. He lowered his hands to Monty's ass and squeezed, then shoved Monty's pants and underwear down. They moved closer, their erections brushing against each other as Wade moved back to take Monty's mouth. Wade pressed his body into Monty, grinding on him against the counter.

Wade felt a large hand shove between their bodies and then grip his cock. It had been so long since he'd been with another man. When Larry left, he'd taken Wade's libido, too. Depression made it hard to date or hook up because it was hard to find motivation to do much at all. He eventually kept himself so busy with Titan that he rarely thought about what he was missing. His sexual needs being neglected barely bothered him anymore, he was so rarely in the mood. But the closeness and intimacy that came from being with someone like this, he craved it. He missed it. The fact that he had it now, with Monty, made Wade weak at the knees. He didn't want this moment to end because he knew as soon as it did, it was another moment closer to Monty's departure from Titan and from his life.

Monty's hand then wrapped around his own dick, too. He worked them together, slowly at first, but then with increased urgency. His frantic breaths and tongue were hot against Wade's neck. He licked the shell of Wade's ear, which elicited another groan. Wade felt Monty's dick swelling against his own and the feeling made him lose all remaining composure, sending Wade over the edge. Monty was following close behind, grunting into Wade's ear.

"Oh, shit," Wade panted. He bit down on Monty's shoulder, his cum pouring over Monty's fist. He sucked on Monty's pulse point, letting go only when his pleasure began to fade.

Monty swiped up Wade's cum and spread it over his own dick, using it as lube and increasing the speed of his fist.

"I'm gonna - I can't - shit, Wade," he mumbled gibberish and shot onto Wade's stomach, their releases mixing over Monty's hand.

They held onto each other before they stepped apart slightly. Both of them were breathing hard and then Monty kissed Wade sloppily. He was wobbly. When Monty finally let go of Wade's body, Wade grabbed some tissues from the countertop and handed some to Monty.

"I'm sorry," Wade said as he cleaned himself up.

"What? What are you sorry for?" Monty looked at Wade, his face worried.

"It's just been a while for me, you know. All the times I imagined this in my head, I lasted a lot longer."

Monty looked down at his still-visible dick, which was covered in cum, then he looked back up at Wade. "I don't know if you noticed, but uh…" he said, pointing at himself. He gave it a dab with a tissue and laughed. "That was so…wow. I promise I didn't come over here with a plan to give you a hand job, but I won't pretend I'm sad it happened. And don't think I didn't catch that you've imagined this a bunch of times."

"I don't mind," Wade smiled. He pulled both of their pants up and pulled Monty into his chest, wrapping his arms around him. He squeezed Monty and planted a sweet kiss to the side of his head.

"You know who probably did mind?" Monty said, looking over at the counter. "Oh, poor Jojo."

Wade barked out a laugh and pulled his head back to give Monty another soft kiss.

"Thank you for coming over here. Thank you for worrying about me. I'm sorry I've been such an idiot. I'm not good at… this," Wade said.

"What's 'this?'" Monty asked.

"Talking about my feelings, handling jealousy in reasonable and mature ways. I'm trying. I want to do better, for you. I know it's not fair to punish you, or us, for my own baggage, and I'm trying to do better. Just please know that I like you. A lot. And I am so glad you're braver than me."

"I like you a lot, too."

Still tangled together against the counter, Wade raised his hand and brushed Monty's hair off his sweaty forehead, tucking a few strands behind his ear. "Do you have to go right away? Or do you have time for another beer?"

"I have time."

They broke apart and Wade directed Monty to the living room. Monty grabbed Juliet and flopped on the couch while Wade turned on the marine life docuseries he had been watching in the evenings, hoping Monty would be into it. He chose the octopus episode, which started with a clip of a purple octopus using its arm to open a door and let itself out of its tank. He went to the kitchen to grab two beers while the show started up.

While he was opening the beers, he peeked through the doorway to look at Monty watching the show. He looked so cute, with his eyes wide and mouth hanging open. Wade smiled thinking about what they'd just done in the kitchen and he shoved the lasagna into the fridge, too nervous to eat and too unwilling to be unkissable.

"I love octopuses! Wait, is it octopi? I think I read once it's not, but people say it all the time anyway," Monty yelled from the living room. "I also read that people always call them 'octopus tentacles,' but they're actually *arms*. Hey, would you rather have arms with suckers, but you're way weaker, or arms like you have now, with no suction power?"

Wade walked in slowly, trying to think of a suitable answer to Monty's ridiculous question.

"I guess I'd want the suckers? I could use them in the ring. And then I could probably make money off of it once I'm retired."

Monty looked up at Wade with a look of sympathy that made Wade feel silly for saying anything.

"Are you nervous about the match?" Monty asked him.

"I am a little nervous, sure. I really want it to go well. I'm afraid of retirement, to be honest. I wish I could keep going forever."

"Why can't you?"

Wade looked at Monty dismissively and set his beer down on the coffee table harder than he meant to. He leaned forward, putting his forearms on his knees and letting his hands dangle.

"I'm serious, Wade. Why can't you?" Monty repeated, scooting closer to him.

"I don't know. I kind of go back and forth. Right now, I think I've done what I can. The new talent is young and creative, like you and Amit. And that's how it should be. I'm not upset about that. I just keep thinking that if I moved to CWA, I could have a fresh start. Maybe change my name. But then self doubt comes in and I think, if they wanted me, they could have poached me when they took Larry."

"Did you ever find out why you didn't get to go with him?"

"No, Mike tried to find out, but they were close lipped about it all. They just said I could try again the following year, but I was a mess when they came around."

"Of course, yeah."

"So, I don't know. I think I probably messed up my chances with them, and that's why I'm feeling so anxious about the match. I want to do well for myself, and I want to do well for you, but I'm worried I'm going to fuck up and ruin both of our chances. I don't know if I can handle that, being let down twice."

Monty hummed, grabbing Wade's hand to play with his fingers.

"And, if I'm being totally honest…" Wade started, then hesitated.

"What?"

"No, nevermind. Forget it, please."

"Wade!"

"Well, okay. What if you move to CWA some day and I don't? Like, okay, I'm jumping the gun here. I know, I know, we just met. But I have to admit that the idea of that happening has been on my mind since I realized I had feelings for you and I don't really know what to do about it."

Monty didn't say anything, which was unlike him. Wade realized then he'd been desperate to hear Monty say something reassuring, or to hear that he'd made an impact on Monty's life too, and that they could figure this out together. But that was way too intense for one hand job in the kitchen, so he pulled back.

"You know what, nevermind. You don't have to say anything. That was unfair of me."

"Wade, listen. I want to move to CWA someday, obviously. But, I'm also very excited about this," Monty said, waving his finger back and forth between the two of them. "Both are true. Why spend our energy worrying about what unlikely series of events could happen, when we could spend our energy learning about octopodes and making out?"

"You're right. I think that's a good plan," Wade smiled and leaned in to kiss Monty again. "Wait, octopodes?"

"I don't know. Google has a lot of conflicting information, Wade. I'm trying to cover my bases."

∼

MONTY HAD LEFT Wade's apartment around midnight, after they'd watched several episodes of the docuseries and got each other off again on the couch. It was the best night Wade remembered having in years. He'd wanted to ask Monty to stay the night, but before he'd finally worked up the nerve, Monty said something about having an early morning.

After a short, but surprisingly aggressive make-out session at the door, Monty finally left, looking disheveled and adorable, with flushed cheeks and a smile on his freshly kissed lips.

When Wade had gone into the kitchen to clean up, he found a small rubber snake in the bag Monty brought. He squeezed it in his hand against his chest and put it on his nightstand. He took a picture of it and sent it to Monty with a text that said "sweet dreams, Romeo," and then he slept better than he had in years.

WHEN WADE WALKED into Mike's office and sat down, he was obnoxiously peppy and ready to go over the match schedule Mike had put together. He looked at Mike across the desk and grinned.

"Hey, Wade," Mike said, not looking up from his papers.

"Hey, Mikey."

Mike looked up. "Excuse me?"

"Just trying something new. You don't like it. Noted."

Mike set his papers down and narrowed his eyes at Wade.

"No, I don't like it, Wade," Mike said. "What is your problem? What is that look on your face? Oh, my God. Did you have sex?"

"What the hell, Mike?"

"Well, don't come in here spewing weird bullshit like 'Mikey' and I won't say things like that to you."

"Jesus, fine," Wade said, looking anywhere but Mike's face. "Can you please ask Linda if I can bring those stuffed onions again this year?"

"Yeah, no problem. Bring enough for twelve," Mike replied. His face lit up as he noticed his opening and he asked, "Is it just you, or should I put you down for two?"

Wade glared at him. "It's just me, Mike."

Mike put his hands up in surrender. "I was just asking!"

"Can we move on, please? What's the schedule?"

"Fine," Mike said. "So, based on engagement, I'm thinking Amit and Niall will lead next Saturday. They're polling pretty well but I want them fresh before the scouts. Amit is still pretty green. After that, I'd like you and Monty to go. Your numbers aren't as strong as Monty's, but he's on fire, so the two of you combined have a big draw. Some of Limpet and Viper's old fans are excited to see what you're up to."

"Yeah. I'm sure they'd like to see my burial confirmed," Wade said, unimpressed with Mike's excitement.

"Hey. Wade. This is a good path for you. It's fresh, it's new. That's what you wanted," Mike said defensively. Wade didn't respond, so Mike added, "It might be what they're looking for."

"Okay. So who's next?"

Mike hesitated before he continued. "Anthony and Don. The night will end with Will and Castro, who just flew in from Vegas. I owed someone a favor. I don't expect much traction for them, but it's good to get them used to the attention. I'm not scheduling Kenji, Curt, or

Dicky this time, but the scouts will come back Monday so we can always add them at the last minute."

"This all sounds pretty good to me. When do we find out what happens on Monday?"

"Let's see how Saturday goes. We'll go from there, okay?"

"Sure."

"Okay, now that we have that out of the way, can we get back to why you're in such a good mood? Seriously, did you meet someone?" Mike asked.

"Kind of. Yes."

"That's awesome. I'm happy for you, bud."

"It's new," Wade said, attempting to manage Mike's expectations.

"New is okay. Sometimes you just know, huh?"

Wade shrugged one shoulder and smiled a small smile. "I guess so. It's sort of complicated."

"Ah, I'm sure you can figure it out. Are you sure you don't want to bring him to Thanksgiving?"

"Mike, seriously, I've known him for a month. Thanksgiving is, like, four weeks away. That seems a little rushed, even when you 'know,'" Wade said, using air quotes to stress the end of his sentence. "Not that I'm saying I know."

"Well, if you decide you know, he has a seat at the table," Mike smiled.

CHAPTER 14

MONTY ARRIVED AT THE ARENA A FEW MINUTES PAST NOON AND DID HIS best to not look for Wade immediately, but when he walked by the offices, he spotted him talking to Mike. Mike saw him through the window and nodded in acknowledgement. Monty waved, and when Monty and Wade's eyes met, he broke into a huge smile, but then looked at his feet and kept walking. When he turned to glance over his shoulder, he saw a questioning look on Mike's face, whose eyes were darting between Wade and Monty.

Monty sped up and walked to the locker room where he changed into his workout clothes and made his way to the gym. It was empty aside from Amit and Niall, who were by the squat rack arguing about something, like usual. Monty ignored them and hopped on a treadmill to warm up.

After a while, a familiar face walked through the double doors and Monty smiled at him in the mirror. Wade dipped his head towards an alcove on the opposite side of the room. Monty looked at Amit and Niall, who were still arguing, but now also watching something on Niall's phone. He took the opening and hopped off the treadmill and grabbed his water bottle, walking towards the water fountain near the alcove Wade was standing in.

As soon as he got close enough, Wade grabbed Monty's waist and shoved him up against the wall, hidden from Amit and Niall's line of sight. Wade pressed his lips against Monty's and kissed him, long enough to leave Monty a little breathless. His hands squeezed Monty's ass.

"Wow," Monty breathed. "What was that for?"

"Just happy to see you," Wade said, pecking another kiss on Monty's mouth. "Um, I realized we didn't really talk about how open we were going to be about this at work. I don't want to do anything to make you uncomfortable."

"I'm not worried about people knowing, but—" A lightbulb went off in his head and he laughed. "Ohh. Mike knows we had sex."

"I'm sorry," Wade said. "I didn't tell him it was you. At first. But when you walked by… I don't know. I probably had a dopey look on my face or something."

"Well, that's cute." Monty patted Wade's cheek gently.

Wade grabbed his hand and pinned it above his head before kissing down the side of Monty's neck. He shivered, and goosebumps spread over his arms and scalp. His body's reaction must have motivated Wade to go lower, which was hot and sensual and he thought he'd never felt such a mix of affection and desire. He wanted nothing more than for Wade to–

"Oh my God, stop! I cannot get a boner in gym clothes!"

Wade stepped back and looked at Monty, doing his best to school his expression. His eyes scanned down Monty's body and he smiled. "You can't?"

"Fuck off!"

Wade cleared his throat and adjusted himself in his pants. "I am sorry," he said.

"Well, that's just not true," Monty said. "But that's okay. So, tell me what Mike said."

"He didn't say much. He asked me if I'd met someone. I told him I had, and he told me to invite them to Thanksgiving. I told him to mind his business. That's all."

"Do you think he's upset that the guy you met is me?"

"No. Not upset. I do think he's worried, maybe," Wade said. "Not because it's you, just…"

"I'll try not to take it personally," Monty replied. "I know he loves you. But I'm not Larry, okay? None of us know what is going to happen, but I like you. I like this. You can trust me, Wade."

He squeezed Monty in his arms and gave him a peck on the cheek and said, "Thank you. I promise I won't maul you at work anymore. I have some stuff to do before we practice today, but do you want to come over again tonight?"

"Yes. I do."

"Okay," Wade said. "See you in an hour or so?"

"It's a date. A date for me to kick your ass, but still a date."

"You wish, Romeo."

MONTY HAD STASHED a ladder under the ring earlier in the day, ready to break it out during today's practice. They got through the two thirds of the fight before Wade jumped out of the ring to grab the ladder, delighting Monty. He tossed it into the ring which made the guys gathered on the mats erupt into cheers and beat their hands on the floor of the ring. Monty looked across the ring and saw Wade unsuccessfully trying to hide a smile. Wrestling with Wade was so fun and easy. He hoped Wade felt the same way. If he did, maybe he wouldn't retire this year after all, and Monty could keep doing what he loved most with the guy he... really liked.

"He's going to Giant Jim Monty!" Kenji yelled. The rest of the guys cheered. "Get him, Viper!"

Monty stood in the corner of the ring, taunting Wade with a "come here" motion. He leaned forward, placing his hands on his straining quads. He narrowed his eyes at Wade when he slid back into the ring.

Wade was wearing the outfit he'd be wearing for the scouts and he looked surprisingly sexy in bright green spandex. They had shimmering scales down the lines of his long, muscular legs and a single coiled snake on the butt. He was shirtless, and his chest was smooth and shiny from sweat. His full calf boots were black snake-skin with gold tipped laces, an embellishment Monty had encouraged. Wade was a walking wet dream, and this was the worst timing.

Monty shook his head and ran at Wade full speed, drop kicking him before he was able to set up the ladder. Wade writhed on the ground, giving Monty much needed time to get set up. Once the ladder was open and secure, Monty climbed on it and jumped on top of Wade in a frog splash, a nod to Giant Jim. The fall was painful, but laying on top of Wade wasn't.

Wade flung Monty off of him and the two continued brawling for a few more minutes. Eventually, Wade signaled to Monty that the match was ending by putting him in a cradle pin. Monty kicked out, but knew he would need to remain on the ground, catching his breath, while Wade moved the ladder into the corner and climbed to the top.

Monty opened one eye to catch sight of Wade's face once he reached the top. He raised his arms above his head and roared before he launched himself off the ladder, tucked his knees to his chest, and completed a backflip before landing on top of Monty.

The "ref," who in this case was Mike, counted Monty out and Wade won the match. Mike raised Wade's hand above his head and the guys all cheered. Well, except Dicky. For whatever reason, he rolled his eyes and stormed off towards the locker room. That was the first time Mike had seen the whole match Monty noticed he looked like a proud dad.

Monty got up and hugged Wade hard, trying his best to make it look like a manly bro-hug and not the hug he was giving his… boyfriend? Friend with benefits? He should probably ask.

"That was awesome!" he said, close to Wade's ear. "You are amazing."

"It was. You are. God, I can't wait until next week," Wade said, his eyes bright and clear, like the clouds that normally lingered behind them had finally floated away. Monty loved seeing this happy, excited side of Wade and would do anything to keep it around. Before he could react, Wade grabbed Monty's arms and pulled him into a brief kiss in front of all the guys. They hollered, some of them shouting *I knew it!* before Wade pulled back and placed his hand on Monty's cheek, petting his jaw with his thumb. "Um, sorry. I know I just said I wouldn't do that. I just… needed to."

Monty just smiled. He grabbed Wade's hand and squeezed before they hopped out of the ring.

"Wade, stay here for a minute?" Mike shouted across the ring.

"I guess I'll see you later. Do you want to meet at my house at like seven?" Wade asked Monty, walking backwards towards Mike.

"Sounds good. I'll bring dinner," Monty said.

He headed down the hall towards the locker room, Curt and Kenji jogging to catch up to him.

"Holy shit, that was so great. I loved that entire match. I can't believe how smooth it was. The scouts are gonna eat it up. Man, I bet we lose you *and* Wade this year," Kenji said, bouncing with enthusiasm as he walked next to Monty.

His heart fluttered at Kenji's suggestion. That would be incredible.

"No shit. I've never seen Wade wrestle like that, dude. You must do something to him for him to pull that off. And… I guess now we know what it is you do, huh?" Curt added with a laugh.

"He's always been good," Monty snapped, feeling defensive of Wade. He turned his head to look at Curt, glaring in his direction. "Just because he's not with CWA doesn't mean he's not a great wrestler. He's been good since before we got together. And that's all new, anyway, not that it's any of your business."

"Alright, alright," Curt said. "Sheesh. It was a compliment to you, anyway! You have the magic touch."

Monty clenched his fists. He picked up his pace as the three of them turned into the locker room. Kenji headed to his cubby to escape the tension.

"I like Wade, like I said. It all just seems convenient."

"What's convenient?"

"That he does so well the one time Mike is there to see it, and now he's hooking up with golden-boy Romeo," he said, laughing. "He's finding relevance wherever he can."

"What does that even mean?"

"Nevermind, dude. No ribbing Monty's old man, got it."

"No, not nevermind. This is the second time you've talked to me about him being some underperforming, flop wrestler. Everybody hears that shit, Curt. It's not ribbing if he's not here to defend himself. It's cowardly."

Curt rolled his eyes. "Sorry."

"Wade is good. He's always been good. You *just* saw him."

"Right. I've seen him lots of times, that's the point," Curt said, clearly trying to goad Monty into a bigger reaction.

It worked. Before he could stop himself, he turned and shoved

Curt into the wall with his forearm pinned against Curt's chest. Kenji's eyes widened with concern, but he said nothing.

"What the fuck, Monty?" Curt raised his hands in a calming gesture, but Monty was too angry to stop himself.

"You and Dicky aren't even on the scout schedule this year, or did you forget that?" Monty said, raising his forearm to Curt's neck to hold him in place. Curt's neck stretched unnaturally and his jaw pressed shut. "Get a few matches under your belt where Mike doesn't have to redirect you before you run your mouth. Do me a favor, Curt, and tell Dicky the same. Get fucked, and keep Wade's name out of your mouth."

Monty pushed off Curt's body, causing him to stumble slightly. Curt had the decency to look ashamed of himself, but stayed quiet. He snatched his backpack out of his cubby and rubbed his jaw. Monty watched him leave, probably going to look for Dicky to tell him about Monty's bereft sense of humor and unhinged reaction to his joke, but Monty didn't care. He had a dinner date with Wade.

WADE WAS FLOATING after the match. It was Mike's first time seeing it start to finish and it had gone well enough that he was actually *excited* to hear Mike's thoughts. The last several times he'd been in Mike's office unexpectedly it was to be given less than stellar feedback, but he was doing better over the last month or so. Today's match was his probably his best in years. Plus, his engagement was up, and people were loving the rivalry dynamic between Romeo and Viper.

He walked into Mike's office expecting positivity, but when he got there, Mike looked… strained. Wade started to panic.

"Mike?" Wade said, rushing over to the desk.

"I'm fine, Wade," Mike chuckled.

"You looked upset. Did I do something?"

"Yes, bonehead. You did something awesome. I'm so proud of you. I haven't seen *that* Wade in two years. It's such a sight, seeing you like that. I wasn't sure I would ever see it again."

Wade must have made a face because Mike walked around the desk to be closer to him.

"Hey," Mike said. He placed his hand on Wade's shoulder and squeezed. "This is great news. You guys were unbelievable. You really made the right decision working with Monty, and I think the scouts are going to be thrilled with what they see. I just wanted to tell you that. It's exciting."

"Oh. Thank you," he said, unable to form any other words. He was just so grateful Mike took a risk on him ten years ago, and two years ago, and every day since.

A WEEK LATER, Wade hadn't seen Monty outside of the arena since the dinner they shared after their big practice match. They went to a restaurant Wade's friend owned that served upscale sandwiches, which Monty claimed was "not a thing." Wade bet him five dollars that he'd be blown away by them, and Monty counter offered sex, figuring it would be win-win.

By the time they got home, they'd both been so full of fancy cheese, meat, and fruit that neither one of them could handle putting anything else in their mouths, including each other. Monty acknowledged that he lost the bet, Wade generously offered to postpone collection, and they fell asleep on the couch watching an HGTV show about a log cabin renovation.

Since then, he'd been staying late at work to help Mike with online scheduling and video releases. They were filming and releasing promos and vignettes, uploading clips to social media and long form videos to YouTube, and the CWA film crew had been around more often. He got home late every evening and still had to show up to practice every morning, so he was exhausted.

On the Wednesday before the match, Wade paced the office, anxious about Saturday.

"Will you get out of here? You're distracting me," Mike said. "You can't just walk around in here, it's annoying. Please take the day off."

"But I have things to get done!" Wade said. He felt Mike's hands shove him towards the open office door. Wade was always shocked by Mike's strength, considering he was retired and Wade was almost a foot taller than him. "Ow, asshole!"

He tried to get back in, but Mike closed the door in his face. He knocked on the door.

"Mike!"

The door opened slowly, much to Wade's relief, but instead of letting him in, Mike thrust Juliet's soft carrier into his chest and closed the door again.

He stared at the closed door in disbelief before giving up. He held Juliet's carrier under his arm and turned to walk down the hall towards the locker room to gather his things.

"Boo!" Monty yelled, jumping out from behind a corner. Wade jumped back and screamed.

"Jesus, Monty," he said, gripping his chest. "What is wrong with you?"

His terror appeared to delight Monty, who was walking toward him with a giant smile on his face, but it fell dramatically when he saw Juliet.

"Oh, my God! I must have scared her so much," he said, reaching for the carrier. "Why didn't you tell me you had her?!"

"I'm fine, if you were wondering."

Monty ignored him and unzipped the carrier, pulling Juliet from her slumber. She yawned and he hugged her before turning his attention back to Wade.

"Where are you guys headed?" Monty asked.

"Mike is kicking me out. Said I was too annoying."

"I'm done with my workout. Do you want to hang out? I've missed you this week."

"That sounds nice. I was thinking about taking Juliet to Linda's to hunt for bugs."

Monty bit his lips between his teeth and breathed slowly. "I would really, really like to do that. If I'm invited."

THEY WALKED hand in hand through Linda's back lot, which wasn't so much a yard as it was a long, forested two acre plot lined by water. The rainy weather had replenished the dry creek bed, transforming it back into a full stream with small rapids and deep pools. Its banks were full of lush plants and the damp air smelled earthy and musty from the wet leaves that had begun to fall.

They watched Juliet weave in and out of the grasses with her nose on the ground, searching for snacks in the rotting vegetation. All of it was beautiful and comfortable and a little too close to perfect. Wade had to force himself to reel in his emotions, nervous he'd scare Monty off if he shared them.

"That is just so darn cute," Monty said, pointing at Juliet with his free hand. "How do they know how to do that? Is she looking for slugs?"

"Instinct, I guess? And yes, they eat slugs. Good for gardeners."

Wade watched Monty take a deep breath and look out towards the forest in front of them. He looked pensive. And really beautiful, with his hair blowing in the breeze.

"This is really nice. I want this someday," Monty said.

"You want what? A forest?"

"Yeah, or like, land. Something peaceful like this. I also want cows. At least two, because I read once that they have best friends and their happiness depends on friendship."

"That sounds nice. I like cows, too," Wade said.

"I've always wondered what that means, though. Like, if you have two cows, are they automatically best friends? Or do they pick a best friend and settle for acquaintances if their best friend lives on some other farm?"

"I… don't know. I'll try to find out for you, though."

"I also want a big farmhouse. And a garden. You know, for all the free time I'll have when I'm full time at CWA," Monty said, grinning.

Wade's stomach tensed, but before he could focus on it too much, Monty continued.

"Ooh, and dogs, of course. At least two. Hmm, and a trophy spouse."

"This list is really growing."

Monty just smiled.

They kept walking and Juliet strolled out of the grass, chewing on something gray and slimy they couldn't identify. Monty looked horrified.

"Oh, God. What is that? Juliet, no!" He started walking towards her with his hands out, like a parent ready to dig bark chips out of their toddler's mouth.

It made Wade feel a certain type of way.

"It's okay. They're like garbage disposals. They eat everything," Wade said, pulling Monty back towards him.

"Ugh. I love her, but I do not like her right now," he said, shuddering.

Monty stopped to put his hair up in a bun. The damp air had made it frizzy and unruly, which Wade loved, but Monty complained about it enough that he knew his compliments wouldn't convince him to leave it down.

Bun secured, a lock of golden hair dangled by his eye, and Wade reached out to play with the ends. He must have had a goofy look on his face because Monty started laughing.

"What?" Wade asked.

"What's that look for? You look like you're about to say something... profound."

"No. Just enjoying the moment," Wade said. "I'm glad we got the day off."

"Me, too."

"So, um," Wade said, hesitantly, "say you had that farmhouse. The one with a forest, cows, garden, dogs, and trophy spouse. Would there be anyone else there? Like... kids?"

"I think so. I always imagined I'd have kids. I haven't really met anyone I've felt serious enough to think about it much, but I think I want some," he said.

He said it so nonchalantly but so confidently. Like he didn't worry about how he'd get there because he just assumed it would happen. Or not. Wade envied the effortless way he seemed to approach life. It was different from Wade, who worried and fussed and panicked over every decision and timeline.

"How about you?" Monty asked. "Any baby Wades in your future?"

"I hope so," Wade said. He ducked his head, suddenly embarrassed about the conversation he'd started. Monty squeezed his hand and Wade forced himself not to overthink it. He could see it, though. A future with Monty and gardens and dogs and kids.

"Of course," Monty said, walking again, "that's all in the future. I don't know where I'll be in one year, let alone five."

The reminder of their impossible future was like a splash of cold water in his face. It ripped him from his daydreams just in time.

"Right."

"Same for you, right?" Monty said, nudging him with his shoulder. "But hey, maybe we'll both be in Boston next year. You can help me scope out Boston-area farms."

CHAPTER 15

WHEN WADE FINALLY GOT HOME FROM THE ARENA THE FRIDAY BEFORE the scout match, it was already six o'clock. He was expecting Monty at seven, so he ran to the shower to wash the day's grime off of his body, making sure to get extra clean, scrubbing all his creases and sweaty spots.

After he finished in the shower, he was already worked up because he'd been thinking about Monty so much and anticipation of what the evening would bring, so he walked to his bedroom and laid on the bed. He grabbed a bottle of lube and touched himself just enough to get the edge off. Now that he finally had Monty for himself but was still required to touch him aggressively all day, it was nearly impossible to function without some level of arousal. He decided not to touch his dick, but he did prep himself a bit, hoping to be ready for Monty when he arrived, and was hoping Monty would fuck him. When he checked his phone and saw that it was close to seven, he washed his hands, put on some clean clothes, and sat on the couch to wait anxiously.

He heard a rap on the door at 7:02 and jumped off the couch. He pulled the door open, and when he saw Monty, his heart leapt. God, he looked good. He was wearing an old Viper shirt from Wade's early years at Titan and he had a book shoved under his arm. Wade burst into laughter.

"Where did you get that shirt?!"

Monty gave him a brief smile and stepped inside the door.

"Wade, I need to tell you something before we have dinner. You have to promise not to kick me out right away," he said.

Wade laughed again, but Monty didn't.

"Wait, you're serious? Why would I kick you out?"

He tried to think of what Monty could possibly say that would make Wade kick him out of his home, and none of the stupid ideas he came up with were things he could even begin to imagine. Like, did he sleep with Mike?

"I think I made a big mistake. I came over here thinking this was going to be very funny, but as I was driving, I realized it's *not* funny, it's weird, and you're just going to think I'm a freak and not at all someone you should voluntarily spend time with. And now I'm here at your door, and you've seen me in my Viper shirt so I can't go back now, and to be honest, I feel a little panicky. I fully expect you to fake a stomach ache to get out of our date, and I'm going to deserve it."

"Hey, relax. That all seems very unlikely," Wade said, stepping to the side so Monty could head into the living room. "Do you need to sit down, or…"

Monty headed for the couch and sat down, then pulled out a notebook. Wade looked down and saw scribbled letters spelling out *MONTY'S WRESTLING JOURNAL*. He looked at Monty with a smirk, but Monty's face was worried.

"Okay, so," Monty said, opening up the journal slowly, then closing it again as he continued. "I'm usually a very open and honest guy, and this has been sort of looming over me since we met. I should have told you when we first met because now it's… well, with our relationship changing, it felt wrong to keep it from you. I mean, not that I'm expecting anything from you and our relationship. Which I know isn't even a relationship, or whatever," Monty said, his eyes briefly looking up to Wade's face, hesitating, waiting for… something. "But I asked my mom what she thought about what I'm about to show you, and she said I should share it with you. She's always been a stickler about honesty, so I kind of knew what she'd say when I asked her. Maybe that's *why* I asked her, honestly…"

Wade took a deep breath and pinched the bridge of his nose. He usually found Monty's inability to efficiently get from Point A to

Point B charming. The way his brain took little jaunts, introducing Wade to new pieces of Monty Trivia made every conversation unpredictable in the best way. But this time, he had an urge to grab Monty by the shoulders and shake him until the truth came out.

"Um, you're making me nervous. We can work through it together, whatever it is," Wade said. "I mean, if you want to."

"Okay, so," Monty started again, slowly, then paused, causing Wade to clench his jaw. "You know how I told you I got into wrestling when I watched that WrestleTalk interview with you, and that your career has been sort of motivating for me?"

"Yeah?"

"Well, that's… Okay, maybe it's easier if you just look at this," Monty said, handing over his journal.

Wade flipped to the first page. There was a list titled *GOALS*, and it had three bullet points. One, he was to become a professional wrestler. Two, he was to become friends with Wade Donovan, and three, written in a different pen, he was to have sex with Wade Donovan some day. He put four question marks next to that one, which made him laugh.

He blinked and looked up. Monty's cheeks were bright pink and his eyes were glued to his hands. He was picking at his cuticles.

He flipped through the rest of the notebook, still unsure what had sparked Monty's panic. The first part of the notebook was just training outlines, his favorite moves, and moves he wanted to learn. There were pages dedicated to rules and illegal moves. There were magazine photos of wrestlers cut out and glued to the pages, Monty's teenage handwriting listing their stats and signature moves and finishers. He noticed Monty had also drawn chili peppers by each wrestler, some wrestlers earning one chili pepper and some earning up to five. He could guess what that meant, and chuckled.

He turned the page again and saw about a dozen photos of himself, spanning almost the entirety of his career. The updates had stopped several years ago.

He counted the chili peppers on his page: *ten!* His pages also listed fun facts, like how he grew up in Minnesota and had a childhood dog named Reggie. Monty had drawn a little poodle next to Reggie's name. Wade cracked up and stroked the drawing with his finger.

"Oh, my GOD, Monty!"

"I stopped doing this years ago!" Monty said defensively. He looked mortified and Wade felt bad for him, but this was too cute. "I was just a kid when I was doing that."

"Monty, is this seriously what you were afraid to tell me? That you had a crush on me when you were a teenager? It's cute that you think I didn't know that." Wade was still laughing. He couldn't stop. He just remembered the shirt Monty was wearing and laughed even harder. "Oh my God, how long have you had that shirt?! Why would you start the evening by making me think you were ending things? That was mean as hell."

"I've had this shirt for, um, eight years. And, yeah, I did have a crush on you as a teenager. But I sort of… kept having a crush on you? And I applied to sign with Titan because I've always had this dream that we'd become friends, or whatever. God, this is really embarrassing. Why did I think this was funny?"

"I mean, it's kind of funny."

Monty glared at him. "I wanted to work with Mike, too, to be clear. But you were my motivation to get good enough to move out here. It's given me this awesome opportunity to be here and to meet you. It has been beyond even the best-case scenario I imagined for the goals in that notebook. And now that you've seen my deepest shame, I need you to know that I like you for *you*, not for whatever I imagined when I was a weirdo teenager."

"Of course I know that. So what's the problem?" Wade asked. His face softened. "I feel like you're a lot more upset about this than you need to be. This is adorable, Monty. I love it."

"The problem is now you know I'm an obsessive freak and that my parents know all about you. Like I'm some weird stalker who moved here to be close to you. I have like five enormous plush snakes back at my parents' house." Monty said, mumbling the last part.

Wade pursed his lips and did some controlled breathing so he wouldn't laugh, beginning to feel bad.

"Monty. This is, hands down, the best thing anyone has ever shown me," Wade said, standing up from the couch. He held his hand out and grabbed Monty's, pulling him up so their bodies were pressed together. He reached around Monty's back and clasped his hand at the dip above his butt. "I get why you feel silly, but Monty… listen, my biggest regret in life has always been that I wasted all these years wrestling with Titan, failing to progress to the level I wanted. Knowing some kid out there had a crush on me and used that to motivate himself to become one of the best wrestlers I've ever met or worked with? I mean, fuck me. That is something so few people get to experience. It was totally worth that. You are totally worth that."

"Jeez," Monty said. His hands lightly pressed against Wade's chest.

"I'm serious. You are the sweetest, best person I have ever met in my life," Wade said, giving Monty one final squeeze before he pulled his head back to kiss him. He gave him restrained kisses at first. He wanted to make sure Monty knew he was serious about what he said, and serious about him. But things progressed when Monty ran his strong fingers down Wade's chest and stomach. Wade kissed him deeply, like he wanted to consume him, or share a body, or fuse together.

After a few minutes, their kisses turned frantic. Their breaths got heavier and their hands roamed over each other's clothes and Monty's hands squeezed Wade's ass. He ran his fingers up the seam of Wade's pants, pressing for more. Wade raised his fist to Monty's hair, grabbing it and twisting it through his fist before he pulled Monty's head back to give himself access to his neck. He lowered his head and sucked hard enough to make Monty yelp.

"I love your hair," he said. "It was the first thing I noticed about you. I've wanted to wrap it around my fist like this since the first time I saw you at the arena."

Monty whimpered. "Fuck." His hands fisted Wade's shirt and then lowered to the waistband of his pants. His fingers danced along the front, Wade feeling the touch low in his belly. He was already so hard and Monty's hands were too light. He grunted and roughly shoved his erection into Monty's stomach while he kissed him.

"Do you want to go into your bedroom?" Monty rasped.

"Yes." Wade grabbed Monty's hand and dragged him down the short hallway before stepping into his room. Monty followed, grabbing Wade's waist and backing him up against the bed. Wade fell backwards, pulling Monty down on top of him.

"Too many clothes," Monty said against Wade's open mouth. "Unless you want me to keep the shirt on?"

Wade laughed so hard he coughed. "God, no, please remove that immediately."

They stood up and removed their shirts first, then their pants and boxer briefs. They stood in front of each other naked and breathing hard, scanning each other's bodies. Of course this wasn't the first time Wade had seen Monty naked and vice versa, but it was the first time he'd been able to appreciate every body part belonging to the man he was falling for. Their previous times together after their first time in Wade's kitchen had been hurried hand jobs and quick blow jobs in Titan's supply closets and darkened shower rooms.

Monty was slightly shorter than Wade, maybe by an inch, but he was the same bulk. All of his muscles were visibly defined beneath his smooth skin. Wade couldn't stop himself from reaching out to run his hands down the length of his torso. Monty's waist was narrow, which made his broad chest seem even wider. His arms were strong, the veins in his forearms were close to the surface. He left a patch of pubic hair that stretched up to just below his belly button. Wade felt a pull inside that demanded him to touch it.

He couldn't take it anymore and shoved Monty back onto the bed. He climbed on top of him, their bodies touching everywhere, finally. He kissed Monty again, softly this time, before he sat up and strad-dled Monty's hips. Wade lined their dicks up so they rubbed against one another and it caused them both to moan.

"Please," Monty said.

Wade rolled his hips into Monty's again before he leaned down to kiss Monty's chest, paying attention to each nipple. Monty writhed beneath him.

"God, yes," Monty breathed. He sounded desperate and it made Wade feel desperate, too.

Wade continued making his way down Monty's chest, licking his defined abs and kissing every blemish and bruise. Knowing he put them there was almost painful, each one a visible reminder of the intentional pain he'd inflicted on the man he cared about so deeply. So he took his time, offering gentle apologies to each one.

Monty's dick was leaking and it was pooling on his belly. Wade licked it up on the way down Monty's abs. He found a visible vein that led to Monty's dick and he traced it with his tongue, and then he spread Monty's legs and licked the crease between his thigh and his groin, eliciting a long groan from Monty.

"Please," Monty said. He moved up to his elbows, watching Wade.

"You keep saying that. Please what?"

Wade looked up and met Monty's eyes. He took pity on him and swallowed Monty down all the way to his throat.

"Ah, fuck. You feel so good," Monty groaned, dropping his head back to the pillow.

Wade worked Monty up and down, saliva dripped down the sides of Monty's dick. He popped off and replaced his mouth with his fist, jacking Monty slowly as he flattened his tongue and licked Monty from his taint to the tip of his dick before he swallowed it down again. Wade reached down and started touching his own dick, afraid to come too early but too desperate to stop himself.

Wade sat up and looked at Monty. His eyes were lustful and dark. "I want you to fuck me," Wade said, his voice gravelly.

"God, yes, I want to," Monty replied. He sat up and grabbed Wade, flipping him onto his back. Wade reached blindly for the bedside table and grabbed the lube and a condom from the drawer. He tossed them at Monty. Monty opened the cap and slicked up two of his fingers, reaching for Wade's hole, one finger sliding in easily. He paused and looked up at Wade.

"Wade…?" Monty asked, eyes playful.

"I was optimistic, and nervous… and horny," Wade laughed. "Do you know how hard it is to be required to touch you all day?"

"Yeah, I think I do." He moved up to kiss Wade. They both groaned when Monty put another finger in. Wade's noises became more urgent, and after a while, Monty crooked his fingers, drawing out a long, low groan from Wade.

"Fuck," Monty said, grabbing the condom and rolling it down his aching shaft. "You are so hot. I have to fuck you now. Are you ready?"

"Yeah, please," Wade begged.

Monty spread Wade's legs and bent one thigh up to his shoulder, bringing Wade's calf behind his back. His other leg fell open and laid on the bed. Monty pressed the head of his dick against Wade's hole and applied just enough pressure to slide in.

They both groaned and Monty rested his forehead against Wade's. He kept pressing until he was buried to the hilt, his balls resting against Wade's ass. He moved his head to the crook of Wade's shoulder, kissing the base of his neck, as he pulled his dick out slightly before he started thrusting slowly.

"Fuck, Monty," Wade whined, already feeling his orgasm building. He squirmed, trying to meet Monty's thrusts. "Harder. Please. I can take it."

"I know you can," Monty said, breathless. "You're so strong. Watching you own the ring makes me so hard."

Monty rolled his hips, then fucked into him hard and fast. Both of them were panting and moaning, Monty's breaths were hitting Wade's ear. Monty grabbed Wade's other leg and bent it up, folding Wade in half. He leaned back to kneel in front of him and kept going, fucking Wade hard until his rhythm got jerky, slamming into Wade even harder. It had been so long since he'd been fucked that he couldn't believe he hadn't come yet.

"Fuck. Yes," Wade said. He was barely able to think of words.

"Do you want my cum inside you?"

Wade groaned and his face looked pained. "God, yes. I need to come."

Monty grabbed Wade's dick with his and jerked him hard and fast. Wade felt his balls tighten immediately and he shot cum all over his chest. He could feel himself clenching on Monty's dick and he watched intently as Monty closed his eyes and rolled his head back. His mouth opened and let out a hoarse cry as he stilled, buried inside Wade, his orgasm washing over him. When he came down, he fell forward onto Wade, who lowered his legs and placed his hands on Monty's back. He rubbed up and down, loving the slick feeling of Monty's sweat.

"Jesus," Wade said, still breathless. He closed his eyes and put his forearm over his eyes.

Monty rolled off of Wade and onto his side. Wade hissed at the loss of Monty inside him but he was too blissed out to complain.

Monty's hand reached out and sprawled across Wade's chest for a moment before he got up to get a washcloth from the bathroom. He came back and wiped the mess from Wade's chest and between his legs. He tossed the rag into the laundry basket at the foot of Wade's bed and crawled under the covers, scooting his body closer. Wade rolled over onto his side so he could look at Monty.

"I don't really understand what I did to deserve you coming into my life," he said, stroking Monty's hair. He took a few strands of it and twisted it in his fingers.

"You're deserving of a lot of great things."

"I think this is the best day of my life," Wade said. He gathered Monty up in his arms and kissed him before he passed out, exhausted by the emotions of the day.

WHEN MONTY WOKE up the following morning, he was crushed halfway under Wade, wrapped up in his arms. Wade was holding him so tightly it felt like he was dying a slow, suffocating death, and he loved it. He pressed his back against Wade's chest and listened to his slow breathing. He tried to reach his phone on the nightstand but couldn't stretch his arm that far. His movement caused Wade to stir.

"Sorry," Monty whispered.

Wade didn't say anything, but placed soft, sleepy kisses on Monty's neck. Well, not so much his neck as the unruly hair *covering* his neck, because he'd been too tired to put it in a braid before they went to sleep, but it didn't matter. It felt amazing, and Monty smiled, hoping he could convince Wade they had time to repeat last night. But Wade's soft snores started again, interrupting his train of thought.

He wondered if their evening had meant anything to Wade the way it had Monty. He hoped it had, but both of them had been dancing around their relationship for reasons he didn't understand, though he assumed it stemmed from Wade's inability to be straightforward about his feelings. It didn't always bother him, and he was figuring out how to pry information out of him. But the uncertainty sometimes nagged at him.

He lay in Wade's bed, surrounded by the scent of Wade and

laundry detergent and the remnants of their evening together, and he felt a confusing twinge of longing. He was physically touching Wade, their legs were twisted together and Monty was still pinned between Wade's ridiculous arms. They'd had a very hot and then very romantic evening, with Wade ordering a fancy dinner and declaring his old Larry superstition dead, then starting a new one involving Monty's lips.

But even with that, he couldn't shake the idea that Wade was holding him at arm's length for reasons he wasn't sharing, and Monty didn't know how to approach it, or if he should even try. Things felt right, and he was afraid to scare Wade off.

"I'm going to head home, if you can hear me," he whispered again. "I have to get my stuff. See you soon."

HE DUG through his closet at his apartment and found the garment bag Lexi from costume design had put together for him. His new pants were royal blue velvet with gold colored, medieval style accents. He chose brand new, very expensive, full calf black vinyl boots. He originally wanted to wear a tunic so he looked more the part of Romeo, but Lexi suggested he go shirtless under his feathered cape. She said online engagement increased when he wore leggings alone, which made him laugh. He didn't argue.

The arena was buzzing with energy when he arrived around noon. The scouts would be there by mid-afternoon, but there was a lot to do to get ready. He was no stranger to the film crews, because matches happened throughout the season all over the region, each wrestler taking on others with minimal overarching plot plot lines, and they were all filmed and posted online. But the level of professionalism needed for those matches was lower than that of the bigger matches involving rivalries and championships.

It was clear to Monty how big of a deal the day really was when he walked down the hallway towards the locker room and was passed by about a dozen people running with cameras and microphones, someone yelling about some parking lot fight that had just sprung up. There was live streaming happening all day, which Monty used to really love when he was just a fan, but now it made him nervous.

He stepped into the locker room and slipped into his new pants and zipped up his boots. He went to the mirror to look at his hair and decided it was a good day to leave his hair dry. Romeo Montague didn't seem like he'd go for the greased-up look, so he put it in a topknot on top of his head. While he was standing by the mirror wondering about the hairstyles of the 1500s, Dicky and Curt walked in, laughing about something. Both grew silent when they noticed Monty. He didn't engage, but glared at them through the mirror.

The locker room door flew open and a camera was shoved in his face. He knew from talking to Wade and Mike over the last few weeks that he needed to be ready to be on whenever cameras were running. He also knew Wade had pre-recorded his cutscenes and he made a mental note to do that next year. Monty's face shifted into an angry frown and he growled before punching the mirror. He walked over to Curt and Dicky and turned to face the camera.

"Today's the day, Romeo!" Dicky said, playfully shoving Monty. "It's time to show Viper what we can do. Out with the old, in with the new, right, brother?!"

Monty grumbled, hating Dicky and hating what he said. He knew Dicky was acting, but it was an act that was totally believable coming from him. He wanted Wade to retire, and was turning the Viper-Romeo rivalry into an all or nothing fight. At least the intense anger he felt towards Dicky served as a source of fuel, enabling him to channel his anger towards Viper.

"That's right!" Monty snarled. He pointed to the camera and scowled. "I am the future of Titan wrestling, Viper! You hear me? I've beat your ass so many times I'm practically yawning, so let's make it official. Today is the end of your pathetic reign. You're yesterday's news, yesterday's leftovers—and feel free to call me the trash man." Monty cringed at how stupid he sounded. *Trash man?*

Dicky and Curt yelled and patted Monty on the back, egging him on and shouting obscenities about Viper. A handful of women in skimpy outfits charged into the locker room, giggling and asking Romeo to keep them busy for a few minutes in the greenroom. He took one on each arm and winked at the camera, taking them to the empty office they'd disguised as a greenroom for filming. As he walked down the hallway, he yelled to the film crew, "If Viper needs me, you bring him here. If he's lucky, maybe I can teach him a thing or two about more than just wrestling today!" He lowered his hands to the women's butts and squeezed as they broke into giggles again.

When he got into the greenroom, he removed his hands from the women who had come with him and smiled at them.

"Thanks, ladies," he said. "Sorry for the butt grabs."

CHAPTER 16

Wade was hiding out in the extra office, surprisingly unprepared for the number of people swarming the arena. He was sitting at the desk and his leg was bouncing with nerves. In just a few hours, he would be done with the match, his last chance at being scouted officially in the past. It was scary.

The last few weeks working with Monty had started to shift his perspective wrestling. He'd spent two years putting less of himself into his brand and it showed in his matches and, of course, his popularity. He regretted it.

He was still firm that this was his last year wrestling with a goal of moving to CWA, but he was starting to warm to the idea of continuing his career with Titan. Maybe part time, if Mike would let him. He still didn't feel confident in who he was as a wrestler anymore, but he did have hope that there was a future for him, somewhere.

A knocking sound pulled Wade from his thoughts. The door opened and Mike poked his head in.

"I have a surprise for you," he sang.

Wade figured it was Monty coming to say hi before the match. He stood up and brushed off his shirt.

"Hey!" Madeline said, bounding through the door.

"Hi!" He was surprised to see her. He'd told her not to come, and she never listened to him, but he still didn't expect her to be there. He extended his arms out to hug her and she cuddled up to his chest. "What are you doing here?"

"Just here to support you. How are you feeling? Are you ready to kick some Romeo ass?"

"I guess so. I mean, I know I'm going to win, so that helps."

"I bet. Hey, the kids drew you some pictures." She removed herself from Wade's arms and rummaged through her bag, pulling out two wrinkly drawings. One of them was of Viper wearing his shiny green pants, flying through the air about 30 feet above the ring. A tiny stick person with long blond hair was on the floor of the ring, awaiting his fate. Blood was pooling by his head. There were snakes in the audience and it looked like they were hissing their support.

"Wow, dark. I bet Ramona did this one," he smiled.

"She's staunchly anti-Romeo, I don't know what to tell you."

The other drawing was of Wade and Jack, side by side, but the scale was way off. Jack was taller than Wade and had bigger muscles than him, too, but the figures were labeled so he couldn't argue. He snorted out a laugh.

"I told him no steroids until he was eighteen," he looked at her with worried eyes. She slapped his arm playfully. They were quiet for a moment and then his eyes grew moist and he cleared his throat to try to stop the tears from forming.

He and Madeline had been friends since he moved to Portland. She'd been there for every major moment in his adult life. She was there when his parents told him they didn't support him, and when Larry left him and the subsequent crumbling of his career. She was even there when he got the news via Facebook that his childhood dog died and then helped him work through the complicated feelings that came from his shitty parents not even texting him to let him know.

Similarly, he'd been with Madeline the night she met Kenny and he was her best man at their wedding. He was the first one to the hospital after she'd delivered each of her babies and he took two weeks off from work to support her when her mom died and she couldn't get off the couch.

She left her family at home to come watch his final scout match because she knew he needed her, even though he told her not to come. It filled him with an emotion he couldn't name and he wanted to bottle it up so he would never forget. He blinked and a tear dislodged, falling onto one of the drawings.

"Shit," he said, wiping his eyes with the backs of his wrists.

"Aww. Come here," she said, forcing him into another hug. "You've done such a great job, sweetheart. You've had an incredible career. You have so much life left. This is just one part of it ending."

He nodded but didn't say anything. He buried his head in her hair and breathed out a quiet sob. She rocked him back and forth and rubbed his back, something she once said she started doing after she had her first babies and she hadn't been able to stop. He'd even see her do it to a frozen turkey in line at the grocery. It made him happy that she was doing it to him now, even though he towered over her and his arms were the size of her thigh. He stood up straight and took her hands, squeezing them in unspoken thanks.

The door opened then, and Monty poked his head around. He caught Wade's eyes and squeezed himself and a cat carrier through the mostly closed door, shutting it the rest of the way behind him. Monty looked so handsome in his new Romeo outfit it made his mouth water.

"Sorry! I didn't mean to interrupt," he whispered with no malice in his tone. "Mike told me you were in here and I wanted to come say hi, but I can come back."

"No, no, stay here. I wanted to see you anyway," Wade said, reaching out his hand to him. Monty took it and walked towards him. "This is Madeline."

"Hi." Monty's voice was quiet and shy. "It's really nice to meet you. I've heard so much about you."

"Likewise," she smiled. "I'm really glad to meet you. I hope today goes great. For both of you. It's 2:30, by the way. I'm going to go find a good seat. I wanna be so close I can feel the sweat, boys. Make it rain!"

"Gross," Wade groaned. "Get out of here!"

Madeline laughed and then left and closed the door. Monty stepped over to it to latch the deadbolt before returning to his spot in front of Wade.

"Ready, big guy?" Monty said, patting Wade's stomach.

"As I'll ever be, right?" Wade replied, dabbing the last tears out of his eyes with his t-shirt. "I don't even know why I'm so emotional about this. It's not even the end of the season."

"I know, but it's still a milestone. It's okay to have feelings about it."

Monty's phone buzzed in his waistband. He pulled it out and opened the text he received from his mom. It was a photo of Becky with what Wade suspected was one of Monty's big plush snakes. He let out a wet laugh. The text said, "Becky teaching Viper who the real alpha is." He turned the phone to show Wade.

"I don't think there are vipers in Boise," Wade said.

"I don't know, our neighbor's house once got raided by Idaho Fish and Game and they took a bunch of illegal venomous snakes out of the basement. Maybe one broke free, tried to live her best life, and got snatched up by Becky. So quick to judge my poor dog!"

"Maybe," Wade said as he leaned forward and gave Monty a kiss. "Well, this Viper is about to kick your ass."

"Which viper? This one?" Monty asked, reaching into the front of Wade's leggings.

"Stop!" Wade laughed, removing Monty's hand. "If I'm not allowed to give you a boner in the gym, you're not allowed to give me one like, five minutes before I have to go on live television."

"Wait, I had a few more puns. Like, show me your one eyed snake. Or, um… unhinge that jaw, baby, and take this viper. Oh! What about, I want to make your viper spit." He recited them all in a deep, breathy voice that was not at all sexy, and to make it even worse, he hissed the "s" every time.

"Please stop."

"I hope you don't suffer from reptile dysfunction later, I have big plans for you after the match."

"Okay, well, thanks for that. I've never been less attracted to you, so at least there's no risk of me getting hard now."

Monty looked pleased with himself. He bent down and removed Juliet from the cat carrier.

"I forgot! Surprise!"

"What is she doing here?" Wade asked. "Shit, I'm too emotional for this."

"Linda is in Mike's office on the way to the clinic. I walked by and saw Juliet's carrier and asked to borrow her."

Wade gave Juliet a scratch behind the ears. "It's almost time for her to go, you know."

Monty scoffed. "Tell your daddy we aren't going to talk about that today." He held Juliet up to Wade's face. "Today is for good vibes only. Say, 'I love you, daddy! You're going to do great, daddy!'"

"Please don't say daddy like that." Wade laughed again and watched Monty snuggle Juliet before putting her back in her carrier. His heart squeezed at the sight, and his stomach sank at the most horrible realization.

The wall he'd built so deliberately was demolished now, and the space it had occupied was fully erased from the earth, driving them unavoidably towards one another. The result was something he'd hoped to avoid, despite how little effort he'd put into it. He *loved* him.

He loved him, and admitting it made panic flood his veins. Because now, no matter what happened after the match, he'd have to deal with this. He'd have to deal with his heart breaking when Monty moved on. But it wasn't possible to ignore it anymore, and he'd just have to get through it when the time came.

He would also have to find a good time to tell him, but this wasn't it. Not before Monty's first scout match, and not before he figured out how he'd gone and done something so reckless.

Monty smiled up at Wade from the ground after latching the cat carrier and then launched himself at him, jumping up into his arms and kissing him over and over. Wade was glad he worked out for a living, Monty's weight a non issue as he shoved him up against the wall and peppered his face with kisses. He slowed down and gave Monty several long, chaste kisses before he set him down, sending Monty on his way to the backstage waiting area.

"Good luck. See you soon," Monty said.

Wade took a moment to sit and digest as he fought the impulse to think of his happiness as something fleeting. He had incredible friends, an amazing guy in his life, a cute baby opossum to care for, and he had a ten-year career with Titan that would change after today, but it didn't have to end. It felt like the weight of his past was lifting off his shoulders, disappearing with the rubble from the metaphorical wall that had kept him from Monty. He was ready to see what came next.

CHAPTER 17

Monty heard the siren sound from his entrance music, *Indestructible* by Disturbed, blaring through the arena. He was used to the lights and sounds that preceded big events, but this was beyond anything he'd experienced. It was exhilarating. It felt like the energy flowing through the arena made a detour through his body, leaving through his fingers and toes. The music and frenzied cheers from the audience sent goosebumps up his arms when he realized the audience was reacting like that for *him*.

He thought about Wade and how he was feeling. It must have been similar on some level. Both of them worked hard over the last few months to get here. But where Monty's future was vast and open-ended, Wade's would be decided, with finality, tonight.

When Monty heard the guitar intro start, he took off running down the aisle, high-fiving fans and planted actors who lined the fencing. He slid on his belly into the ring and jumped to his feet, running around the perimeter with his arms raised up, trying to hype up the audience. He threw his cape into the audience and the young woman who caught it screamed so loud he was a little concerned.

Monty hopped up on the turnbuckle and continued doing his best to energize the crowd, yelling nonsense angrily. Nobody could actually hear what he was saying, but it was fun to yell. He jumped down and ran to the other side, repeating the actions until he heard Viper's entrance music drop, at which point he moved to the center of the ring and tried to look as angry as possible.

Viper entered moments later to Sevendust's *Black*. The arena lights went dim and turned red as the song progressed. He walked out slowly, shooting daggers at the audience and Romeo.

The crowd erupted at Viper's entrance and they jeered and booed and hurled curse words at him. Wade was a professional and knew it wasn't personal, so he ate it up and used it to power his new persona.

But Monty sometimes thought the fans leaned too far into their hate. They got nasty and mean, and even though Monty knew Wade couldn't hear what was being said, it still made him a little sad. For so many years of Monty's life, Wade had been a larger-than-life presence, beloved and popular. Knowing what he knew now about Wade's past, it almost hurt to know the fans were so willing to give up on him. But that was the reality, so Monty took an angry breath and redirected his focus to kicking Viper's ass.

Viper finally entered the ring by hopping up to the apron and using the momentum he gained to hurl himself over the top rope. The crowd kept booing, and Viper walked around mean mugging the audience, scowling and grabbing his groin at them aggressively.

The crowd calmed down as the match began. The first half went off without a hitch. Halfway through, Romeo jumped to the ground and grabbed the ladder from under the ring. Viper used that opportunity to grab an aluminum folding chair from the announcer's desk, a strategically stashed prop that wouldn't injure Monty badly but would make a loud noise and entertain the crowd.

Viper stalked around the outside of the ring, chair in hand. As Romeo pulled the ladder from beneath the ring, Viper slammed the chair over Romeo's head and shoulders, and a loud crack echoed through the arena. The crowd went wild. Romeo collapsed on top of the ladder so Viper used his foot to shove him off, rolling him onto his back. He picked up the ladder and threw it into the ring, sending the crowd into another frenzy.

After a few more minutes, it was time for Viper's finisher. They'd been in and out of the ring for twenty minutes and they were both getting tired. Both Viper and Romeo had successfully landed impressive ladder attacks, and Monty felt confident they'd both done what they needed to impress the scouts and give Wade the final scout match he deserved. The momentum they had built with fans was more than Monty had expected, so even if neither of them got poached after this, the rest of this season was going to be a blast.

Romeo fell on the ground after one final blow with plans to stay there until Viper could climb the ladder for his finisher. Viper pulled the ladder to the corner of the ring to give himself enough room to complete the move. He climbed to the top, raising his fists and roaring before he took the final step to the highest part of the ladder. He bent his knees, leapt from the ladder, and tucked his body as he had every time before.

The flip started normally, but somehow he undershot the degree of rotation needed to complete the backflip and was flying towards Romeo at a concerning angle. He landed, but instead of softening the blow with his knees and chest, his chin and neck hit the canvas at full force, directly beside Romeo. Romeo stayed on his back a few more moments, waiting to get pinned, but it didn't happen. Viper's eyes were closed and he wasn't moving.

Wade's eyes were closed and he wasn't moving.

"Wade?" Monty sat up and touched his arm gently, trying not to jostle him. *"Wade?"* he said, a little louder. Wade didn't move. Then Monty *couldn't* move. He was frozen, like he was watching the events of the last fifteen seconds through someone else's eyes. The arena was still frantic because the audience assumed Romeo was the winner of the match by KO. They chanted 'Romeo!' and he couldn't figure out why. His heart was racing and his panic muffled the sound of the arena.

When he finally made sense of the situation, he jumped up to his feet and crossed his arms over his head repeatedly, a once universal sign in professional wrestling indicating a legitimate injury had occurred. In recent years, other wrestling promotions had used the X as part of the event, faking injuries and hiring "referees" to take bumps by previously "injured" wrestlers. It was divisive within the industry, but most fans nearby watched more than one promotion, so the message of urgency and legitimacy had become muddled. Monty's eyes darted around, looking for Mike or a medic or fucking anyone. There was an entire sea of people in the arena, and not a single one seemed to notice him.

"Help! Help him, please!" he screamed, still raising his arms. It was pointless. He crouched down by Wade and told him he was going to get help, just in case he could hear him, because he didn't want him to be alone. Before he left the ring in a rush to find Mike, he kissed his fingers and lightly touched Wade's temple. Mike was nowhere to be found, but he did see Madeline, who was beginning to realize something was wrong. He ran to her with tears streaming down his face.

"Call 911 or something, please! He's really hurt. This is not part of the show. Where the hell is Mike? Where are all the medics?"

Her face was panicked. She made a noise of distress and grabbed her phone out of her purse with shaky hands. Just as she started dialing, Mike came running down the aisle with paramedics who were pushing a stretcher and carrying bags of gear. He rushed over to where Monty and Madeline were standing. His skin was pale and clammy and he looked like he was going to be sick. That's how Monty felt, too.

Four paramedics jumped into the ring with a spinal board. They crowded around Wade, careful not to touch him before assessing his injuries. By then, the audience had finally realized something was wrong because the lights were back on and the music was off. The murmuring audience filled Monty with rage, because moments earlier they'd been cheering that Wade was KO. He tried to run into the ring to be by Wade, but Mike grabbed his arm.

"Stop. Let them work."

"But…" Monty's eyes filled with tears and he looked at the ring.

"Let them help him. They need space." Mike said. His voice was shaky, but Monty could tell he was trying to hold it together.

Monty felt a hand slide into his and he looked over and saw Madeline standing next to him, pulling him closer. She squeezed his hand so hard it almost hurt. He squeezed back.

"I don't want him to be alone right now," Monty said to her, still looking at the ring. "He must be so scared."

"He's really strong. He's going to be okay," she replied, her voice weak.

What did that even mean, anyway? He hated that platitude. Wade was physically strong, but he was still a human being with hopes and dreams and *fears*. He was allowed to be scared when he was lying in a ring, in pain, surrounded by strangers. It didn't make him weak. He wanted to say all of that to Madeline, but he knew she was scared, too, and probably trying to comfort herself as much as Monty.

Monty watched the paramedics move Wade to a spinal board after immobilizing his neck with a cervical brace. One of them hopped out of the ring and slid the spinal board out halfway. She grabbed the board near Wade's feet and another one lowered herself out of the ring to grab the board by Wade's head. Together, they lifted the board onto a stretcher and strapped Wade in. A third paramedic started wheeling Wade down the aisle and the crowd cheered for him. Monty watched Wade as he passed by, trying to see if there were any signs of consciousness. Or life.

"Try to stay awake, buddy," one of them said to Wade. "Keep your eyes open if you can."

Wade's eyes opened halfway and he looked around. The paramedics paused to adjust some straps, so Monty took his chance and ran up to him.

"Hey," he said, swallowing roughly. "I'm here. I won't leave you. I'm going to follow you to the hospital as soon as I can."

Monty lowered his hand to Wade's but he wasn't sure if he was allowed to touch him. His hand hovered above Wade's fingers, too afraid to connect and hurt him further. Wade locked his glazed eyes on Monty's. Monty felt one large finger wrap gently around his thumb. A weak, cold, but very much alive finger. Monty's eyes filled with tears again, but he blinked them away and smiled down at Wade.

Monty thought he saw Wade's mouth move, but no sound came out.

"What? I couldn't hear you. What did you say?" Monty asked, frantic.

"I love you," he said.

He said it so quietly Monty was only eighty percent sure that's what he said.

Instead of telling him he loved him too, his brain betrayed him, only coming up with a question."*What?*"

The paramedics shoved Monty out of the way before tossing a blanket over Wade's body. They wheeled him down the aisle, asking him again to stay awake.

Monty's shaky knees barely kept him upright as the paramedics rolled Wade to the parking lot, and when he heard the doors to the ambulance slam shut, he threw up all over his brand new boots.

MONTY AND MADELINE drove to the hospital in silence. He didn't remember getting to the car and he had no idea how much time had passed, but eventually they were walking side-by-side to the hospital entrance.

When they got to the emergency department, Madeline went to find them somewhere to sit while Monty went to ask for updates. The person at the front desk guessed he was here to see Wade, probably because of his stupid velvet pants, but she told him there were no updates yet and that details were reserved for family. He wanted to yell at her that Wade didn't have any family here. That Madeline and Mike and Monty were all he had, and they all needed to know how he was way more than either of his parents did. But he didn't.

Monty found Madeline and sat down. They stayed silent for a long time. Madeline tapped her fingers on her knee in an annoying pattern and the sound filled Monty with rage. He closed his eyes and breathed deeply, trying to calm himself down. His phone vibrated in his waistband.

"Mom?" he sniffed. He walked into a stairwell, the door closing behind him.

"Monty. Are you okay? I saw the match."

"No."

"What happened?"

"I don't really know. Something happened with his backflip. He landed wrong. I haven't been able to see him yet. I don't even know if he's alive, but they can't tell me anything because I'm not family."

"I'm so sorry this happened. I'm especially sorry this happened in a match against you."

"I think it's my fault," he said.

"How could it be your fault? You didn't touch him."

"He wanted to do the finisher off the turnbuckle. I said a ladder would be cooler."

"Monty, you know that doesn't make this your fault. It's nobody's fault. Sometimes bad things happen. All you can do is support him now. He's going to need that."

"I know. I'm at the hospital right now. I already said that, sorry. Ugh, I'm losing it." Monty cried harder then. "Mom? What if he dies?"

"He's not going to die."

"He could."

"Okay. I'm going to remain optimistic enough for the both of us. He's in good hands, sweetie. You'll see him soon," she said. Monty knew she was trying her best, but there wasn't anything anybody could say right now that would help him.

"Okay."

"Do you need me to come out? I can get a flight out tomorrow."

"No. But I'll let you know if I change my mind." Monty sniffed again.

"Are his parents nearby?"

"No," he said, quietly. "I have to go, mom. I want to be out there if they give us any information."

"Okay. Call me tomorrow if you can."

"I will." He hung up the phone and shoved it back in his waist-band. He left the stairwell and went to sit back down by Madeline, whose fingers were still drumming.

Mike rushed in through the front doors and went directly to the front desk. Monty got up and walked towards him.

"I'm here for Wade Donovan. He came in an ambulance? He came from Titan Arena," Mike said. "Can I see him?"

"We can't let anyone back who's not family, sir," she said.

"I'm his father," Mike lied. He turned to Monty. "Monty, hi."

Monty didn't say anything, he just pressed his lips together in a polite smile and waited for the person at the front desk to respond to Mike.

"Okay, sir. He is still in imaging. It'll probably be another hour or so. When he gets a room, I can bring you back. Only two people are permitted at a time," she said, looking between Monty and Madeline, who had joined them in front of the desk.

"Thank you. We'll just go over there and wait."

The three of them sat at a table in the back of the waiting room, none of them wanting to be the first to speak.

"Does anybody want coffee? I can go to the cafeteria and get some," Madeline offered.

"Yes, please," Monty and Mike both said. Madeline got up and headed to the cafeteria, leaving Mike and Monty sitting next to each other at the table.

"Mike, I…" Monty started. He could barely see Mike through his swollen eyelids.

"Monty, if you apologize to me right now because you think this is somehow your fault, I will take you into the ring myself and kick your ass. You didn't do anything wrong. Wrestling can be very dangerous. There's a reason a few promotions have banned that move. Wade is good, but he's not invincible."

Monty nodded. He knew that, of course. But it was hard to reconcile that with his guilt. Monty laid his head down on his folded arms and closed his eyes. He breathed out a long, shaky breath. Mike reached over and rubbed Monty's back for a while, and before he knew it, he had fallen asleep, exhausted by the day and endless stress of the last several hours.

When he woke up a while later, it was because a nurse had come to the waiting room to let them know Wade was conscious and ready for visitors. Monty knew this meant he'd have to stay in the waiting room by himself, which he really didn't want to do, but he wanted Wade to be with Mike and Madeline, so he stayed put. When they were led to the back, the nurse sat down next to Monty and placed a finger to the back of his hand.

"It's unlikely he will remember anything from tonight," she said. "He won't remember if you went in first, last, or not at all."

"I just want to see him so I can know he's alive, you know?"

"I know. I promise he's alive. I saw him wiggle his toes," she said, smiling at him softly. "They think he'll be okay. The doctor will come in and talk to his dad soon and he can share details with you."

"Thank you," Monty said, laying his head down on his arms again.

CHAPTER 18

IT WAS SUNDAY AFTERNOON WHEN WADE FINALLY WOKE UP ENOUGH TO stay lucid longer than twenty minutes at a time. The doctor handling his care stood over his bed, pointing out injuries in various images of his neck. The words felt heavy, but Wade only understood about half of them.

"You're extraordinarily lucky, Wade," she said. "You have a concussion, two fractures here and here, and you have a compressed spinal column, which is putting pressure on your spinal cord. It can be very dangerous. You'll need to wear this for six weeks, minimum, but maybe longer."

Wade blinked at the doctor, his mind not allowing the words to solidify into anything he could comprehend. The doctor repeated herself, slowly, emphasizing the limitations he'd face for the next couple of months. He wasn't allowed to drive or exercise, couldn't lift anything over the weight of a grocery bag, and for the next two weeks he needed someone nearby to help him prevent falls.

"Even a minor jostle can make the injury worse, and we really want to avoid that. In severe cases, this can lead to paralysis."

Wade frowned. "Okay."

"I'm going to leave some information here. Don't try to read it yet, but it will be here when you're ready. If you have questions, your nurses can help you. They can call me if anything comes up."

"Okay. Thank you."

He understood enough to know this was bad news, but he was so tired and his mind was so fuzzy. He couldn't remember the match with Monty. The last thing he remembered was seeing Madeline in Mike's office, but even that was a bit of a blur. He was pretty sure Mike and Madeline had visited him at the hospital, but he'd be lying if said he wasn't a little disappointed he hadn't seen Monty yet. He wanted to text him, but the phone hurt his eyes. So did the TV and, frankly, pretty much everything else. Like keeping his eyes open. He closed them again, sure he was going to stay awake. He didn't.

When he woke up, he kept his eyes closed as long as he could, not ready to deal with the pain from the light. He stretched his fingers, spreading them wide. His left hand nudged something unexpected. It felt hard beneath his touch, but strangely familiar. He opened one eye and peeked down as far as he could, unable to move his head or neck. He saw a blond mass of hair resting on the edge of his bed and it felt like he could breathe again.

He opened his other eye and looked around the room for a clock. It was 11:39pm. He wondered how long Monty had been here. He stroked his long hair, twisting the ends in his fingers. Monty lifted his head slowly at first. He must have been orienting himself, trying to remember where he was. Then he reached up and felt Wade's hand and jerked his head up quickly.

He gasped and jumped out of his seat, standing up over Wade's bed, his hands suspended in the air over Wade's arm. Wade thought he was going to lean in for a kiss, but Monty stopped himself, probably afraid to hurt him.

"Hi," Wade said with a sleepy smile on his face.

"Hi. God, Wade. I've been so scared," Monty said, sitting back down in his chair but still leaning onto the bed.

"I'm sorry. I would say 'same,' but I can't remember much of anything," Wade chuckled. Laughing hurt, so he squeezed his eyes shut. "Ugh, ow."

"Can I get you anything? Would a cool washcloth help?"

"Sure."

Monty got up and walked to the sink. He grabbed one of the rags folded off to the side and let the water run for a bit, probably trying for whatever he thought was the perfect temperature. Wade heard

Monty squeeze out the excess water and then he came back, placing the washcloth on his aching head.

"That's really nice," Wade said with a wince. "Thank you, Monty."

A few moments passed before Monty blurted, "I'm coming home with you."

"What?"

"I talked to Mike. He said you need someone to help you at home for two weeks to help you prevent falls. I'm going to come home with you for two weeks."

"I… Okay. I don't have the energy to argue, but I don't want you to feel obligated to do that," Wade said, closing his eyes.

"Can I… am I allowed to touch you?"

Wade waggled his eyebrows and immediately regretted it, groaning from the pain he'd inflicted on himself. Monty rolled his eyes.

"That's what you get. I just want to give you a kiss and hold your hand." Monty flipped the washcloth to the cool side, setting it back on Wade's forehead. He reached up and scratched Wade's scalp gently, then leaned forward to give him a peck on the lips. When Wade yawned, Monty stood up. He stroked Wade's cheek with the back of his finger.

"I need to go home. I wanted to wait until you woke up and I keep missing you. But I've been here for like over 24 hours and the velvet-leggings-and-scrub-shirt combo has really run its course. I smell terrible," he grimaced. "I'll come back tomorrow, okay? As early as you'll have me. You should get some more sleep."

"Okay," Wade said. He closed his eyes again.

CHAPTER 19

Between working at the arena, visiting Wade, learning how to care for him, and trying to sleep when he could, Monty felt like he hadn't stopped moving in days. His body was tired and his mind was in pieces that he was just now starting to put back together. He knew Wade would be okay, but even with the confidence he had in the medical team, he was constantly worried about Wade becoming paralyzed or having some secondary injury they hadn't found yet.

The match, his inability to be with Wade during his recovery, admitting he was in love with him, the realization that Wade could have died without ever knowing Monty felt that way... it was all so heavy. And now Mike had asked Monty to meet him at the arena on Saturday. It was almost too much.

On Saturday morning, Monty opened his eyes to his chaotic apartment and groaned. He could hear his mom's voice in his head saying "cluttered house, cluttered mind," but it didn't help him find the motivation to do anything about it. The exhaustion he felt was almost paralyzing. He just had to make it a few more hours before he could get Wade from the hospital and take him home to care for him over the next couple of weeks. Maybe then he'd be able to relax.

He hauled himself out of bed, took a quick shower, and drove to meet Mike at the arena. A quick detour to walk down the hallway allowed him to enjoy the moment a bit longer. He kissed his finger and tapped the photo of Wade as he passed it—maybe for luck, or maybe just to send Wade love any way he could. Wade being out for the time being meant several of the matches they were involved in would need to be adjusted for both timing and participants. Monty would have to switch up his angle, maybe for the rest of the year, and the idea worried him. His popularity was rising quickly, and any interruption to the momentum could mean destroying his chances of a CWA contract.

He slowed down as he approached Mike's office, hoping to delay hearing whatever potentially bad news Mike had, and then knocked on the office door.

"Come on in," Mike yelled.

Monty pushed the door open and slipped in, then sat down at the chair in front of Mike's desk. He gave Mike a small smile and rubbed his hands back and forth on his knees. His palms were damp with sweat.

"Are you okay?" Mike said.

Apparently, Monty wasn't doing a good job selling how cool and calm he definitely was.

"Yeah, I'm okay." His voice broke. He cleared his throat. "I really am. I swear. I'm happy. I'm taking Wade home today."

"I heard," Mike smiled. "I'll swing by in the next few days with some food Linda put together. Thanksgiving is out this year, obviously, but Linda's gone into overdrive trying to put stuff together for him so he doesn't miss out. He loves her sweet potato pie… or so he says. She learned how to make it just for him because I guess he grew up eating it."

"That's sweet." He picked at a frayed thread on the seam of his jeans. Monty could tell Mike wanted to chat about Wade, but Monty just wanted this meeting over with.

"She loves the guy," he shrugged.

Monty gave him a small smile.

"Anyway, Monty, listen. I got a call today from my buddy Graham over at CWA."

Monty's stomach dropped.

"I know this is weird timing. But they were really impressed with you guys last week. And based on what they're seeing between ratings and online engagement, they're interested in signing you."

Monty's heart pounded in his chest. They looked at each other, silently acknowledging the awkward position they were in. It felt wrong to be happy about anything when Wade was suffering, alone in the hospital.

But it was also exciting. Monty's dream was within reach, and Mike would earn a nice chunk of change if he let Monty out of his Titan contract. CWA would pay for it and everybody would win. All Monty had to do was sign a few forms.

"Did they say anything about Wade?"

"Not on that call, but I'm speaking to them again next week. I was hoping to know a bit more about Wade's prognosis before we talk about him."

Monty nodded. "Okay. Well," he attempted a laugh, "I, uh, guess I'll have my lawyer look at the contract, huh?"

"Yes! This is great news, Monty," Mike clapped his hands together. "Seriously. It's the right decision. I know the timing is awkward, but this is what you've been working for. I'm sorry you won't be working with us longer, but –"

"I won't?" Monty interrupted. "How soon would I have to move, did they say?"

"Not exactly. I know they want you there for the JingleRing."

"Shit, Mike, that's like a month away."

Mike leaned forward on his desk and twisted a pen in his hands, avoiding Monty's eyes.

"I know." He seemed to understand exactly what was going through Monty's head, which was nice. Monty didn't want to say any of it out loud. "I'll take care of him, Monty. He wouldn't want you to turn this down."

Monty left the arena nauseated from both nerves and excitement. Wade was scheduled to be released in the early afternoon, so he headed straight to the hospital after his meeting. He'd packed a change of clothes and overnight bag, ready to move in with Wade temporarily.

WHEN MONTY GOT close to Wade's hospital room, he heard Wade's familiar, rumbling voice. He heard another voice, too, but he couldn't hear what was being said. To give them privacy, he stood outside and flipped through his phone, texting his mom to say hi. She sent a new Becky photo. He noticed the voices inside Wade's room were getting louder, short but not angry. He was in the middle of typing a note asking his mom to give Becky a kiss when he heard a crash and weak shouting. A nurse passed by Monty quickly and jogged into Wade's room.

Monty ran in and saw a woman he assumed was a doctor standing next to Wade's bed. He saw Monty's water bottle, phone, and notebook in a wet puddle against the wall. His tray had been knocked over. Wade's face was distraught, his eyes were red-rimmed and teary.

"I'm sorry, Wade. I'll give you some time. The nurses can page me if you have questions, but otherwise I'll see you next week, okay?" The doctor bent down to pick up Wade's stuff from the floor. The nurse picked up the tray and the doctor set the items on it gently. She handed Wade some printed handouts and put her hand on his shoulder. She murmured something to him and he grabbed the papers gruffly. He stared straight ahead.

The doctor turned around to leave, smiling grimly at Monty as she left. The nurse finished setting the room and left shortly after. Wade didn't say anything to Monty.

"Hey. What happened? Who was that?"

"Dr. Nikolov. She's my neurologist."

"Okay…" Monty said slowly. He looked at Wade, trying to catch his eyes, but Wade continued staring ahead.

"What?" Wade snapped.

"Well, you're obviously upset, and," he gestured around the room, "something clearly made you mad earlier. I was outside texting my mom and I heard you yelling. I just wanted to know what happened."

"Dr. Nikolov just let me know that based on my scans and history of injuries, unless I want to risk paralysis or death, I can never wrestle again. That I might not be so lucky next time," Wade said blankly. "Lucky."

"What?! Shit," Monty said under his breath. He hurried to sit down in the chair next to Wade's bed and grabbed his hand. "God, I'm so sorry. This is awful. I don't even know what to say."

Wade was silent. Monty was used to that, but this time it made him sad.

"Do you want to talk about it?" Monty asked.

"No."

"Okay."

They sat in uncomfortable silence until a nurse came in with discharge paperwork. She was cheery and kind and Monty watched as she took Wade's IV out carefully, taping soft cotton gauze to his forearm using bright yellow tape. The tape matched the flowers on his tattoo.

"You have a couple of appointments lined up next week, Wade. One with Dr. Nikolov and one with orthopedics, okay? The discharge paperwork has the dates and times for those. The numbers you can use if you have questions are on there too," she said, pointing at various things in the packet. "Did you need anything before you head out? Remember, no driving, no sleeping on your stomach, and no lifting heavy things or exercising until you're given the okay by your doctor. Have someone help you in and out of the shower for the first few days, if you can. You're at an increased risk of falls right now and we really don't want you slipping and straining your neck."

"Okay," Wade croaked.

"Good luck, Wade," she said as she left the room.

Monty gathered up the stuff Mike and Madeline had dropped off and put the bag down on the chair while he searched for Wade's shoes in the gym bag he brought. When he found them, he sat down on Wade's bed and put socks and shoes on his feet since Wade couldn't bend to do it himself. He stroked Wade's calf up and down and said, "Okay, time to go, I guess." He smiled at Wade but didn't get one in return.

A hospital tech showed up with a wheelchair and transported Wade outside while Monty got his car. When he pulled up, Monty watched Wade carefully wipe fresh tears from his cheeks while he sat alone outside the automatic doors. He had to raise his arms up at an unnatural angle to reach them and it made Monty's heart ache. By the time Monty got Wade and his stuff situated in the car, Wade was quiet again, having wiped all signs of emotion from his face.

After about ten minutes of mostly silent driving, disrupted only by Monty's occasional one sided attempts at conversation, Wade reached over and grabbed Monty's hand.

"Thank you," he said. "For everything, I mean. Keeping me company and picking me up and staying with me. I hate being a burden."

"Of course," Monty said, turning to Wade briefly before looking at the road again. "There's nowhere I'd rather be, okay? I'm not going anywhere." After Monty said that his stomach lurched. That wasn't true at all, was it? He didn't want to lie to Wade but had no clue how to approach any of this.

The closer they got to Wade's apartment the more anxious Monty felt. Not because he was going to be with Wade for two weeks, he was excited about that. But he wasn't sure what would happen at the end of the two weeks. It could be the end of their relationship, depending on how Wade handled Monty's contract news and learning he'd be moving shortly after. Even with the excitement around moving to CWA, the thought of not being near Wade anymore made him queasy.

Monty used the continued silence to imagine every scenario for how Wade would handle everything, and each one was worse than the last. He figured the best case scenario would be that Wade was happy for him and willing to have a semi-long distance relationship for a while, but that seemed so out of reach. It was going to be hard enough for Wade to handle being forced into retirement. Being forced into retirement while watching his boyfriend live the dream stolen from him by one bad jump? He didn't see how they'd make it through that. The entire situation made Monty want to throw up, but he didn't want to do anything that would make Wade hurt his neck, so he swallowed it down and ignored his thoughts.

Monty pulled up to the front of Wade's building and put his hazard lights on so he could get Wade inside and settled before he parked for the night.

"I can walk upstairs by myself. There's an elevator," Wade grumbled.

"No sir, you cannot. Come on, big guy."

Wade held onto the crook of Monty's elbow and they walked to the elevator leaning into each other. Once they got inside, Monty leaned forward to kiss Wade.

"I missed you. This has been the worst week ever," Monty said. His mouth opened and closed and he sputtered. "Um, I mean, of course you know that… It was obviously worse for you. Boy. It's been a while, huh?"

Wade laughed carefully and squeezed Monty's elbow. Monty was happy to hear that sound again.

"I missed you too. All of you, even that part," Wade said.

They got to Wade's door and opened it up. Monty was glad Wade was so much tidier than him. He imagined what his apartment would be like if he returned after abandoning it for a week and cringed. Then he remembered he was leaving his apartment for two weeks and groaned quietly to himself.

"I need to feed Jojo. God, I hope he's still alive," Wade said, ambling into the kitchen. "Hey, little guy."

The type of brace Wade was required to wear covered part of his head, neck, and torso. It was rigid and heavy and didn't allow him to turn his head at all, so when Monty peeked into the kitchen he saw Wade turning in circles trying to find the fish food.

"Would you stop? You're at an increased risk of falls, I don't think making yourself dizzy will help. Go sit down," Monty said. "I'll feed Jojo and get some dinner started."

After he fed Jojo, who did survive, Monty helped Wade get settled on the couch sitting upright with pillows wedged around him.

"Comfy?" he asked. "Warm enough?"

"Yeah. Thanks," he said. He looked at Monty and smiled.

When Monty returned twenty minutes later with two bowls of pasta, Wade was asleep sitting up. Monty set the food down and pulled Wade's blanket up. He gave him a kiss on the head, grabbed his dinner, and watched the TV on mute until his eyes got heavy. He laid down on the far end of the couch and closed his eyes, one foot pressed into Wade's warm thigh, the touch providing a reassuring reminder he was alive.

CHAPTER 20

MONTY HAD BEEN AT WADE'S APARTMENT FOR OVER A WEEK, AND THEY'D settled in well together. He was still sleeping propped up on the couch but was hoping Monty would help him move into the bedroom soon. Monty helped him with a seated sponge bath in the shower each evening because Wade couldn't get his brace wet. They took short walks around the block when Wade was feeling restless and engaged in lots of movie watching and couch cuddling.

If he didn't occasionally remember that he no longer had a job, any career prospects, the ability to care for himself, or that one wrong move could paralyze him, he would think he was pretty happy. He was in love with a great guy! And he was pretty sure they were on the same page. Their circumstances hadn't changed, and Wade knew their relationship likely had an end date. But regardless, he wanted to embrace the one good thing he had going for him before life threw him any more curve balls.

"Monty?" Wade called.

Monty was washing the morning's dishes, which was sweet. He'd said he was messy, but he'd been cleaning so often that even Wade was afraid of leaving stuff on the ground.

Monty poked his head out of the doorway. "What's up?"

"Can you come sit for a minute?" Wade patted the couch.

"Sure," he said. Monty sounded nervous, which made Wade nervous.

Monty sat down next to Wade and turned towards him. He fidgeted with his fingers.

"I wanted to talk to you about something. Um, you've done so much for me over the last week or two, I just don't even know how to say thank you," Wade said.

"You don't have to say thank you. I'm happy to do it. You're important to me."

"I know. You're important to me, too. So important. That's kind of what I wanted to talk about. I just…" Wade paused for a moment and looked at Monty carefully. "I think crossing paths with you that first day you arrived at Titan is the best thing that has ever happened to me."

Monty huffed out a small laugh. "Okay…"

"You reignited something in me that had been dormant for two years. You helped me remember what wrestling means to me, and on a level that has been missing from my life for so long. And I know, that part of my life is over. And that sucks. But that match was a great ending to my career. Well, before I almost died and everything."

Monty was clearly unamused.

"Sorry. But… I love so many things about *you*, too. The way you ramble every time you feel shy and nervous. Or your face when you teach me a weird fact about marine life or spend time with Juliet. How you come to my defense at Titan even though you think I don't hear about it. My knight in spandex armor."

Monty smiled and grabbed Wade's hand. "Well, Dicky is a jerk."

"I hope this isn't too much," Wade continued. "Maybe it's the near death experience talking. Is that a thing? I survived something scary and I just want to… I don't know. Be a little reckless. And I know we've been dancing around our relationship, so maybe we just call it what it is. Be my boyfriend, or whatever."

"You want me to be your boyfriend?" Monty said. He sounded surprised.

Had Wade really been so stingy with his feelings that Monty was surprised he had strong feelings for him?

"Yes?" Wade said, worried. "I mean, only if you want."

Monty's face brightened slightly. "Of course I want," he said, grabbing Wade's other hand. The angle required Wade to shift his entire torso awkwardly. "Oops."

"It's okay," Wade smiled. He held on with his closer hand and scooted closer, unable to move his neck in the direction required to kiss him, but Monty got the idea. He straddled Wade's hips and gently held his neck brace, then kissed him softly. Wade moved his hands down the back of Monty's pants and squeezed.

"I'm looking forward to five to seven weeks from now when I don't have to wear this thing all the time," Wade murmured against Monty's mouth.

Monty pulled away, surprising Wade.

"What? You're not hurting me. I just miss touching you. It'll be easier when I'm allowed to take this off occasionally."

"No, I know. It will be great," Monty said, his eyes distant.

Before Wade could consider Monty's behavior, there was an unexpected knock at the door. Monty slid off Wade's lap and walked to the door, opening it slightly.

"Hey, Monty!"

It was Mike and Linda. Wade rolled onto his side so he could stand up. He was getting pretty good at getting off the couch by himself. He would feel smug, but he still had to have Monty wash his legs and feet, so he kept it to himself.

Monty walked back into the living room with Mike. He was carrying two bags, presumably Linda's incredible feast. He was sad to be missing the party this year. Over the years, it had grown to include over twenty people, Madeline and her family included. He was grateful to be part of it, and even more grateful that Mike and Linda loved him enough to make sure he didn't go without now. Linda trailed behind him carrying a covered pie pan, and held it up to Wade's nose, waggling her eyebrows at him.

"What'd you guys bring me?"

They all walked into the kitchen to unload the bags. Mike pulled out two roasted quail, which Linda explained she chose because there was no way she was cooking two turkeys in one year. He also took out containers of stuffing, mashed potatoes, yams, greens, kale salad, and a couple of Tupperware containers that contained surprises.

Linda set down her sweet potato pie next to the rest of the food. Wade's eyes were huge and sparkling.

"Oh, my God! Look at him!" Monty laughed.

"He gets like this every year. He likes food," Mike said, patting Wade's flat belly.

"Do you guys want to stay for a while? We can play cards or something. I'm so bored. Please say yes," Wade begged.

Monty scoffed. Wade leaned over and kissed Monty on the cheek while whispering a quiet apology. He loved being alone with Monty, but he'd been desperate for more company during the day because Monty was at the arena for big chunks of time and he could only take so many naps.

"I mean, um, it's just been a while since I've seen you two. Please join us," he said.

"Nice save," Monty grumbled and Linda laughed.

"We can stay for a bit, but I have to get home soon and do some stuff at the house. You two go get everything set up and Wade can point out where I can find drinks." She reached into her hoodie pocket and pulled out Juliet, who was holding a kibble in her paw. "I also brought you this."

Monty squealed. "My baby!"

He grabbed Juliet and put her on his shoulder, then headed into the other room with Mike to set up the cards.

"Well, I'll spend time with her soon, I guess," Wade laughed. "When do you think we'll release her?"

"Probably within a couple of weeks, unless her balance issue starts acting up again."

"Monty is going to be crushed."

"It's a hard lesson, but a good one. She knows what she's doing out there. She's going to be just fine. It'll be a slow release. I'm not going to kick her out and hope for the best. I'll take care of her, but she needs to learn to be away from people."

Wade gave Linda a poignant smile, both of them knowing what lay ahead.

They were interrupted by arguing in the other room and gathered up lemonade for the table. For the last week, "cards" meant Uno, because

Monty didn't know how to play poker or spades or any standard-deck card game besides war. He would have found it cute, but he was really sick of Uno, especially with two people. Based on the squabbling coming from the living room, Mike seemed to agree with Wade that Uno didn't count as cards, but Monty ignored him and dealt everyone's hands.

One thing Wade had learned was that Monty was a dirty Uno player. He added a dozen ridiculous rules that often resulted in Wade having a hand of 20 cards because he'd never heard of "Spicy Uno" and constantly got hit with penalties. *I get that you're an Uno purist*, he'd said, *but this is Idaho style. Take it or leave it.* He tried to *leave it* but Monty had looked so sad that Wade subjected himself to at least two games a day since they got home to avoid seeing that face again.

Linda and Wade carried lemonade to the table and Wade felt embarrassingly proud to be useful for the first time in weeks. Monty directed Linda to go first, since she was their favorite guest. They made it through two normal rotations, but on her next turn, Linda played a three. Monty played a three immediately, shoving Mike's hand out of the way.

"What the hell was that?!" Mike asked. "It's my turn!"

"You snooze, you lose, Mike. I got there first, so I can play my three."

Wade rolled his eyes. "I'm telling you, Monty, nobody plays like this."

"I can name at least five people who play like this."

"Do they all have the last name Hill?"

Mike played a six next, and Wade slapped the deck. Monty slapped the deck next and yelled, "Linda! Slap the deck!"

"Seriously, what the hell is going on?!" Mike yelled. "If you're going to add rules, can you at least explain?"

"Okay, I'll explain. You slapped the deck last, so now you have to draw two," Monty said. Then he winked at Linda and she laughed.

"It was my card!"

"I don't make the rules," Monty shrugged.

"You literally made these rules."

"It's called Spicy Uno, Mike!"

"Nobody has ever heard of Spicy Uno!"

"I told you, Monty!" Wade laughed.

"Alright, boys, relax," Linda said, chuckling. "Boy, I bet Mike's blood pressure is going to go way down when you move to Boston, Monty."

Monty froze. He looked at Linda with a look Wade couldn't quite decipher, and all the color drained from his face.

"What?" Wade asked, puzzled.

"Um…" Monty stuttered. He grabbed Juliet off his shoulder and started petting her. "I…"

"Oh, shoot," Linda whispered and put her hand to her mouth. "Monty, I'm so sorry. I didn't know it was a secret."

"You didn't know what was a secret? Can someone tell me what is going on?" Wade asked. Monty was still pale and he looked panicked and sweaty. "Monty?"

"Um. Maybe you guys should head out," he said, turning to Mike and Linda. "I should probably talk to Wade."

Mike and Linda nodded and excused themselves from the table. When they got to the door, Wade was behind them. Mike placed his hand on Wade's upper arm and looked up at him.

"Don't be too upset with him, okay? It's been a hard time for all of us. Nobody is thinking straight."

"Yeah. I'm really sorry this has been tough for all of you," Wade spat. His face softened when he turned to Linda. "Thank you for the food, Linda."

Mike looked down at his feet. He gave a short nod of understanding. Linda grabbed Juliet from Monty and gave them a sad smile before ushering Mike out the door. Wade closed the door behind them. He turned around and saw Monty standing by the table, his hands twisting as they often did when he was nervous.

"Why don't we sit?" Monty said.

"Why don't you explain what Linda is talking about? Are you moving?"

Monty stepped closer to Wade, but he backed up and crossed his arms, closing off his body from Monty. Monty swallowed hard, and Wade could see the tension in his neck.

"Okay. So, last Saturday, Mike asked me to come to Titan to talk to him about something. When I got there, he said his friend Graham from CWA called and wanted to offer me a contract." Monty's twisting hands were trembling. "I wanted to tell you, but it was the same day you were being discharged and I just never found the right time. I feel terrible now. I always meant to tell you."

Wade hated seeing Monty upset. Every instinct he had was telling him to reach out and offer comfort, but the weight of this news was paralyzing. The feeling of betrayal was so strong he couldn't think straight. It twisted in his gut, nauseating him. But it wasn't just Monty's betrayal making him sick. He was angry at his own stupid body and that fucked up landing and this devastating reminder that his career was over, and Monty's was just beginning.

He was also embarrassed that apparently everybody knew Monty had been offered this opportunity, and nobody thought to tell him. As if a couple more weeks would have made it easier for him to watch someone else live his dream for the second fucking time.

"I'm so sorry, Wade. I know it was wrong to keep this from you. Every day I wanted to tell you, but—"

"But what?"

"I was scared. Of how you would react, and what it would mean for us."

"Wait. Oh, my God. So earlier today, before Mike and Linda came over, when I asked you to be my boyfriend, you *knew*. You knew you'd been offered the contract, and you didn't think maybe that was a good time to tell me? Actually, forget even finding a good time. You didn't think I deserved to know my *boyfriend* had already accepted this opportunity that requires him to move to the fucking East Coast?"

Monty hugged his arms around his middle. He looked up at Wade with tears in his eyes, the physical evidence of Monty's pain making Wade feel even worse.

"How long were you going to keep this from me? Were you just going to let me know before you moved out there, like, 'Hey babe, I gotta go catch my flight! See you in a few months!'" Wade tried to pace to rid himself of some of his anxious energy, but it hurt his back and he reached back to rub a knot next to his spine. "I can't believe this. I'm such a fucking idiot. Did you already sign your contract?"

"No, I haven't signed it," Monty said quietly. He tried to approach Wade, tried to rub his back.

"But?" Wade asked, moving away from Monty again.

"But… it's with my attorney."

Wade exhaled sharply and a sardonic laugh escaped him. "I think you should go." The anger had left his body, because it was pointless. He'd known this was an inevitability. He'd been expecting it, but was clearly under some sort of spell when he asked Monty to be his boyfriend. And now he was heartbroken. His eyes stung. "Please, Monty. Go."

"I can't leave you here alone," Monty said.

"I'll call Madeline."

"Can we talk about this, please? I didn't hide this from you for any nefarious reason, Wade. It's been a stressful week." He visibly winced at his own comment. "Please, please don't make me leave right now. You can call Madeline and she can come stay here but I really want to discuss this."

"Why does it even matter? You're leaving. When are you leaving, anyway?"

Monty looked at the floor and said nothing.

"When, Monty?" Wade said, his voice cracking.

"They want me there in two and a half weeks."

"Two and a half weeks."

"They want to debut Romeo at the JingleRing."

Wade gawked at him. Monty let out small, squeaky sob.

"Then why does it matter if we discuss this? You'll be gone in two weeks. So please just get your shit and leave. You owe me that much, at least." Wade pulled his phone out and texted Madeline.

"Why does it *matter?*"

Wade's phone rang. He told Madeline he couldn't explain right now, but he needed her to either come over or come pick him up. When he hung up, he turned back to look at Monty's tear-stained face. His cheeks were blotchy and pink, and not in a cute way like when he blushed. It was in a sad, pitiful way that left Wade feeling even more miserable.

"We need to discuss this because I can't leave here not knowing where we stand," Monty said.

"Well, just imagine it's three weeks from now and you're on a plane to Boston. That should help you know where we stand."

Monty was crying big, miserable tears. He had the heels of his hands pressed into his eyes and Wade could see his desperation. It made his stomach hurt. He wanted to punch something, or throw up, or punch things for so long that he threw up.

"I want to be with you. I was going to figure out how to make it work!" Monty said through his tears. "I even asked Mike if I could postpone my contract transfer until spring. I love you, Wade. So much. And I—"

"Don't," Wade snarled. "You don't get to say that to me now. You don't get to keep this from me and then tell me you love me in some attempt to get me to forgive you. That's not fair. It makes a mockery of the way I feel about you, and if you actually loved me, Monty, you'd go pack your shit and go home. Please."

Monty stared at Wade for a moment before he nodded and went to gather his things. Wade sat down on the couch and tried to breathe, wishing he could curl into a ball but being physically unable to.

Wade watched Monty gather his things from around the apartment and shove them into his backpack. He disappeared, then came out of the bathroom, zipping up the front pouch of his backpack and sniffling. The quiet of the apartment was deafening, and a stark contrast to the sounds of Monty's usual cheer and energy Wade had silenced.

Monty looked up at Wade like he was about to say something, but Madeline pushed the door open, interrupting whatever it was. Wade watched as Monty threw his backpack over his shoulder and cast a sad smile at Madeline. He wiped his eyes before slipping out behind her and closing the door. The click of the door echoed in the apartment, and Wade tried to ignore the retreating sobs he heard coming from outside.

CHAPTER 21

The door shut behind Monty, and Madeline's eyes went wide. Her mouth opened slightly in confusion. She walked through the living room and rushed to Wade's side, touching him gently, like she was feeling for injuries.

"What's going on? Are you okay?" She asked, still running her hands over his face and arms.

"Well, no, but… I mean, I'm fine, physically. Um, would it be okay if we don't talk about it right now? My head is killing me. I'm off the narcotics now and I think if I had to rehash everything I'm upset about I'd lose my mind. I need sleep, maybe." He grabbed her hands and lowered them to her sides.

"Of course. Whatever you need. Do you want to come home with me? The kids miss you."

"Yes, please. I'm not allowed to be alone, but I don't want to be here. Can you help me pack a bag? I can't bend," Wade sighed.

Madeline followed Wade into his room to help him get sweatpants and other stretchy clothing items from his drawers. He grabbed a book from his nightstand and saw the small rubber snake Monty brought him the first night they got together and his body slumped. He picked it up and squeezed it between his fingers so its head flattened out. How could a day that started out so wonderfully unravel into such chaos? Monty had lied to him. Hadn't he? It felt like Larry all over again, but instead of just losing the man he loved, he was also losing every version of the future he'd laid out for himself. Without Monty and without wrestling, he had nothing.

He sat down on his bed gently and leaned back to rest his hands on the mattress. Madeline held things up, silently asking if he wanted her to throw them in his suitcase. He really didn't care what she brought since he couldn't imagine moving from his bed much over the next few days. What was the point? His career was gone. His now ex-boyfriend, with whom he'd been in an official relationship for three fucking hours, was moving to Boston. Not even Juliet needed him anymore.

While Madeline packed his suitcase, he let his mind wander. He thought about Monty at CWA, meeting new people, maybe getting a new partner. His stomach rolled imagining it being Larry. What if Larry and CWA spun it to humiliate him? First Larry left Viper behind, then stole his partner. They'd be thrilled with the drama. His mind flashed with images of Monty and Larry in the ring and locker rooms together. He thought of them becoming friends and talking about how pathetic he was. Maybe they would even be right for each other romantically. They were both handsome, beloved, and *good enough* in a way Wade never would be. He accidentally imagined them in bed together and his mouth went dry. He coughed in an attempt to clear his mind, but that just made Madeline worry. She forced him to drink some water, which was a hassle because she had to tilt the glass for him and he felt like a child. He just wanted all of this to end.

He watched her clear out his bathroom and grab his toothbrush and toothpaste, hair products, and razor. She even grabbed his shower chair, which shouldn't be embarrassing, but he felt stupid anyway. Once again making him feel like a child, she bent down to tie his shoes before grabbing a pair of slides, then gave him a kiss on his head and carried everything to her car.

"You sit here. I'll be right back. Do not move," she warned.

"Okay, mom," he said, turning one side of his mouth up.

When she came back, she threw Jojo some fish biscuits and turned off his light. Then she took Wade's arm and led him to the porch. She walked him to the car with such deliberate slowness that it took all of his remaining emotional strength not to scream.

"For the love of… I think a snail just passed us."

"Excuse me! I don't want you to hurt yourself!" she snapped. "What would I tell Mike if I broke you?"

He grumbled until they finally got to the car. She sat him down in his seat and buckled his seatbelt. Wade rolled his eyes, but after she closed his door, he smiled while she walked around the car.

She didn't force Wade to talk on the drive to her house and he was appreciative, but he knew his time was running out. He spent the drive reliving the argument he had with Monty and his stomach burned. He was so angry that he'd allowed himself to fall for him. He knew the implosion of their brief relationship was inevitable, but he'd let himself be swayed by Monty's sweet demeanor, eternal optimism, and silky hair. He'd let Monty fool him into thinking they'd do this together, one way or another. But now it was like everything in his life—his very public burial as the leftover half of Limpet and Viper and ensuing professional stagnation, his family's disapproval of his career choices, his struggle to pass his rehabilitation test. They were all failures that created a huge pile of shit and his injury was a can of gasoline dumped over the top. Monty's lie was the lit match that blew it all up.

"Okay, let me help you into the house and then I'll come get your stuff. I warned the kids you're not a jungle gym anymore," Madeline said, breaking up Wade's internal pity party.

"Okay," he said sadly.

"Hey," she said, touching his arm. "This is temporary, right? Dr. Nikolov said after six or eight weeks you should be okay for normal living. I think that probably includes fifty pounds of child hanging on each arm. We'll double check."

"I know. Everything is just changing so fast. It's hard," he sighed. "I'll be fine. Let's just get inside and put those kids to work. I want a beer."

She gave him a look.

"I just said I'm off the narcotics. I can have one beer, Madeline."

She grumbled under her breath as she walked around the car and helped him up the front steps. When they got inside they were greeted by Ramona and Jack bouncing around, holding up cards they'd made for him.

"Hold on, guys, let's get Uncle Wade situated before you show him your drawings."

Ramona and Jack were vibrating with anticipation as they watched Wade sit down slowly in Kenny's recliner. It was like a salve on his heart.

"Dad said you can use that as long as you need it," Jack yelled from the edge of the rug, apparently unable to modulate his voice.

"I'll have to tell your dad thank you," Wade smiled. "Okay, I'm situated. Come on, let me see what you got."

The kids showed him their get well soon cards and told him all about their days and did their best not to touch him. Eventually he invited them onto his lap one by one to give them gentle hugs. He's missed them over the last couple of weeks. Being around them was healing in a way he didn't know how to find elsewhere. He was looking forward to having more time to spend with them now that he was retired. Silver linings.

Madeline, Wade, and the kids watched a movie and ate pizza to pass the time. When Kenny came home with Gavin, he passed the baby off to Madeline to feed him. Kenny caught up with Wade for a bit and offered his condolences, but Wade wasn't in a chatty mood so there was more awkward silence than any of them were used to. He and Madeline seemed to have some psychic connection because Kenny looked at her and suddenly stood up.

"Well, we'll leave you to it," he said, grabbing Gavin from Madeline's lap.

Wade narrowed his eyes at Kenny. He tried to look at Madeline by moving his eyes but she had managed to scoot over far enough that she disappeared from his line of sight.

"Move back over there." He pointed to the other side of the couch. "I can't see you. I know you and Kenny are doing some weird married-person communication to get me alone."

Madeline scooted back to the other side of the couch. Kenny bounced Gavin on his hip and told the older kids to follow him for ice cream sundaes.

"Their bedroom is going to be a war zone tonight with all that dairy," Wade said. "Yikes."

Madeline laughed loudly. "It's Kenny's night to get up with any bedroom interlopers so it's not my problem."

They smiled at each other. The air was thick with Madeline's obvious curiosity. Wade knew he should talk to her about it it for no other reason than she'd taken him in and he owed her an explanation as to why he was now her burden instead of Monty's.

"So… what's up?" she asked, casually running her fingers along the arm of the sofa.

"Oh, my God, Madeline." He rolled his eyes again. "Fine. I broke up with Monty."

"Um, yeah, I figured that out when he left your house sobbing."

"Well," he shrugged slightly, wincing and grabbing his shoulder, which only hurt his other shoulder. He groaned. "Shit."

"Be careful. Do you need to lay down? Do you want medicine?"

"No. I'm fine."

"Okay. So…"

"There's not much else to say."

"That can't possibly be true. Tell me what happened. Because last time I spoke to you, things were really good and you were happy, even with all of this going on," she said, waving her hand around at his body.

"I was. But I found out he got signed and didn't tell me. He's known for a week and just didn't mention it. He let me make a fool of myself, confessing my love to him and asking him to be my boyfriend, and he still never mentioned it. I had to hear it from Linda, who now feels like total shit because she let it slip not knowing it was a secret."

"Oh. Shit," she said.

"Yeah."

"What did you say?"

"Not a lot. I told him to leave. Then I texted you," Wade said.

"God, you are infuriating," Madeline said, pinching the bridge of her nose. "Okay, then what did *he* say?"

"He just said he was sorry and that he didn't know when to tell me. That with my injury and everything it never felt like the right time. But apparently half the guys at Titan knew, even Linda knew. They were all keeping it from me."

"I'm sorry," she said.

"When I told him to leave, he told me he loved me. It made me so angry. It just felt like a last ditch effort to get me to forgive him. I feel stupid and embarrassed. And sad. I really love him."

Madeline hummed.

"What?"

"Well… Okay, just hear me out before you tell me I'm wrong," she said.

Wade sighed dramatically and closed his eyes. "Go on."

"What if Monty was telling the truth about why he didn't tell you?"

"What, that there was no good time? We've been together for pretty much all of my waking hours for over a week since he found out. I don't buy that there was no good time."

"Maybe there were times he could have told you, sure. He definitely should have told you earlier today when you guys talked. But, Wade…" She sighed and leaned forward on the couch. "You had a devastating injury. We all thought you were going to die. Or at the very least, lose the ability to walk. You didn't see him that night at the hospital, he was beside himself. I know for sure he loves you. Put yourself in his shoes. Can you honestly say you would have been, like, *eager* to tell him something you know would have broken his heart? Something that not only risked your relationship with him, but reminded him of everything he's lost? All while he was dealing with pain and uncertainty about his future?"

Wade frowned, but didn't say anything.

"I'm not saying he didn't mess up, Wade. He did. But I bet he knows it and regrets it."

"Well, it doesn't matter anyway. He's moving to Boston in three weeks. Once he gets there and gets a taste of what he's been after, he won't care about Portland or Titan and he certainly won't care about me. I've been through this before and don't need to do it again. I told you this when I first met him, and I didn't go with my gut."

Madeline stood up and walked over to Wade's recliner and sat one side of her butt down on the arm. She put her arm around his neck and back and pulled him into a gentle hug.

"Monty isn't Larry," she said, stroking his hair.

"I know. He's so much better, which is even more reason I can't do it again." He lifted his arms to rub his eyes and whimpered at the pain. "Can you please just help me to bed?"

"Of course," she said. She helped him up the stairs and got him tucked into bed. He looked at his phone and saw a text from Monty but didn't read it. He squeezed the rubber snake he'd brought from his apartment and closed his eyes.

As he drifted off, dreams took hold. He saw visions of botched aerial moves that sent him crashing to the canvas and heard the sound of his body hitting the ground. In his dreams, he could smell the sharp scent of hospital room air that filled his lungs, and he could hear the low murmur of Monty's hushed voice, just beyond his reach. It was comforting at first, but eventually his traitorous brain showed him Monty. He was laughing, happy, beautiful, and with someone who looked like they belonged in his life more than Wade ever would again.

MONTY DROVE HOME IN A DAZE. His emotions were so heavy it felt like he was choking on them. It was an excruciatingly quiet drive, and he was so miserable being trapped with his own thoughts that he was actually relieved to see his building, even though seeing it was evidence Wade had kicked him out. He kept replaying Wade's words, and knowing he had caused such pain was almost unbearable.

He walked up the steps to his apartment and frowned as he opened the door. Disgusting, as expected. Instead of dealing with it, he threw his coat and keys on the table by the door and went straight to bed. He texted Wade once, apologizing again and telling him he was serious about wanting to be with him, but he didn't pressure him to discuss it any further.

He tortured himself by scrolling through their messages and managed a smile at their inside jokes and flirting. But then he thought about how there may never be more of that, so he shoved his face into his pillow and cried himself to sleep.

. . .

HE WOKE up the next morning earlier than usual because he'd tired himself out by crying. When he opened his tender, dry eyes, he immediately grabbed his phone to see if Wade had reached out. He hadn't, of course. He wished Wade would yell at him or cuss at him or send him a gif of a flaming middle finger. Anything would be better than silence.

He tried to call his mom but remembered after dialing that his parents were in Canada. He groaned and rolled over, pulling the covers over his head. With the tone of his day set, he double checked that the local coffee shop was open and then put his coat on and headed out. It was cold and sunny, which was his favorite weather. The sky was blue and bright, and his feet crunched the dry leaves as he walked, a rare treat in such a damp and rainy place. He smiled and opened his phone, scrolling to the video Wade sent once of Juliet stepping on a crunchy leaf for the first time. She jumped up in the air, all four feet leaving the ground, and ran to Wade's hoodie pocket. His rich, deep laugh came through the speaker. It was like a punch to the gut.

He texted Aaron on the off chance he was up and invited him to meet him at the coffee shop. He'd missed the last two D&D sessions and he wanted to catch up to see how the group's campaign was progressing, plus Aaron had turned into a pretty good friend, plus he just really didn't want to be alone. He waited impatiently for Aaron to reply and was disappointed when he didn't see the three dots appear. But he figured a crisp walk and a warm drink might elevate his mood anyway, so he lumbered on.

When he walked into the shop, he looked around for Aaron but didn't see him. He swallowed his disappointment, but he really didn't want to be alone. He ordered a latte, sat down at one of the booths, and tried to avoid looking at his phone. The temptation to text Wade was intense, and every glance at his phone picked away at his resolve a bit more. He turned his phone over and slumped in his booth. The door opened a few moments later and Aaron walked in with a big smile on his face, but as soon as he saw Monty, his eyebrows furrowed and he picked up his pace. Monty was embarrassed, realizing he must look worse than he thought.

Aaron came to the table after ordering his coffee and slid in across from Monty.

"Hey, man."

"Hi," Monty croaked.

"What's up? We've been missing you at our sessions," Aaron said, kindly avoiding any comments on Monty's appearance.

"Yeah, I missed you guys, too. Just kind of a crazy couple of weeks."

Neither of them said anything for a moment, and Monty bit his lip, eager to share his problems with Aaron but unsure where to start.

"So, um. I guess I'll just say it, because I'm thinking you texted me for a reason. You look awful. What's going on? Your eyelids are so… big."

Monty laughed. "Thanks," he said. "I guess it's pretty obvious, huh?" He pressed his cold fingers to his hot cheeks.

"I'm sorry. I'm not trying to make fun of you. But you're clearly upset. Is it Wade? I read he's going to be okay, but I'm getting that information from the internet, obviously." Aaron said. He gasped quietly and his eyes opened wide. "Oh, shit, is he…"

"Oh, no, he's okay! He's home. I've been with him for the last week. He's feeling pretty decent now, physically. Very sore, but the break itself wasn't too severe. No surgery or anything."

"Oh! Well, that's great news," Aaron said, blowing out a relieved breath.

"Yeah, it is." Monty gave a wistful smile.

"But…?"

"I, uh… Well, it's not official yet, but I got offered a buyout on my contract from CWA. They want me to move there in a few weeks."

"What?! Holy shit, dude!" Aaron leaned forward in the booth and slapped his hands on the table. "That's incredible news. So fast, huh? You just got here!"

"Yeah, it's really cool. I'm happy. But I fucked up with Wade and I don't know what to do now. He broke up with me last night."

"Wait, he broke up with you because you are moving to CWA? What the hell?"

Monty's chest warmed at Aaron's misplaced loyalty.

"No, no. Well, it's kind of a long story. But basically, I didn't tell him I got a contract buyout, and he found out from someone else. It just sort of snowballed. He's upset because he feels like I lied to him. I wish I could turn back time."

"Shit," Aaron breathed, leaning back in his seat. "I'm sorry, man."

"It's okay. I'm glad you were around. I needed to get out of the house."

"Oh, yeah. I never go anywhere. Hey, do you have anything to do today? You're welcome to come with me to my family's big monthly dinner. My stepmom is a great cook," Aaron said.

Monty smiled at Aaron, his puffy eyes narrowing to the point of vision impairment. "Thanks for the offer, but I'm definitely not going to be good company today. I have a lot of stuff to figure out, both emotionally and, like, logistically. I guess I have to start packing?"

"Sure. Well, text me if you change your mind. I'll send you the address."

They chatted about D&D, and Aaron filled Monty in on the campaign. Some homicidal cultists had approached their party, but they'd managed to escape, ending up in a small, dimly lit tavern where they'd left themselves at the end of their last session.

Monty smiled sadly, wishing he'd been there or that things could just be different.

"I'm sorry," Aaron said, noticing Monty's gloomy face.

"It's okay. It has to be, right? This is what I've been working towards."

"That's right! And Ronnie is an even bigger fan of CWA than he is of Titan. Um, no offense. But maybe when you get settled, we can fly out?"

"I would really love that," Monty said.

After an hour, they stood up and Aaron held his arms out. "Come here, buddy."

Monty stepped into his hug and let out a shaky breath, squeezing Aaron around the ribs.

"It's going to be okay, Monty. No matter what happens. Don't give up."

Monty smiled into Aaron's shoulder, his words providing the comfort he needed.

· · ·

As he walked up the stairs to his apartment, he thought about Wade and what he might be doing. Everything in Wade's life was falling apart, but at least he had Madeline. He loved her family, and Monty had heard the kids adored him. He imagined Ramona and Jack playing nurse, taking care of Wade and bringing him snacks and drinks. Wade was obsessed with Gavin, so he could focus on that. Wade was obsessed with most babies as far as Monty could tell, which was sweet. He thought about their date at Linda's house and how Wade had asked him if he saw kids in his future. At the time, he thought it was just conversation, but it wasn't. It never really was with Wade.

He sat down on the couch and grabbed his laptop to search for moving supplies nearby, but that was boring, so his mind drifted back to Wade. He knew Madeline had a spare room for him at her house and that he'd be in good hands. He'd once told Monty that Madeline and Kenny took care of him after Larry moved to Boston because he didn't want to be alone at his apartment, and... *Oh, shit.*

Monty stood up from the sofa abruptly, his laptop cord snagging under his foot and yanking the laptop to the floor. On its way down, it knocked over two glasses of water. It was classic Monty, forever living in filth, hating his inability to function as an adult. He scrambled to pick up everything he'd dropped while also dealing with the horror of knowing he'd done exactly what Larry had. He cursed under his breath, berating himself for being a moron in so many ways.

Wade wasn't just dealing with the traumatic end of his career or his relationship ending, he was reliving a terrible moment from his past with the first person he'd opened his heart to in two years. Monty couldn't believe he hadn't realized this. He felt like a fucking asshole. He stood up to take the two glasses to the kitchen, tempted to throw them against the wall. And when he stepped in a puddle, soaking his sock, impulse won. He threw both glasses at the wall in a rage, half from his mistakes with Wade and half from his disgusting sock. The glasses shattered, creating an even bigger mess.

Unsure what to do, he paced his apartment for a while before forcing himself to sit down on the couch. He took out his laptop and after confirming it still worked, then he checked his email. His lawyer had sent him a DocuSign agreement for his updated contract. The email attached said they'd agreed to all the changes Monty's attorney had requested, minus the delayed start date. Bile rose in his throat as he submitted his signature, knowing the act may very well serve as a death knell to his and Wade's developing relationship. He swallowed hard and sent a text to Mike letting him know it was done. Monty was now officially expected in Boston, which meant Monty had exactly two weeks and two days to fix things with Wade. He had no idea where to start.

CHAPTER 22

WADE HAD BEEN AT MADELINE'S HOUSE FOR A WEEK. HE WAS FEELING better about the situation with Monty, mostly because he was pretending none of it happened. Monty hadn't reached out, which was a blessing most of the time, but painful when he thought about it too much.

Even though he'd ended things by kicking Monty out of his house and telling him he didn't want to be with him, and even though the ball was in his court since he'd never actually replied to Monty's previous message, part of him still hoped he'd wake up each morning to a text message from Monty.

Monty talked a lot and loved sharing everything that crossed his mind. He couldn't even decide what to eat without talking it out with someone, but he was equally kind and respectful. Wade knew he'd never disturb him if what he said he needed was time. And when he thought about it that way, Monty's silence was just another reminder of what he'd lost.

Wade did what he could to distract himself. He spent his time doing arts and crafts with the kids, reading books to Gavin, napping, and helping Madeline in the kitchen. Well, helping as much as he could. His pain was well controlled with over-the-counter medications as long as he rested when he felt tired, but he wasn't allowed to lift much and couldn't bend at all. He also couldn't really safely use a knife because he couldn't see his hands at table height. And, okay, he didn't cook very much even when he was healthy, so even if he had been capable, she wouldn't have wanted his help. So he mostly hung out and talked to Madeline while she worked in the kitchen, but that was something.

He'd visited Dr. Nikolov who was pleased with his progress and said he was healing well. He no longer needed to be monitored for falls, so he was cleared to move back home to his apartment. But he still wasn't allowed to drive because he couldn't turn his neck, and Dr. Nikolov reiterated that he could never wrestle again and that doing so would put him at risk of paralysis or death, so it wasn't all good news. He knew that would be the case, but a small part of him had held out hope that maybe new scans of his neck would show something different. A different injury, or maybe miraculous healing. They didn't, of course, which confirmed it was time for Wade to hang up his boots.

Madeline dropped him off at the arena where he planned to clear out his locker and record his farewell message to the fans and wrestling industry at large. She squeezed his hand and told him she loved him and that she was proud of him, but none of it helped.

Retirement was bad enough, but retiring at his current level was worse. It felt meaningless, like nobody would actually care. At one time, he'd been the most popular wrestler on the West Coast not signed with CWA. He had the magazine articles to prove it. So did Monty, come to think of it—his fanboy wrestling notebook had a photocopy of the article pasted next to a photo of Viper ripping his shirt off.

But his retirement *was* big news, even with his lack of popularity, which meant he'd have to endure people talking about him and bringing up the most painful parts of his past. The buzz around the Viper-Romeo rivalry had brought him back to the spotlight, and had he not injured himself, he thought he could have risen back to some level of acclaim. But he did injure himself, and he would never be on top again, so it was time.

He walked down the halls of Titan for the first time in weeks and felt bittersweet nostalgia. For Monty, Larry, Niall, and all the other guys at Titan. For all of the belts earned and championship titles held. Limpet and Viper held the tag team championship title for a record 512 days, and he'd never have a chance to break that record.

But he had a lot to be proud of, which was easy to forget when he was wallowing so deeply. He stopped and looked at a new photo he hadn't seen before, one Mike must have framed recently. It made his chest tighten uncomfortably. It was a candid shot of Monty and Wade in the ring, with Wade bent over a supine Monty, his hands on his knees. He was smiling and his eyes crinkled from his laughter. Monty had his arms out to his sides and he was laughing too. They were wearing sweats and hoodies, which meant it was early in their friendship.

Wade remembered that day and felt a pang of sadness. He had just laid Monty out with a clothesline and it was the first time they'd done it together. It was basic, but Monty had landed hard and hit his head on the canvas. Wade bent over to check on him when Monty looked up at him and told a terrible joke. *Hey, why did the wrestler bring a clothesline to the match? To hang his opponent up to dry!* Wade had burst out laughing at how stupid it was, which must have been when Mike took this photo. He remembered the moment now so clearly, because it was the first time he'd felt really good inside the ring since Larry left.

Wade's reminiscence was interrupted by the squeak of Niall's shoe at the other end of the hallway. He looked like he was in a hurry going the other direction, but when he spotted Wade, he started jogging toward him, grinning.

"Wade! Shit, I'm so happy to see you, brother!" he said. He went in for a weird, too-gentle side hug.

"Hey, brother. I'm happy to see you, too. I wish it was under better circumstances, I guess."

"Yeah, yeah. Me too, man. This sucks dick," Niall sighed.

Wade laughed. "Yeah, for sure. I knew it wouldn't last forever, you know? It's earlier than I was hoping for, but I'll be okay."

"You will be. And we still need you around here. Please don't leave us with Mike," Niall joked.

"Hey!" Mike interrupted. Wade and Niall jumped.

"Ah… hey Mike! Well, that's my cue. Gotta hit the gym. Amit looked up some weird new fitness regimen he wants us both to follow and I am…" he squinted at his watch, "shit, a minute and thirty-two seconds late. He will kick my ass if I don't get there now."

"See ya," Wade said, laughing.

"Hey, Wade," Mike said.

"Hey."

"You ready to record?"

"Yeah. I'm ready."

They made their way to the ring together. Their footsteps echoed and Wade stepped on something crunchy. Probably popcorn, but he couldn't see it. It was dark by the ring, but Wade wanted it that way. Seeing the entire arena would have been painful. The darkness was like a protective shroud, shielding him from images of the last time he was there. Even being inside the arena made him anxious and he felt sweaty and nervous, but he pushed through, because the only thing worse than doing this once would be doing it twice.

When they got to the ring, Wade noticed Mike had set up a wooden stool and tripod inside the ropes. Wade wouldn't be able to balance on the stool and he wouldn't even be able to get in the ring without multiple helpers. It was yet another depressing reminder that he was no longer made for this.

"Hmm, I didn't think about this. I'm sorry. Is that going to work for you?" Mike asked.

"I'll just sit on the steps," Wade said.

"Sure. I'll be in my office. Come see me when you're done, okay?" he said.

Wade gave him a thumbs up, and Mike moved the tripod to the mats by the stairs. He squeezed Wade's arm, then left to give him some privacy.

Wade cleared his throat and took his beanie off. He folded it a few times before he set it on his lap, then he rubbed his eyes one final time and looked at the camera.

"Hi, everyone," he started, waving awkwardly at the camera. "Um, I have some news to share. It may not come as a surprise, but it's something I want to share with you in my own words, now that I'm confident in my decision.

"The first time I watched wrestling on TV as a kid, I knew this was what I wanted to do with my life. I've been given so many incredible opportunities throughout my career and I want to start by saying I owe everything to all of you, the fans, for the support you've given me over the last ten years. Every bump, every bruise, every strain was worth it because it meant I got to do what I love. Your support carried me through some of the darkest times in my life, and you've made every sacrifice worth it.

"While my retirement was already on the horizon, the injury I suffered in the ring recently moved the timeline up. Um, I'm here to announce that I'm hanging up my boots effective immediately, and will no longer be wrestling professionally.

"Um… I also wanted to say that the camaraderie I've shared with my fellow wrestlers, and the connections I've had with fans, they'll stay with me forever. For better or worse—looking at you, Romeo— you've all made an impact on me.

"It's been an honor and a privilege to work for Titan, and I'm excited to see what this new era of wrestlers brings. Stay venomous!"

Wade got up and walked to the tripod, turning off the video. He heaved a heavy sigh and shook his arms to rid himself of the emotions he was feeling. It shot pain up his neck, and he instinctively reached his hand up, hitting his brace. He kicked the corner post on the ring, cursing, and then he heard a noise echo in the empty arena. He turned around and his breath caught. Monty was there, looking handsome, warm, and a little bit tragic.

CHAPTER 23

"I WASN'T EAVESDROPPING. I PROMISE," MONTY SAID. HIS VOICE WAS A little shaky.

"It's okay if you were. It wasn't private," Wade said. He grabbed Mike's camera from the tripod and walked towards Mike's office. Monty grabbed his arm and Wade went stiff.

"Sorry. I'm sorry, I shouldn't grab you with your neck and stuff. I just really… Can we please talk? I can't stand this."

Wade seemed hesitant and Monty wasn't surprised. He knew it was a risk coming here, but he didn't know what else to do. In two weeks, he'd be in Boston. Every day that passed was a day closer to never talking to Wade again, and that just wasn't an option. So, when he'd heard from Mike that Wade was coming in to record his retirement announcement, he threw his shoes on and ran over, finally ignoring Wade's request for space.

Monty waited in the hallway during Wade's speech and only started walking towards the ring when he heard his farewell. His heart raced, and when Wade turned around and spotted him, he got lightheaded. He couldn't fuck this up.

He'd spent much of last night working on bullet points for his apology. One, he would reiterate that he was sorry for not telling Wade the truth. It was a bad call, and if he could do it over again, he'd tell him immediately because Wade deserved to make life decisions with all available information. Two, he would tell Wade that he wanted to make it work between them, no matter what he had to do. If he had to use all of his paychecks to fly Wade back and forth, he didn't care. And three, he loved Wade, and nothing anybody said would change that.

Unfortunately, the instant he laid eyes on Wade, every word he had written and memorized vanished from his thoughts, leaving behind only an empty void of panic and longing.

"I have to go meet with Mike, but maybe we can go get a cup of coffee after that. Can you give me fifteen minutes?" Wade asked.

"Yes, of course. Anything."

Wade gave him just a glimpse of a smile and Monty breathed in. That was a good sign. He remembered to smile back, thank God. Monty sat down on the steps to the ring and bounced his leg. He tried to remember what he wanted to say to Wade, tried to figure out how to phrase it perfectly so Wade wouldn't turn him down, but it didn't work. He sat there for ten minutes, picking at his nails, until he heard Wade's footsteps approaching. He jumped up from his seat, filled with ridiculous hope, and hurried towards Wade.

"Do you want to just go to Sacky's? I think they have shitty coffee on their breakfast menu," Wade said.

"Yeah, sure. It's close."

They walked next to each other but didn't touch. Neither of them spoke the entire two block walk, and Monty's heart broke even further with the reminder of the distance between them. Just a few weeks ago it was completely different. Monty talked too much and Wade listened to every word, and that was the way it was supposed to be. But he couldn't think of a single thing to say that wasn't his rehearsed apology, and the words to that were missing too.

Monty walked quickly to get ahead of Wade to open the door, and he held it as Wade walked in and headed for a booth. Monty ordered two coffees at the bar and then slid in on the other side of the booth Wade picked out.

It was dark inside Sacky's even during the day, but some sunlight was shining in through a small window above their table. The light illuminated Wade's handsome face and the scruffy beard he'd been unable to shave. Seeing him again looking gorgeous, but also sad and weak, was painful. He took a deep breath and blew it out slowly, trying to lower his heart rate before he started talking. Before he could open his mouth, Wade spoke.

"I'm sorry," Wade said.

"I—what?" Monty's mouth gaped. *What the hell?*

"I'm sorry. For what I said the other night. I wish I hadn't been so cruel last time I saw you. I once told you my biggest regret in life was wasting my time at Titan, but now I think my biggest regret is acting like a jackass."

"You were upset. It's okay. I deserved a lot of it," Monty said.

"Yeah, maybe. I wish you'd told me, of course. But… I spoke with Madeline and realized you were between a rock and a hard place. I'm sure it wasn't easy getting that news and dealing with me and my injury at the same time," Wade said. "I'm just so sorry for hurting you, even though I was hurting too. I never want to be the reason you're sad."

"First of all, I wasn't *dealing* with you. I was caring for you because I love you and that's what you do for the people you love. Second, yes. It was difficult. But I should have been honest with you. You are the most important person in my life, and I don't want to do anything to risk that ever again."

Wade gave Monty a small smile, but his eyes looked sad.

"I had all these things I wanted to say to you today, but at the end of the day I just need you to know that I want to be with you. Even though I'm moving to Boston. You can come with me, or I can fly you out until I have more flexibility. Now that you're retired, you'll have some flexibility too, right? I mean, I know you'll have to get a job eventually, but Boston has—"

"Monty," Wade interrupted.

"What?"

"Um…" Wade's eyes looked wet, but no tears fell. "I… can't."

"You can't what? Move to Boston? That's okay, we'll figure it out. We can figure it all out. I'm not going anywhere, not really. Just my body. To Boston. But my heart is here, with you." Monty reached his hand across the table and put it on top of Wade's. He smiled up at Wade, but Wade's face didn't soften. If anything, it was… anguished.

"No, I mean, it's not about moving to Boston. Not really. I mean I can't be with you. After my injury I thought maybe I could, but the contract stuff has brought up all these old feelings and I realized it wouldn't be fair to either of us."

"What?" Monty said, his hand limp against Wade's.

"I've been through this before, Monty. And losing you after *really* having you would be even worse than this. I wouldn't survive it." He looked at Monty and flipped his hand over to rub Monty's palm with his big thumb. "I want you to go to Boston with nothing tying you down. You have your whole career, your whole life ahead of you. You're going to meet people and do things and see places most people only dream of. Having a sad, busted boyfriend four thousand miles away will only hold you back. I can't do that to you, and I can't do it to myself."

Monty stared at Wade in disbelief and withdrew his hand. Never in a million years did he expect this would be the outcome of their conversation. He assumed Wade would tell him to fuck off or tell him good luck and good riddance. The hopeful side of him imagined Wade would be so swayed by Monty's incredible apology that they would get back together and live happily ever after.

But he never imagined the outcome would be more painful than anything, that Wade would tell him they still couldn't be together, no matter how much they might care for each other. He didn't know what to say. They were silent for a few moments while Monty scraped his brain for some fragment of a coherent thought.

"I don't understand," was all he came up with. "I don't… accept that. There has to be some way for us to be together."

A server dropped off their coffee but Monty's stomach was so sour he couldn't imagine drinking anything.

"If you want to stay in touch, I'd like that," Wade said. He poured some cream into his coffee.

"You'd like that," Monty repeated.

"Yes. Even if we're not together, I still care about you and want you to be successful. I've worked with a lot of those guys. I could give you pointers."

"Okay."

"So, we'll stay in touch?"

"Okay."

Wade took a sip of his coffee and grimaced. "Oh, man. This is not good."

Monty tried to smile at Wade, but he couldn't force it. He couldn't force himself to sit there with Wade, who had just broken his heart *again*, and be pals who joke around about shitty coffee. He stood up and walked over to Wade. Wade turned in the booth so he could look at Monty. Monty crouched down so they were eye level with each other, and he put his hands on Wade's arms.

"I love you." He leaned forward and kissed Wade, never progressing beyond a few gentle pecks that released a painful warmth through Monty's exhausted body. "I, um. I have to go now. Please say goodbye to Juliet for me if I don't see her again before I go. I'm really going to miss her."

Wade didn't respond, and Monty didn't beg. He didn't even try to find a glimpse of regret or sadness in Wade's face. He just stood up, wiped his damp eyes, and walked out of Sacky's.

Wade didn't go after him, and Monty hadn't expected him to, but that didn't stop him from shoving all of his clean laundry to the floor to lay on his couch in silence. He listened to every creak and step in the hallway and hoped that one of them would be from Wade. But Wade never appeared, and when Monty finally gave up, he fell asleep to the octopus episode of the marine life docuseries. Again.

CHAPTER 24

Monty's move date came and went. Dr. Nikolov said Wade could work part time as long as he wasn't lifting or climbing anything, so he was back at work, handling all the administrative tasks he'd taken on in past years. Being at the arena but not wrestling was harder than he thought it was going to be. For the first time in his entire career with Titan, he felt like an outsider. Even at the depths of his depression after Larry left, the guys at Titan all respected and looked up to Wade. But now his presence was not only unnecessary, but embarrassing. The jobs he worked could have been completed by anyone with a semi-relevant background. But, as pathetic as he felt, he would rather be there than home, pining for the man he let go.

He sat in the office he now shared with Mike, Juliet resting on his lap, and continued working on Titan's social media accounts. He took over scheduling duties from Mike indefinitely and even started working with the writers Mike contracted from CWΛ. He was helping develop story arcs for Dicky, Curt, and Kenji because they were new enough that Mike was willing to let Wade give it a shot. He should have felt proud of himself with how much he was learning, but everything still felt sort of dull without Monty and wrestling. He really didn't want to become a shell of himself again like he did after Larry left, but he wasn't sure how to stop it.

He and Monty hadn't seen each other again after that day at Sacky's, which was mostly Wade's fault. Monty had been busy packing and finalizing his release from Titan, then he left early to go visit his parents before he headed to Boston. By the time Wade realized he should ask to see him before he left, it was too late.

Well, that wasn't entirely true. He hadn't forgotten to reach out to Monty, of course. He lived every day wishing he was with Monty, but he'd been too afraid to see him. He was afraid he'd change his mind and risk opening himself up to fresh wounds.

They had communicated occasionally via text, though, with Monty taking the lead on maintaining their friendship. He must have thought Wade was never going to do it and that made Wade feel like shit. It wasn't that Wade didn't enjoy their new friendship, really. It was his suggestion at Sacky's after all. But the reality of communicating with Monty on a platonic level, knowing he was out there living his new life in Boston, was more agonizing than Wade had anticipated.

He never asked Monty if he'd met anybody or if he planned to date because he didn't think he could handle the answer, not that that stopped his imagination from running wild with ideas. Monty was gregarious and sweet and magnetic. Any person in Boston would be lucky to score even one date with him. And Monty's new partner Dom, whose stage name was DarkWing, was really cute. Wade knew they spent a lot of time together since they lived and worked together, and practicing involved a lot of time touching each other. He didn't need to be reminded about his relationship with Monty starting in a very similar way.

So, okay, maybe Wade didn't enjoy their *friendship*, but it was only because it wasn't enough. But the thought of not talking to him at all felt even worse, so he was learning to accept that this was just what his life was now. A constant battle against himself for making this stupid, but safe, decision.

When Monty first arrived in Boston, he sent Wade endless text messages. He imagined Monty was lonely and bored and had no social outlets, but he never complained. Monty mostly sent stuff like CWA backstage drama, a photo of a tiny pink thong with a note about it being his debut match outfit, or a photo of a stuffed octopus he saw in a storefront. His favorite message was a photo of Monty and Dom standing next to Plymouth Rock. They were both wearing giant winter coats, beanies, and exaggerated, unimpressed frowns. He sent it with the note, "*smallest glacial erratic boulder I've ever seen irl.*" Wade loved it, of course, because he loved him.

But when Monty's frequency of communication dwindled, he had no one to blame but himself. And now he was at work, watching his phone, waiting for a text that probably wouldn't come, all because he'd forced Monty to move on.

Wade looked down at the pad of paper he'd been writing on and realized he'd doodled about a dozen flowers and snakes on the script he'd been working on, which he took as a sign he should call it for the evening. He crumpled the paper up and threw it in the direction of the recycling bin next to his door. He didn't realize the door had opened and the crumpled paper bounced off of Niall's groin and onto the floor.

"Nice."

"Sorry. My muscles are atrophying."

"Bah. They look pretty good to me," Niall said, sitting down on the edge of Wade's desk. "What's up? Wanna go get drunk?"

Wade laughed. "No, not really. But it'd be good for me to socialize, so if you want to go out, I will go with you. As long as we go somewhere near my place. I'm not about to be stranded at Chopsticks with no way to get home after you leave with someone else."

"That happened one time! And I'm sorry, but he was hot. You would have done the same."

"Maybe," Wade smiled. He got up from his desk and grabbed his coat. He pursed his lips and tapped the chin of his neck brace. "Should we invite Amit?"

"Fuck off," Niall said.

Wade laughed again and enjoyed the feeling of it. It felt like proof that even without Monty, life would continue to have bright spots. They were dimmer than they'd be if Monty was there, and Niall was an annoying replacement, but they were still bright.

They got into Niall's car and Wade pulled out his phone to see if Monty had sent anything. He opened Monty's Instagram and tried to avoid tapping on his tagged photos but failed. He frowned when he saw a few new photos of Monty tagged at clubs and parties around Boston. He was always with Dom or other guys from CWA and always with a gaggle of really beautiful women. Wade shifted in his seat uncomfortably and tried to hide the phone from Niall, but his stupid neck brace made it impossible because he had to hold the phone in front of his face to see it.

"Put that shit away before you ruin our evening, Wade. This is not what we're doing tonight. I am taking you out to have a good time and stop wallowing. Hey, maybe you'll meet someone!"

"I don't want to meet anyone."

"You don't have to fall in love with them. Just see where the night takes you." Niall grinned at Wade.

Wade glared at him and shoved his phone in his pocket. "You are really annoying, you know that?"

"Yes, and I've accepted that. It's time for you to accept it, too. Can you walk a few blocks? Can that thing get wet?"

Wade mumbled an affirmative and Niall parked the car. They put their hoods up and headed towards a bar near Wade's house called Catch & Release. It wasn't his favorite because it was always packed and had a younger clientele than he was used to these days. But Niall chose it because Wade whined about wanting to be near his house, so Wade kept his mouth shut.

When they walked in, they looked around for somewhere to sit and landed a table near the pool tables. He sat on one side of a booth with cracked leather seats and a sticky tabletop and waited for Niall to join him with their first round.

He picked at the peeling vinyl, his fingers grazing the edges while his mind wandered through old memories of times he'd been to this bar. In his early twenties he'd loved it because it was like a meat market with an endless sea of hot, available men. Later, he and Larry would walk down for a nightcap after work and people watch while talking about their matches.

It was hard to believe how long ago that was and how different his life had become. Back then, he was in love, happy, and healthy; life felt easy. Now, he found himself single, broken, retired, and pathetic.

He glanced up at the TV. It was showing reruns of CWA's summer specials. Monty wouldn't be on tonight, which was a relief, but the endless promos for the JingleRing meant he saw Monty's face several times before Niall even got back from the bar.

Niall slid into the booth and passed Wade a Coke. "Sorry, the line was pretty long."

"All good," Wade smiled. He took a sip of his soda and looked at the TV for what turned out to be a few seconds too long.

"What are you looking at?" Niall strained his neck and looked at the TV. "Oh, hell no. Nope. Switch sides with me. This is a CWA and Monty free evening."

Wade rolled his eyes but got out of the booth. Niall's heart was in the right place, and he didn't want it to feel like a waste of an evening.

"That's better," Niall smiled.

"So," Wade drawled. "It's a Monty free evening, but not an Amit free evening. What the hell is going on with you guys?"

"Nothing is going on with us. He's irritating as fuck."

"Irritating, maybe, but he's pretty cute, right? Good wrestler, too. Good hair. Amazing body…" Wade looked at Niall, whose face flashed something Wade couldn't make out.

"He's a child," Niall scoffed. "I'm thirty-seven. I'm divorced."

"Who cares if you're divorced? People get divorced. And he's not a child, Niall. He's twenty-five. Monty is twenty-four."

"Aht! No Monty talk."

"I noticed you guys have been spending a lot of time together outside the ring, that's all." Wade swirled his straw around in his drink and raised his eyebrows in Niall's direction.

Niall glared at him. "I do not have feelings for Amit. He's not even my type. He's too short. And his hair is dumb. And like, he follows me around. Not attractive. Do you want to date him? You can date him, Wade."

"Hmm. The lady doth protest too much, methinks," Wade grinned.

"Okay, you know what? This is now a Monty and Amit free evening." Niall squinted and scanned the bar. His eyes zeroed in on a pair of guys standing together. They were handsome in a finance bro sort of way, which wasn't Wade's usual type. But maybe that was okay for tonight. "I'm going to go see if those guys want to sit with us."

A few minutes passed before Wade was gently shoved to the inside of the booth by Niall who had returned with two guys he found by the pool tables. Niall spoke out of the side of his mouth and said he called the one wearing the striped polo shirt. Wade could not have cared less, since he had absolutely no plans to go home with anybody they met tonight, especially these clowns, but it was good to know which one he could talk to less.

The four of them chatted for a while, and the crypto bros (not finance, they clarified) told them about what they did for work. Wade understood about twenty percent of what they said, and one hundred percent of it was incredibly boring. They talked a lot about how much money they earned and how nice their cars were, and they talked about how many people wanted to fuck them because of it. They eventually said something about maximizing return and minimizing risk, and that was about the point Wade dug his thumb as hard as he could into Niall's bare thigh through the stupid, giant holes he had in his jeans. Niall made a pained noise and somehow managed to change the topic of conversation.

He and Wade shared stories about Titan and wrestling and talked about some of their most memorable matches. The guys seemed to think it was pretty great, probably because they were also gym bros, and apparently that meant they knew everything about wrestling. Or something.

When the topic landed on Wade's injury, the vibe of the conversation shifted. It sank Wade's mood and he started looking for an excuse to leave. Unfortunately, the crypto bros started telling Wade about investments he should consider for retirement, and Wade dug his thumb into Niall's thigh again. Brilliantly sensing Wade's annoyance, Niall sent him to get another round. Wade shot daggers at him while he walked away.

When he got up to the bar, he ordered a round of drinks and waited for the bartender. He felt someone slide up next to him, closer than he would expect from a stranger. He jumped back slightly and turned his body, only to find Amit standing beside him. Amit was shorter than Wade, and he was lean and sinewy and tight all around.

He could probably get any guy in this bar, but Wade suspected that wasn't his goal.

"Hey, Wade. Um, are you here with Niall? I thought I saw you guys walk in together," Amit said.

"I am, yeah. We're sitting over there." Wade pointed at the table with his thumb. Amit looked over Wade's shoulder and his eyes got wide. "I don't know those guys and they have no idea who I am, but they're all crying over my retirement anyway. I needed some space."

Amit breathed out a small laugh. But then he looked crestfallen. "Is Niall, like…"

"I don't think he knows them any more than I do," Wade said in a soothing tone. Amit peeked over his shoulder again.

"Okay."

Wade could see the worry on Amit's face. Niall put on a front about Amit, he was sure. He was positive there was something going on between them. He just had to figure out how to make Niall stop being an idiot. He leaned towards Amit awkwardly. "What's going on between you two?"

"Nothing."

"Uh huh. Hey, take these drinks to the table?"

Amit looked up at Wade, dubious, but he took them and headed off towards Niall and the crypto bros. Wade took the opportunity to sneak out of the bar through a side door.

On the walk home, Wade pulled his phone out. Monty had texted him earlier in the evening, just a photo of a club he went to. He was feeling loose and silly after escaping what had turned into, well, not a fun evening, but an evening worth talking about, and he couldn't think of anybody he wanted to talk to about it more than Monty. He glanced at the time. It was after ten o'clock, which meant it was after one for Monty. He tapped the FaceTime button anyway and hoped Monty would still be awake.

CHAPTER 25

MONTY'S PHONE BUZZED ON HIS NIGHTSTAND, PULLING HIM FROM HIS light sleep. He opened one eye and tried to see who was calling, but his phone was face down. When he reached out with his arm and wiggled his fingers, trying to will the phone into his hand, he knocked a book over and it bumped the phone onto the ground. He groaned and pushed his face into his pillow.

He was still a tiny bit drunk after a wild night out with some guys from work. Dom and his friend Angel, a big-name wrestler with CWA, rented a huge VIP booth at a club near the arena and invited Monty. Dom and Angel were well known in Boston, and Monty was learning their fame meant special treatment pretty much anywhere they went.

A group of women had joined them in their booth and they all shared many, many bottles of champagne, each of which cost more than Monty's monthly rent. Their booth had been thick with the mixing of perfumes and colognes and sweat, each scent belonging to a different person who had felt emboldened to touch and flirt with him in the safety of the dark. He'd mentioned his discomfort to Dom and Angel, but their solution was to drag him to the dance floor where they danced and drank for hours. By the time he left, he'd felt overwhelmed and touched out, and despite the hours they'd spent together at the gym and club, he felt like an outsider.

Monty still felt like an imposter at CWA and evenings like this, where Angel and Dom used their money and fame to party, only made it worse. He'd been in Boston a couple of weeks, and he'd often lay down at night in the apartment he shared with Dom and wonder how long it would take before CWA realized they'd made a huge mistake.

He was slated to have minimal ring time at first, of course, but if his debut match went well—and all the buzz online pointed toward that possibility—they hoped to have him written into existing angles as the long-lost son of the Duke, a popular wrestler signed to CWA. Eventually, with luck and popularity, Monty would dethrone the Duke just before his retirement. It was a lot of pressure, and his career hadn't even started yet.

While a VIP booth at an intense club had been a strange way to spend an evening, he supposed it had provided a necessary reprieve from nonstop training and stress. That didn't mean he wasn't going to regret it tomorrow. Or today. Whenever he woke up.

Monty rubbed his eyes and leaned off his bed to pick up his still-buzzing phone. His blurry eyes finally focused and his stomach tensed when he saw Wade's name. They never called each other. He wanted to talk to him so badly, but he was tipsy and trying to wake up, and he didn't want to say anything stupid. Then again, he'd rather say something stupid than miss a chance to talk to him… His thumb slid to answer the call, but it was just a second too late because the phone stopped ringing.

"Shit! Shit, shit," he said, scrambling into a sitting position. He took a gulp of water to wet his mouth and called Wade back. He drummed his nervous fingers on the mattress and muttered to himself. "Please answer."

His phone lit up and Wade's handsome face filled the screen. He was intermittently illuminated by street lamps while he walked, and it looked dark and drizzly outside. He was wearing a black beanie and had a light blue scarf wrapped loosely around his neck brace. Monty doubted it actually helped him retain any heat, but it looked really good on him anyway. He wished he could reach through the phone and feel how soft it was against Wade's skin.

"Hi, Monty," Wade said.

"Hi, you."

They both quietly looked at each other and it felt… good. But weird, too. They hadn't really spoken since their last meeting at Sacky's, just exchanged text messages. Monty was worried he'd been forcing this new version of friendship on Wade, but as long as Wade kept replying, Monty planned on continuing.

"I'm sorry I called so late. You were probably sleeping. I was just hoping to catch you on my walk home."

"I'm awake. I was in bed, but I'm up. I'm really glad you called," Monty said. He shifted so he was sitting against the pillows on his headboard and he pulled his blanket up over his lap. He smiled at his screen and patted his frizzy hair down. "I'm kinda drunk."

Wade laughed a little, and Monty smiled at him.

"What did you do tonight? Where are you walking from?" Monty asked.

"Oh, man. I went out with Niall tonight and we met these guys at Catch & Release. They were probably the worst people I've ever had the misfortune of spending an evening with, but after a rocky start it ended up… well, still rocky, but whatever. I escaped."

Monty tried to keep his face neutral, but he knew Catch & Release was a bar people went to when they were looking for a sure thing. He grumbled at Niall internally, guessing their evening out had been an effort to get Wade laid, and that was his right or whatever, but Monty still didn't want to hear about it.

"Oh?"

"Yeah," Wade said, looking downright giddy, "and guess who showed up? Amit!"

"Amit just… showed up at Catch & Release, where you and Niall happened to be?" Monty grinned. "That seems like a suspicious series of events."

"Poor guy is pining hard," Wade chuckled. "Remember when they used to fight all the time? Man, I would pay a hundred dollars to be a fly on the wall of their training sessions."

"Ew, voyeur!" Monty gasped.

Wade laughed and made a gagging noise. "God, no! Niall is like my weird gym teacher or something. And have you seen how hairy he is? His brother used to work at Titan, and he was so smooth."

"Well, maybe Amit could help shave him. Or wax? Imagine what the strips would look like," Monty said, laughing.

"God, stop!" Wade squeezed his eyes shut.

They talked for a while longer about Amit and Niall. They placed wagers on how long it would be before they ended up in bed together and how long Niall would try to keep it a secret from everyone. Wade told Monty about everything he'd been working on, and he gushed over how brilliant Wade was.

Easy conversation flowed and they lost themselves in laughter as if no time had passed. It almost felt like Monty was just on vacation, like he'd go back to Portland and they'd pick up where they left off.

But he wasn't on vacation. They were still four thousand miles apart and there was no reason to think that would ever change. But talking to Wade and remembering how much sense they made him feel hopeful. And frustrated. He was kicking himself for allowing the distance between them to grow.

"So, um. You met some guys at Catch & Release?" Monty asked. He wasn't sure why he was asking.

"Well, kind of. I mean, *I* didn't," Wade stressed. "Niall did and brought them to our table."

"Ah," Monty said.

"What?"

"Nothing. I said, 'ah.' That is generally a noise of understanding. Or... comprehension."

Wade rolled his eyes. "Okay. The guys sucked, for what it's worth. I didn't even want to go there but Niall was trying to, I don't know, get me out of my funk."

"You've been in a funk?"

Wade didn't say anything for a moment. He kept walking, his warm breath forming little white fog clouds.

"Wade?"

"What?"

"I said, you've been in a funk?"

"I heard you. I'm... thinking."

"Okay."

Monty didn't press. He would wait for Wade to respond before he started talking again. He knew Wade needed time to gather his thoughts, but his silence was sometimes so frustrating for Monty, because he couldn't comprehend the need to mull over *anything* before speaking.

"I don't know. This is hard to talk about," Wade said.

"Maybe we should talk about it anyway."

Wade continued walking silently for a few moments. He climbed the stairs to his apartment and unlocked the door. He took a deep breath and sighed as he shrugged his coat off. Monty braced himself for… well, he wasn't sure what. But whatever Wade was about to share didn't seem good.

"I'm just… Well, can I be honest?"

Monty's stomach sank. "Of course."

"There was just so much more I wanted to experience with you. What we had will never be enough for me. What we *have* will never be enough for me, but I just don't see an alternative. I'm trying to make peace with it, but it's been harder than I thought it would be."

"Okay…"

"Without you around, my world just feels darker, or something. My apartment feels colder. Being 'just friends' with you is like torture. Every time I hear from you, I'm simultaneously thrilled and devastated. It's like whiplash. And my neck is very fragile right now, you know," he said, and then gave half a smile. "I keep hoping for a sign that this can be more, but instead, I'm caught in this endless loop of wanting you close and pushing you away. It's exhausting."

"Do you want me to stop texting you?" Monty asked, louder than he meant to. His heart sped up, almost painfully.

"No, no," Wade said reassuringly. "Not at all. But it's been hard. Niall noticed, that's all. Everyone has, I guess. I'm not exactly great company these days."

Monty stared at Wade through the phone for a beat before an unexpected surge of rage washed over him. He was suddenly so angry. Angry at Wade's reluctance, angry at the distance between them, angry at Wade's stupid neck injury, angry at the fact that it was after one in the morning and he was recovering from drinking and he was exhausted.

But mostly, he was angry that Wade was the one who broke up with *him*. Monty never wanted any of this. And now Wade, what, wanted Monty to comfort him? To reassure him that he'd get over Monty at some point if he just went out with Niall and slept with some crypto douche who wore a checkered Oxford shirt and khaki slacks to a dive bar?

"I'm not really sure what you want me to say here, Wade," Monty said, surprised by the lack of emotion in his voice. "I never wanted to end things or change what we had. You broke *my* heart. *Twice.*"

"I know," Wade said. "I'm sorry."

"*I* am here. *I* am waiting," Monty said, pointing at his chest for emphasis. "I already told you I'd do anything to make this work, and you turned me down, twice. You don't get to call me and wax poetic about the heartbreak that *you caused*." He clenched his jaw so Wade wouldn't notice his trembling.

"I know, Monty. I…"

"No, stop. Let me talk. I'm out here, living the life you told me to live. I'm experiencing everything you told me to experience. I'm meeting people, and training, and existing, and it sucks without you. It's new, and different, and truthfully, it's kind of awful and really fucking lonely sometimes. But I'm doing it because I have no other choice. Because you broke up with me!"

"I *know.*"

"So, I'm sorry, but I don't want to hear about how your night went with the crypto bros, or how Niall took you to Catch & Release, or how dark and cold your life is without me. Stop punishing me for loving you. I can't do it anymore, it's too hard."

Wade didn't say anything, but Monty noticed he'd stopped pacing. He watched Wade's jaw work and waited for him to say something. *Anything.* But of course, he didn't. The silence between them stretched on and Monty was getting restless. He needed to pee and get a snack or maybe write in a journal and cry.

"Listen, um. It's after two and I'm exhausted. I think I'm going to go."

"Of course, yeah. I'm sorry I woke you."

"Goodnight, Wade."

"Night, Monty."

CHAPTER 26

THE DAYS FOLLOWING THEIR ARGUMENT WERE A BLUR. HIS PHONE WAS miserably silent, but his mind worked overtime, repeating Monty's words on a loop. Being forced to face the pain he'd inflicted on Monty was heavy in his gut—raw, nauseating, and entirely deserved. He wallowed for a while, but eventually felt so pathetic that he forced himself to get off the couch to visit Linda and the animals.

In a bid to put himself together, he stood in front of the mirror, struggling to trim his beard around a painful, ingrown hair. Grooming these days was a challenge. His brace was always in the way, trapping itchy whiskers beneath the foam-lined metal. Madeline had offered to shave him while he laid down with his brace off, but he'd declined, fearing an ingrown hair would form under the brace. To avoid rocking the follicular boat, he was avoiding razors entirely, using scissors and picking at his beard in the mirror.

Wade laughed at the analogy forming in his mind—Monty was not an ingrown hair—but just like his fear of ingrown hairs led to behaviors that ultimately caused one, his fear of Monty leaving him led to self-sabotage that ultimately caused Monty to pull away. His idiotic behavior had jeopardized any chance he had at having a meaningful relationship with Monty.

Part of him couldn't believe Monty had put up with him as long as he had, which made the guilt even worse. He'd prolonged Monty's pain for purely selfish reasons: too afraid to take a risk with a man who would have made it far easier than he deserved, and too greedy to cut him out of his life and let him truly move on.

In that way, the silence between them should have been expected. Wade's surprise only illustrated how much he'd taken Monty's affection for granted.

A Lyft driver dropped him off outside Linda's clinic. A storm days earlier had caused the oak trees lining the parking lot to drop thousands of leaves and acorns. The resulting fallout was a thick layer of slimy decay coating the asphalt. Tiny acorn landmines awaited their chance to roll an unsuspecting ankle.

Wade stood pathetically in the center of the lot, looking around for the least treacherous path. He tried taking a step towards the door, but his foot slid on the wet leaves. He froze, afraid to move, his balance mediocre at best in his brace. He took a calming breath and tried again, shuffling his feet without lifting them from the pavement. When he looked up and saw Camila peeking at him from behind her blinds, he gave her a sheepish wave. She disappeared from view but reappeared moments later, directly in front of him.

"Hi, Wade," she said. She moved towards him with what was, in his opinion, an awful lot of bravado. "Can I help you to the door?"

"There was a time where leaves didn't scare me, you know," he said, smiling at her. "But yes, please."

"You'll get back there someday." She patted his hand and took his elbow, supporting him as he slid gracelessly across the parking lot.

By the time he got into the clinic, he was sweaty and damp, despite the cool temperature outside. He shed his warm coat and hung it on the rack by the door. The clinic was full, and he was suddenly on the receiving end of the wide-eyed stares of half a dozen patrons. He gave them a small smile before walking towards the back, not asking for permission.

He was used to people recognizing him, though his level of celebrity paled in comparison to someone like Larry or, soon, Monty. He assumed the stares he received today were because of his brace, which was a lot less flattering.

Linda was swamped, unsurprisingly, so he helped out with some cleaning and feeding of resident animals for a couple of hours. Bending was still difficult, but he made it work as best he could. When he reached the rehabilitation animals, he peeked into Juliet's cage. She was napping. He plucked her from her bed and held her to his chest with one big hand.

"Hey, Wade! I didn't see you. Thanks for your help." Linda dabbed at her forehead with a tissue. "I just had to wrestle the biggest dog you've ever seen in your life. I am exhausted. And it was just for a nail trim! It took three of us to hold him down."

Wade chuckled and turned his body towards the door, hoping to get a peek at the dog before it left. But the window was up too high, and the thought of going back to the waiting room was overwhelming, so he changed the topic.

"Do you think Juliet misses her mom?" Wade asked. He didn't like the idea of that.

"Where is this coming from?" She laughed before glancing at Wade's distraught face. "Juliet is several months old now, Wade. If she was in the wild, she might not even be with her anymore. So if I had to guess, she probably doesn't remember her mom."

Wade sighed. If she didn't need her mom, that meant she didn't need him. And that meant it was time to release her.

"I'm just thinking about her release. I don't know. Nevermind."

Linda walked over to him and sat down. She put her hand on his knee.

"I had an idea about that," she said, patting gently. "I think we should release her on my property. I know it's not near where she was found, but she doesn't know that anymore. And she likes it there. It's like an opossum paradise. It'll be a gradual process with her because she's young and grew up in captivity, and we have to give her time to learn to fear humans, right? She can learn that nearby, so I can keep an eye on her. Leave her food, and stuff like that. Plus, she'd have her doctor right there if anything went wrong. You can feel good about that and worry less."

"Oh. Yeah, that would be good," he said. He knew it was the right thing to do and that Juliet would be fine, but he never should have allowed himself to grow so attached to her. He hated that he had done this to himself. An annoyed sigh escaped him as he realized this was a prevailing theme of his life. He'd known he was holding her too much and babying her too much, just like he'd known getting attached to Monty was a bad idea. And both relationships had an inevitable end he'd chosen to ignore.

When he broke up with Monty, he'd justified it by blaming it all on the contract, using it as proof that he'd been right all along. He'd said he wanted Monty to experience CWA alone, to meet his new coworkers and learn the ropes without the distraction of a boyfriend or caretaking requirements. He'd said he knew Monty wouldn't have time to nurture a brand new relationship while dealing with a chaotic tour schedule. And for weeks, whenever a nagging thought entered his mind about the breakup being a mistake, he found a reason it wasn't, even when Monty's words and actions said otherwise.

Trying to distract himself, he massaged Juliet's tiny paws the way Monty used to. He thought of how Monty's nervous energy manifested in his hands, always twisting them and picking at his skin. God, he was doomed if even Juliet's paws were a reminder of Monty and the sweet, anxious bits he tried to hide.

After what had turned out to be a torturous day full of realizations, the worst one came moments later.

Wade was seated behind the curtain next to Juliet's kennel, invisible to those entering the back room of the clinic. Linda had returned to her desk, entering notes from the day's appointments.

He heard a familiar voice. Mike had arrived with lunch for Linda, and as he sat down with her, Wade overheard mention of the watch party they were planning to share Monty's CWA debut. Not realizing Wade was around, he told Linda he'd spoken to Monty and that he was "struggling" in Boston. He stayed still, hoping Linda would forget he was there.

"Struggling how?" she asked.

"I don't know. In a lot of ways, I guess. He's just an old farm boy at heart. I think he's just scared being out there all alone. Um, don't tell him I said that," he said, chuckling.

He heard Mike eat a chip and mumble something else. Linda made a sympathetic sound.

"Did he call you?" she asked.

"Yeah, he said he had some questions about his Titan contract but I think he wanted to catch up, I guess."

"Poor guy. He's such a sweetheart."

"Yeah," Mike said, quietly.

"He'll be okay. He made friends at Titan pretty easily, right? Maybe he just needs to make some friends."

"He has, yeah. I think he just wanted someone familiar to talk to. His new friends are a little overwhelming. It's intense out there."

"Oh, I remember," she said, laughing. They switched topics, reminiscing about several surprisingly risqué adventures they'd had during Mike's professional peak.

Wade cringed and squeezed his eyes shut, but he remained silent and rubbed Juliet's paws gently.

He felt sick. Not just from hearing far too much personal information about Mike and Linda's younger years, but hearing Mike's comments about Monty. Instead of remaining friends like he said he wanted, Wade had started phasing Monty out of his life as some sort of fucked-up attempt at self-preservation. It was cowardly, sure, but worse than that, it was heartless. It meant he didn't just hurt Monty's feelings by breaking up with him, he'd ruined Monty's entire experience of moving to Boston.

Instead of moving to a new city with an engaged safety net, Monty moved alone, without the emotional support he'd needed. Wade hadn't even given him a proper goodbye. And Monty even told him once how difficult it had been to move to Portland on his own, without anyone but his mom on the other end of the phone.

Wade had assumed Monty would flourish socially in Boston if he'd been freed of Wade's endless baggage, but Monty's only available social circle was an alcohol-and-drug-fueled mob of professional wrestlers. What Monty really needed was a reliable, steady presence in his life. Someone who could anchor him when he felt like a tiny dinghy floating in the vast ocean of CWA.

Wade had really fucked up. Multiple times. And he had no idea how to fix it, or if Monty even wanted him to at this point. But he had to try.

Mike left, and Linda finished up her paperwork. She peeked her head around the curtain with fresh food for Juliet.

"Oh, crap. I forgot you were here! Sorry," she said, grimacing. "Hopefully you weren't traumatized by our little trip down memory lane."

"Only a little." He smiled and stroked Juliet's scaly tail.

Linda glanced down at Juliet and gave her a sad smile.

"Come by early the day of the match. That gives us what, a week or so? We'll say goodbye together. Okay?"

He nodded. Then he looked up at Linda and said, "Do you have any clay?"

CHAPTER 27

"Yo, Romeo!" Dom was sitting on a weight bench when Monty walked into the CWA practice arena gym. Angel was behind him, racking a barbell with a freakish amount of weight.

"Hey, fellas."

"You ready for tomorrow?" Dom asked.

Monty's debut was the next day, and panic was beginning to gnaw at him. He was excited, of course, because he'd made it. The culmination of all of his hard work over the last several years had resulted in his dream—a major debut at CWA. But it was almost too much. It felt too big, or too final, like he'd been hiking up a mountain for the last six years of his life and had finally reached the summit, but now he was alone and without any idea how to get down. He'd spent so many years working to get to this point and he'd spent very little time thinking about what came next.

Technically, he had people at CWA to talk to about this. He was sure this wasn't an unusual feeling. But the one person he wanted to talk to about it was dealing with a… strained relationship with wrestling, to say the least.

"Yeah, ready to get it over with!" Monty said, trying to sound lighthearted. "I'm, uh, actually pretty nervous. That's probably normal, though, right?"

"Ah, you're fine," Angel said. "Debut is just one night out of your whole life. Hey, Rome. Come spot me."

Angel's pep talks needed work, and he wished the guys in Boston would call him Monty, but he was too new to complain. He was used to responding to Romeo now, so he walked over to Angel without comment.

Dom was now focused on getting the perfect glute pump photo in the wall-length mirror in front of them. He was grateful he'd already made a decent friend in the short time he'd been in Boston, but Dom was a huge dork. Literally, he was massive. Monty snapped a photo of Dom's ridiculous pose and let him know he'd send it later.

"Just post it, Rome. I trust you."

Monty gave him a thumbs up and turned back to Angel. He had zero plans to post that photo anywhere.

When he found out they were going to be living together, Monty was nervous. Dom was big and burly, but his appearance hid a surprising warmth that Monty had come to appreciate. They'd since fallen into a superficial, but comfortable friendship. Sometimes *too* comfortable. Dom was wildly unashamed of his body, which meant Monty had seen every square inch of it for a plethora of non-sexual reasons.

Monty's phone vibrated in his pocket, but he ignored it to focus on Angel for the next few minutes. When it was Monty's turn, Angel's obnoxious coaching dragged on longer than necessary and ate into the time he planned to use for running. When he started encouraging Monty to demonstrate stretches that bordered on ridiculous, Monty cut his losses and headed to the indoor track.

He needed to clear his thoughts before the match tomorrow. He missed the easy camaraderie he'd had with the guys at Titan, however short his time there had been. They took themselves less seriously and didn't have money to throw at clubs and women. He missed how easy it had all been.

Not that he regretted his move. He couldn't regret it. But he did miss… things.

He pulled his phone out to choose a playlist and his heart stuttered when he saw a text from Wade. Things had been off between them since they talked on the phone the night Wade went out with Niall.

The truth was, while Monty felt bad about snapping at him, he was also glad it happened. He'd had a lot he needed to get off his chest, but had been too afraid to rock the boat. Wade was closed off unless he was throwing depressing metaphors around, and Monty had always been too nervous to be truthful about his feelings.

He was done prioritizing Wade's comfort over his own truth. He'd spent so long begging to be let in, and he just couldn't do it anymore. He needed to focus on his future. If Wade wanted to be part of it, great. If not, well, Monty would survive.

Probably.

Old Monty would have panicked at the idea, but New Monty was prepared for either outcome.

Their argument seemed to be the kick in the ass Wade needed anyway, because he reached out pretty often now. Sometimes Monty was too busy to reply, and he'd come back to multiple messages. From Wade! He couldn't deny it was a little fun being on this side of this much attention, but still, he forced himself to be cautious and made sure not to read too much into anything Wade said.

> Juliet is being released tomorrow. I am going to miss her so much.

Monty frowned at his phone. He knew how important Juliet was to Wade and had secretly hoped she would be ineligible for release. Yes, that made him an asshole, but he couldn't help wanting to spare Wade the pain of saying goodbye to her. And Monty was going to miss her, too. He always imagined they'd see each other again, which was probably stupid.

> i'm sorry. <3 i'll miss her too.

> hmm. would a photo of a himbo with a dump truck help?

> ....Honestly, yes.

Monty sent the photo of Dom and laughed out loud after looking at it again.

> Himbo with a capital H. he once caught a
> bumblebee in a glass and set it free outside after it
> rode into the gym on a bouquet he brought in for the
> social media gal when her pet rat died. maybe his
> ass is so big bc he keeps his big heart in there?

Lol. Thank you. It's a nice picture.

Hmm. I think I like the guy in the background more.

Monty zoomed in. The guy in the background was him. He blushed, glad Angel wasn't around to see him. He watched the three dots bounce on the bottom of his phone screen and picked at his lip. Wade wasn't a big conversational texter, so this was fun. And weird. And exciting. He took an anxious pull from his water bottle while he waited.

> Hey, I'm thinking of you. Not sure how much you'll
> be able to talk tomorrow, so just know that I'm
> sending you every good vibe possible. You're going
> to kill it. Wish I could see it in person. Someday soon
> I will.

> And this isn't luck - it's what you earned from the
> effort you put in over the last six years.

> I'm serious, Monty. You are made for this.

Monty felt a little dizzy, but he smiled a big goofy grin, replied with a billion heart emojis, and shoved his phone back in his pocket before he did something stupid, like call Wade and ask him to marry him. So much for not reading too much into Wade's messages.

But still, New Monty would not beg. New Monty would let Wade come to him. He put his headphones in and started running.

He got lost in his thoughts, his feet moving in time to the playlist he'd chosen as he reflected on the whirlwind of the last six months. From Boise to Portland to Boston, the challenges and comforts of each city.

Boise was his anchor, his home. Portland was just a blip in the timeline of his life, and Boston was still a struggle. He'd been at the top of his promotion in Boise and rose the ranks quickly in Portland.

He was used to being a big fish in a small pond, and now he felt like a solitary anchovy swimming around Boston Harbor. The transition was hard.

But he reminded himself it was too early to tell how his life in Boston would turn out. The future he'd worked for lay before him and he didn't have time to get hung up on what used to be. He put on something more upbeat and ran until his thighs burned.

AFTER SHOWERING, Monty headed towards the doors that opened to the parking lot. He planned on going home to take a warm bath, a method of relaxation Dom introduced him to when they first moved in together.

Monty had entered the bathroom with his small box of toiletries and had been assaulted by a thousand layers of fragrance. Dom had all sorts of salts and soaps meticulously arranged on the edge of the tub, over the toilet, and under the vanity. Neither he nor Dom really fit in their small tub, but something about Dom's excitement was endearing, and he couldn't deny that a hot bath that made him smell like lemony lavender wasn't a bad way to spend an hour.

He'd reached the building's foyer when an intern for CWA ran up behind him.

"Mr. Hill! Wait up!"

Monty looked around. *Mr. Hill?*

"Oh, hey, Lizzie," he said, internally squealing at the formality. People weren't *mean* to him at CWA, but he was at the bottom of the pecking order. Very few people even called him Monty, let alone Mr. Hill. But Lizzie was reliably polite in a way that made him feel important.

"Sorry to sneak up behind you. You got this in the mailroom, and I was heading down here to drop some stuff off and saw your car, so…"

He smiled at her as she twirled her hair. She worked in the administrative building across the parking lot, but she *saw his car* pretty often. Whenever that happened, she would inevitably have some swag item or a file she'd be running to another part of the building, a tactic that seemed to ensure their paths would cross. But this time was different. She was holding a package addressed to him in familiar handwriting. There was no return address, but as he looked at it, his stomach rose to his throat.

"Thank you. I wonder what it is. Hopefully nobody is trying to kill me, huh?"

She gave him a confused look.

"*Anthrax,*" he said in an exaggerated whisper.

Her eyes widened and she took a step back, wiping her hands on her pants. She tripped over the oversized doormat and fell into a trophy case before righting herself.

"Oh, no. It was just a tasteless joke," he said, grimacing slightly. He reached out to her and she flinched. "I'm sorry. Are you okay?"

"Uh huh. I'm fine, sir."

He gave her a flirtatious grin to apologize, hoping his charm would distract her from his joke. His thumb slid along the envelope's seal, and when he peeked inside, he saw a small velvet bag and a handwritten letter. His breath picked up and he closed the envelope, quickly tucking it into his jacket pocket. He patted it gently and said, "I'll open this at home. Goodnight, Lizzie."

He rushed to his car, holding his pocket closed to shield its contents from the rain. Every red light on the way home stretched on for an eternity, every pedestrian crossing the street channeled their inner sloth. His fingers drummed on the steering wheel in a failed attempt to expel nervous energy. Normally he didn't mind sitting in traffic because it was still novel. He enjoyed taking in the sights of the skyline, inventing lives for the people he saw on the sidewalk. But when his building came into view, he felt a level of desperate urgency comparable only to the feeling one gets when their destination appears and they really need to pee. His nerves took over as he ran upstairs. He barely remembered getting to his apartment or through the door.

He decided against a bubble bath, figuring he may need one later depending on what awaited him in the envelope. He settled down on the couch and placed the envelope on the coffee table in front of him. He rubbed his sweaty palms on his knees and read the name above the address – Montgomery Hill, % CWA. After chuckling at the use of his full name, he felt a quick pang of guilt over neglecting to share his new address with Wade. Not that he knew this package was from Wade. But he assumed it was. He hoped it was.

He pulled the velvet bag out first, then the letter. His mom always said it was important to read birthday cards first before opening the related gift, and he figured the rule extended to handwritten letters attached to tiny velvet bags being sent for unknown reasons.   He opened the letter and started reading.

> Monty,
>
> I hope this reaches you before your debut, but if it doesn't, I hope the Power of the Possum transcends space and time to bring you luck. Not that you need it.
>
> I know you think this new chapter of your life is daunting, and it is. But in the time that I've known you, I've felt your energy and been amazed by your ability to transform every moment into something better for everyone involved, and I know you'll do the same at your debut.
>
> You're embarking on a journey that I know will leave a mark on the world of professional wrestling for years to come. At the risk of sounding cheesy, my heart has carried the same, unfading mark since the moment you walked into my life.
>
> Soon, every person across the country will be captivated by you, the same way I am. They'll be a witness to your spirit and your heart. And when that happens, I hope I'm not too late to show you just how cherished you are.
>
> Love,
>
> Wade
>
> PS: Juliet and I worked on this together. We hope you like it.
>
> PPS: We also had help from Madeline because she used

to make questionable jewelry in college. It involved a LOT of pot leaf decor.

Monty laughed and wiped his wet cheek with his hand. He grabbed the velvet satchel and opened it, shakily pouring the contents out. A small clay pendant wrapped in decorative wire spilled onto his palm. He flipped it over in his hand and saw a tiny paw print with five skinny toes indented into the clay. It was unexpected and perfect, and it made Monty so hopeful for the future that for the first time since his arrival in Boston, he felt… content. He pulled out his phone and sent Wade a heart emoji and his address. He added a note that said, "for when you want to show me."

CHAPTER 28

Wade sipped the coffee he'd let cool too much and coughed at the taste. He'd accidentally let it turn into a tepid, filmy sludge, but he was too lazy to make a new cup or even reheat his current one. His disgusting coffee felt fitting, though, because he was drinking it on the day he'd been dreading for weeks. A perfect coffee would have felt wrong.

He and Linda were meeting up at her house shortly to release Juliet into the wild. She'd be able to live her best life, eating whatever she found and maybe meeting her own Romeo.

He occasionally felt guilty when he thought about her rehabilitation progress, wondering if this was yet another one of his failures. But today, when he watched her crunching on a cricket she found all by herself, he decided he hadn't failed her at all. They'd taken their own path, but he'd helped nurse her back to health, raise her to teenager-hood, and give her a healthy start in life. And in some ways, she'd nursed him back to health as well by giving him something to focus on outside of wrestling, and something to carry him through his self inflicted heartbreak.

She spent the night with him so he could bask in the last hours they'd have together. He did one final photo shoot, knowing Monty would probably appreciate one or two photos to remember her by. He set her up on his couch, surrounded her with the wildflowers he'd picked while she hunted, and snapped several photos. In one, she was eating some viburnum he found. He scrolled through the photos he had of her, starting with the ones from back when she fit in the palm of his hand.

He felt weepy, but he smiled. He was proud and sad at the same time, like a parent sending their kid off to college. When the feelings became too much, he distracted himself by ordering a Lyft to Linda and Mike's house.

WADE SAT in the back of the Lyft, Juliet's carrier on his lap. He asked the driver to stop at the store close to Linda and Mike's house so he could pick up a bottle of wine and some cheese to serve at the party. The driver grumbled something about fees and Wade just nodded and hopped out.

He put Juliet's carrier in the cart, covered it up with his coat, and made his way to the cheesemonger. When he got there, he picked up a wedge of Cotswold and squinted at it. He wasn't sure if the flecks were chives or mold, but he thought either could be good. Every wedge he saw had moldy chives mixed in, so it must have been on purpose. He threw some in his cart, grabbed some fancy crackers, and turned to find the wine.

He leaned on the cart as best he could and ambled through the aisles. He was surrounded by hundreds of bottles of wine, totally out of his element, and he picked up two bottles to inspect their labels. It required such focus that he almost jumped out of his skin when a small hand patted him aggressively.

When he looked down, a kid wearing an old Viper t-shirt very loudly asked him if he was Viper, and could he have his autograph, and sorry about his neck, and did he know that even though he was retiring, Viper was still his favorite wrestler of all time. The kid's dad ran up, apologizing and quietly scolding the kid for running off. Wade just smiled.

"No, no, this is great. It's so nice to meet you. What's your name?" Wade asked the kid, reaching out for the paper and pen he held out.

"Jordan," he said. "My dad said I shouldn't bug you because your neck hurts, but I told him you needed a little support right now because you might be sad."

Wade laughed and looked at the kid's dad, who was blushing and rubbing his forehead.

"You're totally right, Jordan. I did need a little support. Here you go," he said, handing the signed paper back to him. "Hey, are you going to watch Romeo tonight?"

"I guess so. He's okay, but his outfit is stupid."

Wade almost choked on his own saliva trying to hold in his laugh. "Yeah, it is. Hey, you can come say hi to me any time you see me, okay? It was nice to meet you."

The kid skipped towards his dad who had started looking at the cupcakes kept near the wine. He waved goodbye to Jordan, threw both bottles of wine into the cart, and headed towards the checkout.

Wade felt buoyant while he bagged up his groceries. It had been so long since he'd been stopped by a fan out in the wild. Kids were his favorite because their love was unconditional and everlasting. Wade still thought about his favorite wrestlers from his childhood and smiled. He thought *they* were the best wrestlers of all time, and they'd been retired for years.

The driver dropped Wade and Juliet at the house a few minutes early. He sat on the black metal bench in their yard, the seat freezing his legs through his pants. He pulled Juliet out of her carrier and snuggled her close.

"I am really going to miss you. You've been such a source of happiness for me these last few months," he said. She sniffed his jacket, sticking her nose into the pocket that often carried her treats. "And can I tell you a secret? If you ever meet Grubs, don't tell her I said this. But I love you more than I loved her. You'll always be my best girl." He slipped her a kibble and she held it in her paw for a moment before eating it whole. When she was done, she cleaned herself on his lap.

"I hope I'm not interrupting," Linda said, emerging from behind some shrubs near the house.

"No," Wade said, clearing his throat. "You're not. Just saying goodbye."

She smiled and sat down on the bench with them. "Are you ready?"

"I mean, no. But that's what this is all about, right? She's ready. She's more than ready, I think."

"Me, too. But I wanted you to be here for this," she said. She placed a gentle hand on his thigh. "I want to show you something."

Linda stood up and guided them to a freshly fallen stump. It had an open, decaying burrow that would make a perfect den for Juliet. Linda had shoved some straw inside to insulate it from the cold.

"That looks perfect for her," Wade said. He crouched down with Linda's help and set Juliet near the den, hoping she'd sniff it out and make herself a home. He reached in and fluffed up some straw. It felt warmer inside and he breathed a sigh of relief.

"I think so," Linda said. She stepped back to give them some room.

"Go on, 'possum queen," he whispered, "go get your trash cuisine." He patted her butt to encourage her, but she turned back around and tried to climb his leg.

"You might have to just walk away," Linda said, gently.

"Walk away? And just leave her?"

"You're not leaving her. You're releasing her."

Juliet crowded Wade's leg some more and he bit his lip. "I think I fucked this up. I shouldn't have held her so much."

"The babies are always harder, Wade. For them and for us. But she's going to be okay. She knows how to forage. She has a warm den. You made sure she knew how to hunt. I promise I'll keep an eye on her. I want her nearby anyway so I can monitor her."

"Okay." Wade stood up and walked towards the house. Juliet trailed behind him. "Please stay there, Juliet. Don't follow me."

He tried walking faster, but she hopped along with him and her claws caught on his pant leg. He stopped and turned to Linda with wet eyes. "What do I do?"

"I'll take her to the bushes over there. You go inside." Linda bent down and removed Juliet's claws from his pants, but not before he glanced down and saw her with her little arms outstretched, holding on tight. Linda unattached her and held her on her arm. Juliet's tail curled around her wrist, something she did when she was settling in for a nap.

Wade held back his tears and stepped towards them, petting Juliet one more time. "Bye, baby. Be good." He walked towards the house and listened to Linda tromp through the high grasses so she could place Juliet under the bushes. He didn't let himself look back. He walked through Linda's back door and found Mike in the kitchen. Surprised and embarrassed, he squeezed his eyes to rid them of the unshed tears.

"Hey, welcome!" Mike said, kindly ignoring Wade's emotional state. "You're just in time to help me set everything up before everyone gets here. Sucker."

"I'm happy to. In fact, I brought gifts." Wade looked around for the cheese and wine. "Oh, wait, I left my bag outside. I'll be right back."

He walked outside and down the steps, then headed towards the metal bench he sat on earlier. He saw Linda, who put her finger to her lips to signal for Wade to step quietly. She turned and pointed at a tree next to the fallen stump she'd shown him earlier. He scanned his eyes up the trunk and saw Juliet sitting on a wide branch, taking a bath. He smiled up at her and quietly said goodbye for the last time.

AFTER HE HELPED Mike set up, Wade was assigned the task of mixing a salad, which sounded easy enough. Wade took his phone out to send some photos of Juliet to Monty before he got started. He included one of her post-release, up in the tree and captioned it, "our baby, all grown up." After he sent it, he wondered if that was too much. He wanted to be friendly, and nothing more, but it was hard because his feelings towards Monty hadn't changed.

He thought about him all the time. Not even in a heartbroken, desperate way. His presence was just a constant resident of his brain, shoving its way to the forefront of his mind in every waking moment.

He thought about him during his physical therapy sessions because he knew Monty's hands were just as strong, but gentler than his therapist's. When he saw fields of animals, he thought of the pair of cows Monty wanted just because cows have best friends and he thought it was neat. When he was at the arena, Monty was everywhere, but he was haunted by some damage on his office wall that

Monty said looked like a face. It stared at him mockingly every time he sat down to work.

Wade had sort of resigned himself to being in love with Monty for as long as they remained friends, painful as it was. But he knew it was unfair of him to expect Monty to feel the same, so he'd been trying to avoid overt flirtation when they communicated. He pulled his phone out to send another message and was relieved that Monty hadn't written back yet. Good.

> By the way, Jordan (my biggest fan) says your Romeo outfit sucks. GL tonight.

He was surprised when Monty wrote back almost immediately.

> idk who Jordan is, but one, he's a jerk. and two, he's not your biggest fan. that's all me, baby.

> speaking of my outfit, keep your eyes peeled for a sssssurprise tonight.

> so proud of our daughter, btw. her tail reminds me of you.

> take that however you will. 😊

Wade couldn't stop the stupid smile that planted itself on his face. He was still smiling at his phone, preparing to send an eye roll emoji, when Niall walked in the front door.

"Hey, brother. Ooh, who are you talking to?" Niall grinned.

Wade glanced up from the salad he was working on to look at him. His shirt had too many buttons open and his chest hair was peeking out. It was distracting, but he supposed someone could find it sexy. Not Wade, of course, but someone. He also smelled surprisingly good. He was wearing fitted jeans and new shoes and - was that a *bracelet?*

"None of your business," Wade replied, shoving his phone in his pocket. "What is going on here? Why do you look so… nice?"

"Shut up," Niall said. "Linda! Wade is texting someone and smiling. Make him tell me who it is."

"I'm not getting involved, boys. You're worse than Madeline's twins, I swear," she said. She took a grocery bag from Niall and watched Wade, who had finally started mixing the salad on top of a pile of books so he didn't have to bend over. "Look at you! So independent."

"I am very impressive," he grinned at her.

"I'd be more impressed if you let me in on your secrets. Did you meet someone?" Niall asked.

"Yes."

"Where?"

"Titan."

"What?! Who is it? Is it Anthony?" Niall spun around. "Dude, he's married. But okay, maybe you're into that?"

"Will you be quiet? It's not Anthony."

"Curt? He's kind of a dick, but…"

"No."

"Oh, shit. Is it Amit?" Niall whispered. "You can tell me."

"I wouldn't do that to you," he said, winking.

Niall scoffed, then grumbled something unintelligible while he looked around at the other talent. "It can't be Dicky, so… Oh, wait. Dammit, Wade, is this a thing where you pretend it's something new and fun, and then it just turns out to be Monty?"

Wade added more dressing to his salad and tossed in some sunflower seeds. "Could be."

Niall reached into the salad bowl and stole a carrot before pointing it at him. "You suck, dude."

He trailed into the living room and plopped on the couch, and Wade watched Linda go in behind him to turn on the channel showing the match. He moved the salad off the books and set it with the rest of the food, then grabbed two beers and squeezed in next to Niall.

The background segments ramped up and he watched Romeo and DarkWing in the locker room, boosting each other up for their match. The storyline being presented was that the two of them were in a fierce battle with another tag team, one half of which was Dark-Wing's ex-best friend, Vortex. According to the story, CWA purposely restructured the partnerships to punish Vortex for sleeping with DarkWing's girlfriend, who was currently on the side of the ring, crying. The camera focused on her sobs for an uncomfortably long stretch of time, then cut to footage of DarkWing and Monty backstage.

Wade watched as Romeo and DarkWing meditated and shouted affirmations in the mirror together, preparing for a battle to win back his girlfriend's affections. It was so ridiculous that he wanted to laugh, but that was the reality of their industry, and if he was honest, they were *really* selling it. When he and DarkWing broke apart, Romeo looked downright feral in a way that made Wade's stomach flip.

The audience was already rowdy. Monty's debut was expected to be monumental because he was the full package—technically skilled, attractive, and good on the mic. Most talent had one or two of those going for them, very few had all three. When the lights dimmed inside the arena, Wade forced himself to take a deep breath in a pathetic attempt to calm his frayed nerves.

When they cut away to a commercial, Wade listened to the guys prattle on about the latest Titan news. He heard all of the new gossip he wasn't privy to now that he didn't actually wrestle. Most of it was just about some of the guys reacting poorly to pranks, some super fans getting a little too close, someone embarrassing themselves at a regional match, or Dicky denying he said something shitty.

At one point, Anthony mentioned a comment Dicky made about Curt, and it must have reignited some sort of dormant rage in Curt, because he jumped out of his seat and tackled Dicky to the ground. Linda sighed and moved the coffee table. Wade watched them and laughed, even though he still kind of hated them. It was just fun to exist in the wrestling scene without feeling like his world was crashing down around him.

Mike broke up the match in front of them just in time for Monty's match to begin. The arena lights dimmed, and Wade heard the entrance theme for Monty and DarkWing come through the surround sound. He leaned forward, his fingers interlaced and tight, his stomach twisting. He could feel his heartbeat under his stupid brace, thumping too hard and making him uncomfortable.

Monty and DarkWing ran down the aisle and slid into the ring on their stomachs. They worked the crowd and hyped up the audience. Romeo brought roses with him and threw them at women in the audience. DarkWing was even bigger than Romeo, but he managed to land several acrobatic rope maneuvers Wade had never even attempted, causing his anxiety to momentarily change into envy.

The cameras got closer to Romeo, and Wade spotted small green snakes coiling up the gold accents on his pants. He sucked in a quick breath, trying not to draw attention to himself. That had to be a nod to Viper, right? What did it *mean?* Wade looked around, but nobody seemed to notice. Or if they did, they didn't care. But Wade noticed. And cared. A lot.

The match went well. He only mildly worried about him once, when Romeo collapsed on the canvas part way through the match. He heard concerned murmurs from Kenji and Curt who hadn't seen the move before. When DarkWing ran to the ref, both members of the opposing team entered the ring to see what was going on. It was all planned, of course. One of his opponents got close to Romeo's face and he used the guy's moment of fake distraction to flip him and pin him to the canvas. He could see Romeo shout, "possum pin" in the guy's face as the ref counted Romeo's opponent out.

"What the hell was that?!" Kenji yelled from behind the couch. He squeezed Wade's shoulders gently.

"Possum pin," Wade said, laughing. "He was playing dead."

The crowd went wild for Romeo, because of course they did. He was hot and new and really fucking good. After the ref raised their hands in victory, Romeo and DarkWing took a moment to jump on the ropes and work the crowd.

Wade knew from talking to Monty that their win was the intended outcome, but he was still excited to witness it. Well, until he had to watch Romeo and DarkWing embrace each other for a lot longer than Wade felt was necessary. He watched DarkWing ask an audience member for their cell phone and took a few selfies of their celebration. He and Romeo stood cheek to cheek while the arena celebrated. Then DarkWing hauled Romeo onto his shoulders and his big hands cradled Romeo's thighs. Wade shifted in his seat and pretended not to care, but he burned with jealousy.

Monty's immediate success was bittersweet for Wade. He was exactly where he was meant to be, and the over-the-top reaction from the crowd was a testament to the effort he'd put into his training and time with CWA's talent. The qualities that made Monty excel were the same ones that had drawn Wade to him in the first place, and that was all good stuff.

But now that he knew of Monty's initial struggles in Boston, he also knew their breakup was not the reason for Monty's success. Instead, he had to deal with knowing Monty had accomplished all of that while nursing a broken heart.

Between matches, more promos and backstage interviews aired and some of the guys lost interest. The din of the party faded into the background, allowing Wade's mind to drift to Monty. He wondered what Monty was feeling. He'd never experienced what Monty just had, but he knew the high would take a while to fade. He had vowed not to call or text him after the match to allow him to celebrate however he wanted, but he could feel his resolve slipping.

The rest of the guys spread out around Mike's living room and dining room. A few of them were playing cards at the table and they invited Wade to join, but he didn't feel like it. Plus, he'd been on his feet a lot today. His back and neck hurt.

He watched as Niall sent a death stare to the man who had arrived with Amit. He was just trying to grab a seltzer from the fridge, but Niall puffed up his chest at the poor guy, like a cat arching its back to seem bigger. The guy narrowed his eyes at Niall and put a possessive arm around Amit before leading him out to the porch. Niall moved into the living room and angled himself so he could see out a tiny sliver of open curtain. Wade snorted as he watched it all unfold.

God, he wished Monty was there so they could gossip about them again. Maybe Mike would want to discuss it, but probably not.

Wade stayed put on the couch, smiling and taking in the good vibes around him. For the first time in a while, he felt genuinely happy. Juliet making her way up a tree all by herself, personally prepping an *entire* salad, Monty's successful debut... It was all great. The heavy feelings that had plagued him in the weeks following his injury were finally lifting, as long as he ignored the obvious.

Wade's resolve to give Monty space crumbled more as the evening wore on. Eventually, he felt the couch sink as Mike sat down next to him. Wade had been about to text Monty about the match and Niall, when Mike shoved him to the side and offered him a fresh beer. They appeared to have a bit of privacy, which was fine, except Wade knew that meant Mike was about to dive into topics he was not in the mood to discuss. Ever since he found out about the nature of his relationship with Monty, he'd been relentless.

"Monty did great, huh? I know I had basically nothing to do with it, but I still feel like one of my kids is all grown up," he said as he wiped a fake tear from his eye.

"He really did." Wade smiled wistfully. "He's gonna blow their minds."

"How are you feeling about that?"

"I mean, I feel fine. I'm happy for him. It would have been terrible if I'd broken up with him and he screwed the pooch on his debut. Although then maybe he'd be fired from CWA, so..." Wade tapped his chin.

Mike laughed and nudged him with his shoulder. "I'm glad you stayed for the match. I know you were on the fence. But I feel like this has been good for you, huh? A new way to enjoy wrestling. You know, I didn't leave the sport because of an injury, but retirement was still difficult. It took me a bit to find my footing, but running Titan has been great for me. Have you thought about what you want to do next?"

"To be honest, no."

"Have you thought about what you want to do about Monty?"

"What is there to do?" Wade asked. "Don't answer that."

He'd been upbeat tonight, feeling good about wrestling and Titan. But even though he knew Monty was in the right place for his career, he still had regret around his decision to end their relationship. He couldn't talk to Monty about it, and he didn't want to worry Mike or Madeline because he was finally getting back to normal. But if he was honest, his renewed friendship with Monty was a big part of *why* he was feeling so much better. And maybe that meant he shouldn't give up quite yet. Like maybe someday, in the future, it could work out between them. He just had to figure out how.

Mike waited for a beat before he spoke, his voice low. "You know he's not Larry, right?"

"Yes, so I've been told. By Monty, Madeline, and now you. Of course he's not Larry. He's better than Larry in every conceivable way. Even his stage name is better than Larry's."

"I mean, most stage names are better than Limpet…"

Wade laughed. "I know he's not Larry. But I really hurt him, and it's cruel to jerk him around when he's trying to live his life. He made that very clear."

"Well, yeah. It is cruel to jerk him around. What if you didn't jerk him around, though? What if you just… fixed it?"

"How do I fix it? Show up unannounced and tell him I made a terrible mistake, beg for his forgiveness, and move to Boston?" He was kidding. Kind of. But he was also secretly hoping Mike would say "*yes, idiot, that's exactly what I'm saying.*"

Mike laid his head against the back of the couch and turned to look at Wade.

"God knows I love you, Wade. I want you here in Portland with us. But I've known you a long time. And the Wade you've been the last three months—the one you became after you met Monty but before things fell apart? That's a Wade I'd never had the privilege to know before. So, yeah. Maybe that's exactly what you should do."

"I'm scared," Wade said quietly.

"I know. But based on what you've told me, the only person standing in the way of this working out is you. You don't have to stay here and work for Titan. You don't have to wait here and hope he moves back in a few years. You can make it happen. He's told you that. More than once."

"I don't think I could keep going if it didn't work out. Breaking up with him the first time was the worst thing I've ever done, and we'd only officially been together three hours," he said with a sad laugh.

"I think being afraid you won't survive is how you know it's worth it."

CHAPTER 29

Monty rolled out of bed close to noon, which was late for him. The guys at CWA had thrown a party at the Duke's mansion and Monty was out until close to four. It was unlike any party he'd ever been to, which wasn't surprising considering the budget for the party was probably the same amount Mike spent on every annual Titan event combined, plus salaries for three years. Monty had no idea what that type of money meant until he experienced it.

The party had llamas to pet and a lobster tank with a scantily clad mermaid swimming in it. Larry had fallen into a koi pond and destroyed a gigantic lily pad that had not only sentimental value but was also worth over two thousand dollars. When he finally climbed out, he accidentally tripped a wrestler named Macho Mouse, who then *also* fell into the koi pond, killing three fish.

Monty had ordered a drink that came with gold leaf on it. The gold leaf didn't taste good, and it actually made the drink worse because it added nothing and got stuck to his lip. He drank a lot and danced for way too long and got a little too close to a lot of people. He was propositioned more times in a single hour than he had been the rest of his adult life combined.

Everything was bigger at CWA. He'd had a great time; he couldn't deny that. But, like every other thing he did since arriving in Boston, it would have been better without the dark cloud of heartbreak surrounding him.

Shit. Thinking about Wade while dealing with this level of nausea was a terrible combination, and he ran down the hall to throw up.

After recovering, he washed up and made his way to the kitchen, bumping into his door frame on the way out the bathroom.

"Oh, God," he said, grabbing his head. "Dom?"

"Shhhhhh," Dom groaned. "Rome, can you call an ambulance?"

Monty walked to the couch and saw Dom laying there wearing only his DarkWing trunks, which were currently wedged into places he wasn't supposed to see. His arm was thrown over his eyes and there was either smeared lipstick or a very serious injury directly above his too-visible pubes. Honestly, it could have been both.

"Good God, Dom," he said, closing one eye. "I'm going to go make some coffee and maybe pour us both a bowl of saltines. You go… take care of that."

Monty walked, very slowly, back to the kitchen. He was wearing boxer briefs too low on his hips, but he couldn't be bothered to pull them up. He dumped the grounds into the coffee maker and then poured the water in. He spilled a lot of it, and the cool water somehow hurt his skin. That single task was enough exertion for him to need a break, so he sat down on the kitchen floor and leaned against the fridge. It was so cold.

"Dom. Help," he rasped.

He couldn't hear if Dom responded, but he did hear a booming knock on the door. It was like someone was knocking with a billy club made of iron, or maybe whoever it was hired a literal ogre to knock for them. He heard the door open and tried to hear the stranger's voice but couldn't make anything out. He figured if it was someone there to hurt them, he stood no chance, so he laid down on the floor and waited for death.

Monty heard Dom's quiet voice and then faint mumbling. "...Monty… Titan… Wade…"

He crawled closer to the door, straining his ear to hear more of the person Dom was talking to. He heard Dom speak again, "...Kitchen floor… dying…"

Then, Monty wasn't sure if he was hallucinating—*just how much alcohol had he consumed last night?*—but he swore Wade was crouching down in front of him, neck brace and all. A familiar scent combined with the smell of recycled airplane air flooded his nostrils. He sat up and gawked at Wade, the real Wade, who was staring at Monty with concern and amusement. He reached out to touch Wade's face and felt the scraggly beard he'd missed so much.

"Wade...? How are you here?"

"I flew out last night after your match. It was very expensive and I had two layovers. I think I was traveling for ten hours, but I really wanted to see you. Now I see that I probably could have waited a few hours to fly out and we would both be having a better time right now," Wade said, reaching to run his hands through Monty's long, concerningly sticky hair. His fingers got caught in a tangle and Monty yelped. "Shit, I'm sorry." He switched to petting Monty's hair with an open palm.

Monty shifted to his knees and shuffled over to Wade, who was now seated on the floor, leaning against the cabinets. He straddled Wade's lap without thinking and plopped himself down. He stared at Wade for an unknown length of time before he finally spoke.

"I'm so sorry, but I am currently battling the worst hangover I've ever had in my entire life and also trying to process this and I'm... struggling to function here," Monty finally said.

"I had a feeling you'd be hungover based on the many, *many* text messages you sent last night. I loved the photo of Larry trying to set up a lily pad propagation in a wine bottle, by the way," he said, moving his arms around Monty's waist. He clasped his hands and squeezed gently.

Monty remembered suddenly that not only did he smell like a distillery, he'd also recently vomited and hadn't brushed his teeth. He removed himself from Wade's lap and somehow gathered the strength to help him stand.

Dom had gone back to the couch and passed out again, this time on his stomach, which gave Wade and Monty even more of a show than before. The entire right side of his butt and thigh were covered in more lipstick-or-injury confusion. Maybe he would talk to Dom about switching to leggings.

"Come with me," he said. He took Wade's hand led him to the bedroom. He propped up some pillows and helped him get situated on the bed, falling into the same comfortable routine they'd shared so briefly when Wade was newly injured.

Once Wade was situated, he looked around the room to make sure there was nothing too shameful left out, but the rapid movement of his eyes was painful and the windows were so bright it added to his misery. "I'm going to go take a shower, but I'll be right back. Do you want coffee?"

"Yes please. If you can handle it," Wade smiled at him.

Monty used all of his strength to get to the bathroom, brush his teeth, and take the world's fastest shower. He poured two cups of coffee, splashing cream into Wade's, then made his way back to the bedroom. He stood in the doorway for a moment and stared at Wade, propped up on the bed that had felt so lonely since he arrived in Boston. Wade's shoes were in the middle of the floor and his flannel shirt was draped on the end of Monty's bed.

For a split second, Monty let himself believe that could be his life someday. Wade in his bed, his stuff on Monty's floor. But he pushed the thought from his head, forcing himself to focus on their less satisfying reality.

"I'm a little more functional now. Let's start from the top. What the heck are you doing here?"

Wade grabbed Monty's hands and rubbed his knuckles. He took a deep breath and said, "I'm here because... I'm an idiot."

Monty's eyes opened wide and Wade laughed.

"Wait, no. I mean, I *am* an idiot," Wade continued. "But I'm not an idiot because I'm here. I'm an idiot for so many reasons I would like to list, but we don't have enough time. So let's focus on how I let myself destroy what we had. *Have.* I hope." He pushed a strand of Monty's hair behind his ear and brushed his cheek with his palm.

Monty's eyes went even wider and he smiled a big open mouthed grin at him. "Wade, I—"

"Wait. Please. Just, let me finish. I have a whole thing I rehearsed on the plane."

Monty scooted closer. "Okay. My lips are sealed. Promise."

"From the moment you walked into Titan all those months ago and got tangled in those ropes, part of me knew you were it. Your existence felt like this cosmic shift in my life. Like the person I was before I met you ceased to exist, and I've slowly grown into this new version of myself. A version I hope you believe is worthy of your love, even if I haven't earned it yet," he said.

Monty pinched his lips shut with his teeth, eager to say a thousand things but forcing himself to stay quiet. He rested his hand on Wade's chest and trailed his finger along the cool plastic of his brace.

Wade continued, "The pain of our separation has been… Well, it's felt like your absence has turned my blood into a weird, sad sludge that is slowly suffocating me. And I tried to tell myself this was the right choice, that my pain was the cost of your success, and I was willing to pay that because you deserve it. But I was wrong. Your success has nothing to do with me. In fact, your success is in spite of me."

Monty shifted slightly, his eyes still wide. "Jeez. Mr. Poet, over here. Oh, whoops. Sorry." He covered his mouth with his hand and let Wade continue. He felt a warm hand spreading wide on his thigh.

"I told you once that the biggest regret I have in life was that I had wasted my time at Titan. And then I told you my biggest regret was being a jackass. But now I know, without a doubt, the biggest regret I'll ever have is being reckless with your love. Treating your heart like something disposable. It never was. I was scared, and I was stupid. And now, I'm here to ask you to forgive me. For so many things. For being an idiot, for breaking your heart, and for making you feel like any of it was your fault. I'll spend the rest of my life making it up to you if you'll let me."

Monty stared at Wade for a few seconds, absorbing everything he'd just heard. He wanted to say something romantic or poetic, or even just two words strung together, but instead he just… laughed. And not a shy, sweet laugh. He laughed loudly, and for five full seconds. Wade's face flashed hurt, then settled into what Monty read as sad acceptance.

Wade moved his hands to his lap. "Hey, I get it. It was—"

"No, wait, Wade. I'm sorry I laughed. What you said wasn't funny. It was… wow. There is absolutely no way I can come up with anything like that, even when my brain is fully functioning. And I think we both know I'd end up saying something embarrassing if I tried, but I—"

"I love you so much," Wade said. "That's what I want you to take away from this."

"I know," Monty said, biting his lip. "But, um…" He hesitated.

"What is it?"

"You really hurt me, Wade. Repeatedly. It felt like every decision I made, it was the wrong one. And I know I haven't really ever had a relationship, but I don't think it's supposed to be like that. So I'm scared, because if… Well, I just don't know if I can go through that again."

"You won't. I promise you won't, Monty," Wade said, an air of desperation entering his tone. "Mostly because I've seen what happens when I hurt you, and I would never forgive myself if I did that again. I should have been here for you, supporting you, not pushing you away because I was scared. I shouldn't have compared you, the best person I've ever met, to Larry, whose name is barely worth remembering."

Monty looked at him, studying his face and trying to identify where this was coming from. The last thing he wanted was to be made a fool of again. To make this leap and end up back where they started.

"Also, when I left Mike's house and told him what I was doing, he gave me a really scary lecture that made me feel like some horned up teenager taking his daughter to prom. I wouldn't have been surprised if he'd pulled out a shotgun. I will do *anything* to avoid telling him I knocked you up," Wade said, his face hopeful.

When Monty laughed, he felt Wade's shoulder relax against his arm.

"What did you tell Mike?"

"I told him I needed some time off to fix this. He gave me the company card to book a hotel as long as I promised to do some CWA 'research' while I was here."

Monty sat back against the headboard and picked at his finger-nails. He was unusually quiet.

"It's okay," Wade said, recognizing Monty's hesitance. "I mean, if this was too little too late. I don't want it to be, obviously, but I can't say I don't deserve it."

"Is it okay if I take some time to digest this? And the bile eating away at my stomach?"

Wade smiled sadly. "Of course. Take all the time you need. I'm at the Sleepy Inn down by the arena. I have a meeting with Graham later. Not about me, obviously, just something Mike wants me to follow up on. But I'll be back to my hotel by five. I'll wait for you. As long as it takes."

"Okay." He gave Wade a brief kiss before helping him off the bed and guiding him towards the door.

Dom was more awake now, glaring at Wade. He muttered something rude under his breath that made Wade wince. Monty swallowed his smile, touched by Dom's loyalty, but afraid to hurt Wade.

"Down, boy," he said. It was meant to be funny, but neither Dom nor Wade laughed. He turned to Wade. "See you later, okay?"

"Sure." Wade squeezed Monty's hand and headed down the hall, leaving Monty to his thoughts.

WADE'S HOTEL room lamps flickered erratically. The flashing lights blended offensively with the gaudy, swirling colors of the hotel bedspread, giving him an instant headache. He turned the lamps off and left the bathroom door open for visibility, which he supposed meant the room was partly illuminated by light reflecting off the toilet. That felt as fitting to his mood as the expired cup noodle he pulled from the microwave for dinner. He hadn't noticed the expiration date before he left the corner store near his hotel, but he figured the sodium would prevent dangerous levels of spoilage, and he was hungry enough that he just didn't care.

He sat on the edge of the bed and groaned dramatically when realized he'd forgotten to grab a spork from the store. His stomach rumbled in solidarity. If he wasn't so desperate for things to work out with Monty, he'd call the trip a bust and cut his losses. But he was, so he didn't.

Monty's response to Wade's apology was… lukewarm, at best. It was certainly not what he'd imagined or hoped for. He'd hoped he would walk into Monty's apartment and both of them would agree they needed each other and that they could put everything that had happened in the past and start fresh. He imagined there would be a lot of hugging and maybe some makeup sex. Instead, everything was uncertain, and now he was alone in a gross hotel room.

After drinking as much broth as he could, he tipped the cup and leaned back awkwardly, hoping the noodles would slide gracefully into his mouth. Instead, the entire glob of them fell onto his face and the rest of the broth spilled onto his white shirt, some splashing onto the bed. Flecks of herbs and green onion stuck to his collar, and the shirt stuck to his chest. Liquid seeped into the foam padding beneath his brace.

He sat there, embarrassed and irritated, as visions of moldy broth eating away at his skin crossed his mind. He froze when he heard a knock at the door. His shirt was half covered in noodles and broth, but his heart leapt anyway when he realized it must be Monty.

Any concern he had about the state of his appearance vanished as he shuffled towards the door. He took a deep breath, living in this last moment between his apology and Monty's decision, then opened the door. Monty looked so sweet and cozy in his Boston winter-appropriate clothes. Wade invited a flicker of hope to settle in his gut.

"Um," Monty said, looking him up and down.

Wade could tell he was fighting a laugh. "Yes?"

"What… happened? Are you okay? Is that a noodle?" Monty said, plucking one from his chest.

"It's a lot of noodles. Do you want to come in?" Wade said, stepping to the side. Monty passed by him, his arm brushing against Wade. His heart picked up at the feeling.

"It's very dark in here."

"Yeah, it's… I got a kind of cheap room because I felt bad using Mike's money for anything nicer. But maybe I went too cheap."

Monty turned on the lamp, and fortunately the flickering had stopped. Wade watched him sit on the edge of the bed, picking noodles off the bedspread, placing them in his palm. He tried to pick up a dehydrated carrot, and it smeared into the fabric.

"Seriously, what happened here?" he said, laughing.

"I was hungry, but I didn't have a spork. Decisions were made."

"You really went for it, huh?" He smiled at Wade and stood to toss the discarded noodles in the trash before sitting back down. "I've seen you eat. I know you can do it."

"Can we, um, skip this part?" Wade asked. "I'm sorry. That's rude. I just…"

"No, I get it. Yeah. Let's sit." Monty patted the bed and looked up at him.

Wade allowed the flicker of hope in his gut to stay, refusing to tell himself Monty was here to end it. Surely, he could have done that over the phone, or before picking up spilled noodles. He sat next to Monty and felt broth seeping into his shorts. He clearly didn't hide his reaction well enough, because Monty pursed his lips before a laugh escaped from him.

"Listen—" Wade started, trying not to smile.

"I'm sorry! Sorry. I just saw that coming. Anyway, let's move on. First of all, how long are you here?"

"I'm not sure. As long as I need to be. As long as it takes."

"And, um, what would you say if I told you I wanted you to leave?"

Wade's stomach dropped. He scanned Monty's face, looking for any hint of a joke or smile, but he came up empty.

"I… guess I would leave, then. I won't stay here and make you uncomfortable or not listen to what you're telling me. I've made that mistake before, remember?" Wade said, smiling sadly. He turned to look Monty in the eyes. "Is that what you want? For me to leave?"

"No." Monty grinned. "Not at all, to be honest. I was just being a dick."

"What the fuck!" Wade said. His arms felt like jelly and his chest felt hot. "Why would you do that?"

Monty laughed. A little too hard, if Wade was honest.

"Sorry," he said. "Kind of. I am glad you're here. I'm glad you came. It was such a surprise. I'm sorry it took me all day to gather my thoughts. I was overwhelmed and needed to think through things. And like, recover physically from my poor decision making last night. And call my mom."

Monty's mom had historically been supportive of his feelings for Wade. Wade had never met her, but he knew Monty shared a lot with his mom and that she knew everything that happened between them, good and bad. Even so, knowing he called her to talk about Wade's surprise arrival made him feel uneasy.

"Stop panicking. She still likes you," Monty said, sensing Wade's concern. "She didn't tell me what to do, just encouraged me to listen to my heart. And my heart has always been irritatingly pro-Wade, even when it works against me. Even when you do stupid stuff like break up with me because you think I'm destined to leave you."

Wade wanted to argue, but couldn't.

"I think what frustrates me the most is that you didn't just talk to me about it. Like, you clearly had all these anxieties and plans from the beginning and you never thought I'd be a good person to talk to about it. Instead, you just powered through, refusing to believe me when I said I wanted this."

Regret settled over him again, and Wade felt the flicker of hope shrinking.

"I *want this*," Monty said, grabbing Wade's hand, "but I can't see myself being happy in a relationship where my partner can't talk to me about what's bothering them. And New Monty doesn't put up with bullshit like that."

"That's fair," Wade said. "All I can ask is that you give me a chance to show you that I'm changing. Wait, New Monty?"

"Yes. That's the name I gave myself after I yelled at you."

Wade laughed and placed his other hand over Monty's. "I like New Monty. And Old Monty. All the Monties."

They locked eyes and Wade felt the hope he had in his gut morphed into something stronger, like promise. He believed they'd make it work and that he'd keep his promise to Monty. He had to, because that was the only option he was willing to entertain.

He felt a tugging on the bottom of his shirt and cool air nipping at the skin of his stomach. He glanced up at Monty, confused but a little hopeful, so he arched his eyebrow at Monty and grinned.

"No, nothing like that. I'm going to clean you up. You can't have chicken broth in your foam, buddy." Monty pulled Wade's shirt up over his head, stretching the collar to get around the brace. "Stand up so I can pull this disgusting bedspread down, then lay down."

Wade obeyed, and the cool sheets sent a chill through his body. Monty worked to get his brace off, then left to clean it up in the bathroom. Wade closed his eyes and surrendered himself to Monty, who gently wiped the soup from his chest with a warm towel. His hands never pressed too hard on Wade's tender muscles, never crossed any lines. It was strangely intimate.

"Is this okay? It doesn't hurt, right?"

"No, it's good. It feels nice."

"I do love you," Monty said. "I have since I was sixteen. It's just a little different now. A little better."

Wade's breath caught and his eyes opened, and the rest of the world melted away, leaving just the two of them. He pulled Monty down to kiss him, careful not to jostle his neck.

"I love you. So much. Will you stay here tonight? I know this room sucks and you have a nice apartment with a roommate who apparently hates me," Wade said, smiling at the blush spreading over Monty's cheeks, "but I can't really leave. I can't walk around without my brace. Actually, can you grab the softer one I brought? I have to use it if I get the other one wet and can't use it for long periods."

"Of course."

Monty threw the washcloth towards the bathroom door and turned off the lamp. He helped Wade with the brace, then pulled the blankets up over them. Wade wondered how he could possibly get any sleep, but Monty's gentle touches and the warmth of his body pressing against his side tugged at him. Monty slipped his hand into Wade's, who then allowed his eyes to drift shut.

"In Dom's defense," Monty said, interrupting Wade's attempted slumber, "I was a real sad sack when I moved here. He was probably so over hearing about you, so…"

CHAPTER 30

WADE LEFT BOSTON A FEW DAYS LATER WITH THE PROMISE THAT MONTY would fly out in a week and stay for a while. Monty had two weeks with no matches, and after talking to his bosses, he got permission to take off to Portland for the whole stretch. Mike had promised CWA he'd make sure Monty stopped by the gym most days to spar with some of the talent, so Monty made a mental note to send Mike a nice gift for his help.

Maybe a signed, shirtless photo of himself for Titan's hallway.

He was staying with Wade, and whatever clean version of him that existed when Wade was injured was long gone. He'd been there less than a week, and Wade had almost re-broken his neck by tripping over Monty's shoes and getting tangled in a stray pair of pants he took off on the way to the bedroom.

THE TWO OF them pulled up to Madeline's house and Monty's pulse picked up. He didn't know why. He'd met her. They'd spent time together after Wade's injury. But they hadn't seen each other since the breakup, and he'd never met Kenny or the kids. He was worried they'd hate him, and he knew Wade wanted to get Madeline's blessing to move to Boston.

"It's going to be fine," Wade said, resting his hand on Monty's neck. "You are very likable. And Kenny is like, the nicest guy ever, so even if he hated you, you'd never know."

"That… doesn't help at all."

"Come on." Wade was laughing. He'd gotten out of the car and was tugging on Monty's arm, trying to pull him from the driver's seat. "I can't lift anything, so you have to come willingly or I could die."

"I don't know about this new happy version of you," Monty said. "Very jokey."

He got out of the car and walked ahead to Madeline's house, then rang the doorbell.

Kenny opened the door wearing an apron, his hair was up in a messy bun. His eyes lit up when he looked at Monty.

"Hey! Bun buddies!" he said, pulling Monty into a hug before pointing to their matching hairstyles. "I'm Kenny. It's so nice to meet you. I've heard a lot about you. Like, *a lot*, a lot. Like—"

"Okay, let us in," Wade said, interrupting Kenny. "Madeline, come get your husband."

Monty was shoved through the doorway and when his eyes adjusted, he saw three kids in the living room. The one he assumed was Jack smiled and waved at him, and the baby chewed on some bright plastic keys. The girl, who he assumed was Ramona, was glaring at him. Hard.

"Hi, guys," Wade said, stepping towards the kids. The two older ones got up to hug him.

"Do you want me to get you the baby?" Monty asked. "Oh, is that okay? Maybe they don't want me touching him."

"You can touch him," Wade said. "But I can't hold him yet, so it's okay."

Madeline came in and picked Gavin up, bringing him close to Wade's face. Gavin reached out and grabbed Wade's brace, which made all of the adults panic, except Wade, who was laughing. He made animated faces, which only made Gavin want to be closer. Monty watched in horror as Gavin pulled himself towards Wade with the brace, causing more panic amongst the adults and even more laughter from Wade.

"Didn't you *just* make a comment about not jostling your neck in the car?!" Monty said.

"I was kidding. And I think I'm getting this off tomorrow, guys. It's okay," he said, pinching Gavin's cheeks and rolls, making him laugh.

"Well, you've met Gavin, so that's good," Madeline said, smiling at Monty.

He hoped that meant there were no hard feelings from the breakup.

"Yes, and I met Jack and Ramona when I first came in," Monty said. He looked for them, but only saw Jack. He turned around and nearly jumped out of his skin when he saw Ramona glaring at him from the stairs. Her eyes were narrowed nearly to the point of invisibility. "But, um, I don't think Ramona is a fan." He gestured to her, hoping she didn't notice.

"Oh, yeah. Sorry about that. She really hates Romeo and was pretty upset we invited you over. She doesn't totally get Romeo, Viper, kayfabe, all that stuff. Plus, Wade is like her favorite person, so…"

Wade let out an actual guffaw. "That's incredible."

"You're so mean," Monty said. He walked over to Ramona, who was still glaring at him from the stairs. "Hi, Ramona. I'm Monty."

She said nothing. Monty heard Wade and Madeline chuckling with Kenny in the living room and felt a lot of pressure to not fuck this up.

"I know you hate me. And that's okay. But I'm excited to meet you. I am willing to let you pin me, stripping me of my championship title, if you let me stay for dinner." He did not mention he'd never held a title in his entire career.

She appeared to think about it for a moment. Monty watched her eyes dart to Wade and her parents, who he guessed gave her a nod, and she looked back to Monty and took a deep breath.

"Okay," she said.

Monty hadn't really considered that she'd accept the terms, and wasn't totally sure how to make this happen, but he stood up and walked to the middle of the living room anyway. He lay down with his arms out. Wade, Madeline, and Kenny stepped to the side.

"Get him, Ramona!"

Ramona took off running from the stairs and climbed briefly onto a chair, then leapt into the air. She floated for less than a second before she landed directly on Monty's balls.

His hands flew to his groin and a strangled howl escaped his throat as he turned on his side, curling into a ball. Ramona fell to the side, laughing. Wade and Kenny were horrified, making sympathetic noises and cringing.

Kenny crouched down to check on him. "You okay, man?"

Monty responded by letting out a quiet groan.

"I'll go get some ice."

THE NEXT DAY, they left Dr. Nikolov's office, where she had told Wade he was good to start tapering off the brace. He still couldn't lift too much, but he could turn his head, shower, and drive. They celebrated by letting Wade drive home. It was an uneventful drive, but Wade was happy.

When they got to the apartment, Monty closed the door behind him and gave Wade a coy smile.

"What's that look for?" Wade asked.

"I dunno, just thinking…"

"Ah," Wade smiled.

He stepped towards Monty and put his hands on the waistband of Monty's jeans, his index fingers slipping through the belt loops and pulling him closer. He bent down to kiss him, the first time he'd been able to do that in six weeks, and it felt even better than he remembered. But *then* he remembered he hadn't properly washed his neck in six weeks, and the moment was ruined by his own stupid nose.

"Oh, God. I have to take a shower. I want you to keep loving me, but you won't if you smell what's happening under that thing," he said, pointing to the neck brace he had discarded by the door.

Monty smiled and shoved Wade towards the bathroom. Wade stripped out of his clothing and turned the shower on, letting it run until it was hot enough for steam to billow out the top. He hadn't felt water running down his skin in so long, he couldn't wait. He toed off his socks and threw them in the hamper before he stepped into his shower, immediately groaning at the sensation of hot water hitting his body.

"It's sounding a little too sexy in there!" Monty called through the doorway.

Wade laughed and grabbed the clean washcloth he'd set on the side of the tub. He lathered it up with soap and scrubbed his neck, under his ears, his shoulders, his armpits, then his neck again. He moved down his body and scrubbed his back and abs, then moved to his legs before sliding back up to clean his various creases. Eventually, he dropped the washcloth and lingered a little longer than necessary. It felt so good in the warm water that he was honestly feeling torn between leaving to have sex with his boyfriend or standing there under the stream of water.

But he didn't have to decide, because Monty stepped into the bathroom. Wade saw his shirt go flying and then heard his belt buckle hit the ground. He stepped back to peek out of the curtain right when Monty was stepping in on the other side of the shower. Wade looked up and saw Monty's beautiful, smooth skin glistening under the water. His long golden hair was dripping from the ends and he looked like something out of a 1980s lifeguard porn movie. After a few minutes of ogling, Wade was not at all torn between having sex with him or doing literally anything else on earth.

Monty moved towards him and placed his hands on Wade's shoulders, gently kneading the tight muscles. His wet palms glided over Wade's neck with careful balance; firm enough to release the tension Wade had built up over the last two months, but tender enough to ensure there was no discomfort to his sensitive muscles. Wade leaned his head forward and breathed out a deep sigh.

He spun around after a few minutes. He grabbed Monty's waist and crushed their lips together, rougher than he'd been in the past, but after weeks of not touching Monty the way he wanted to, he was desperate. He wasn't sure he'd ever wanted something more than he wanted Monty at that moment. But he felt that way every time he thought of Monty late at night or when he touched him softly during the day. It was on his mind every time they were together. And maybe that was the magic of the two of them. Maybe it would just continue getting better, and each time their bodies met, it would be deeper and more spectacular than the last.

They were touching roughly and sliding against each other, the water lubricating their smooth skin. Their erections brushed against each other and they moaned, in unison and into each other's mouths.

"I missed this so much," Wade said, biting at Monty's lips and jaw. His hands gripped Monty's sides roughly.

Monty grunted in response as Wade moved down to his neck, nibbling the ridges of his Adam's apple. Wade dropped to his knees and nuzzled his face against Monty's thigh, purposely teasing him with languid licks and kisses that brought him no closer to Monty's aching dick. Monty whimpered in frustration and grabbed at Wade's head, trying to move him to where he wanted him.

"Quit being an asshole. I'm dying here," Monty whined.

Wade put a stop to Monty's suffering by taking his balls into his mouth and sucking them, then licking a wide stripe up his dick. Monty groaned. He took Monty's dick into his mouth as far as he could, and Monty's knees bent slightly.

"Oh, fuck. That's so good. It's been so long without you," he said, desperate for more of him. He cupped his hands behind Wade's head, not applying much pressure, just firm enough to feel him. The feeling of Monty's hands behind his head was so intense he felt like he could come just from this. His whole body was consumed with a need for *more*. For anything Monty was willing to give him.

"I want you to use me," Wade said, grabbing Monty's ass and licking another stripe up his dick. He looked up at Monty, who was breathing hard. His lips were swollen from Wade's bites and kisses. Water was splashing off his chest and onto Wade's face.

"I can't. Your neck…"

"My neck is fine. Please, it's what I want," Wade breathed. He kissed Monty's thigh again. He hadn't been able to show Monty just how much he loved him and craved him since his injury and the breakup. The need to give Monty everything was overwhelming.

Monty made a noise of desperation and put the tip of his dick to Wade's mouth. He rubbed it on Wade's wet lips and he breathed out a shaky breath. Wade opened and sucked Monty down before Monty slid himself out and started pumping his hips. Gently at first. Wade used his own strength to guide Monty's dick into his mouth, hard enough that he gagged.

"Christ," Monty whispered, his hands still behind Wade's head. "Look at you. Your mouth was made for me."

Wade knew Monty was getting close, the frantic noises he was making were forever etched into his memory from their previous times together. He sucked harder and deeper and Wade noticed Monty glance down to see that Wade had started working his own dick. Monty made a halted noise, then his dick swelled and he came unexpectedly down Wade's throat with a groan. Wade swallowed it down, moaning from his own pleasure. The suction created by Wade swallowing made Monty shoot again, and he swallowed that too. Wade stood up slowly while Monty caught his breath. He grabbed Monty's hair in his fist and pulled his head back so he could kiss his neck again while he shoved him up against the shower wall.

"Oh, my God, Wade. I think you just sucked my brains out of my dick," he laughed, but he stopped quickly when Wade pressed himself against Monty's thigh and nuzzled his face into his neck. Wade hadn't come yet, though he'd been close. "Oh, poor baby."

He moved behind Wade and got down on his knees. He kissed Wade's cheeks and bit him gently. He licked the crease between his ass and thigh and it drew a groan out of Wade. Wade bent over involuntarily, seeking more contact with Monty's tongue.

Monty moved his big hands up Wade's ass and pulled his cheeks apart. He pressed his thumb gently against Wade's hole, causing him to groan again.

"This is mine," he said, and then Wade felt a tongue swirling around his sensitive opening, strong hands keeping him open and vulnerable. "You're mine now. Okay?"

"Shit," Wade groaned. "I think I'm gonna come in like three seconds."

He felt Monty huff out a laugh against his skin, but it felt so good he couldn't bring himself to laugh with him. Wade bent over even more to give Monty easier access, but also because he desperately needed Monty to touch his dick.

He wanted this to last forever and also for it to end because he could hardly stand it.

He felt Monty's hand reach around to grab him and his body jerked. Monty started pumping Wade hard and fast while still licking his hole. Monty used his other hand to briefly grab Wade's balls, pulling a loud grunt out of Wade. Monty dragged his finger from Wade's balls to his opening and touched his finger there, silently asking for permission. Wade managed to nod his head and whispered, "yes." As soon as the tip of Monty's finger slipped in, Wade came with a shout all over the shower wall.

Wade rested his forehead on the wall, the warm water still pouring down his skin. After he caught his breath, Monty stood up and wrapped his arms around Wade's neck and kissed him. Wade kissed him back, and they stood under the water for another few minutes until they felt the water start to cool down.

They both climbed out of the shower and wrapped towels around their waists. Wade left the bathroom first. He felt loose and dreamy, wishing he could pull Monty into bed and stay there the rest of the day, dozing and touching each other. He thought of what their future held and what Boston would be like. He wondered how long they'd be there and where they'd end up after that. He hoped for Portland, but Monty had to go where CWA told him, at least for the next few years. But Wade knew it didn't matter. He'd be happy anywhere, as long as he was with Monty.

Wade ended up in the bedroom where he put on the clothes he was going to wear to see Monty's mom, Carol. His dad and Becky were driving out separately and would be arriving tomorrow, but tonight Wade and Monty were taking Carol to dinner and later, showing her around Titan where she'd stay and watch a match between Kenji and Anthony, then guests from out of town.

Monty trailed out of the bathroom shortly after Wade, with freshly brushed teeth and his hair wrapped up in a twisty microfiber towel.

"Aw. You look so cute in that thing," Wade cooed.

"Hey, this hair takes work."

"I was being serious!" Wade walked over and kissed Monty again. He tugged at a rogue strand that spilled out of the towel. "I love how you're physically incapable of getting every hair contained. It's my favorite."

"I will shave my head, Wade, I swear to God."

"I'm serious!" he said, tugging again. "I can't believe I get to do this whenever I want. For the rest of my life."

"Me too," Monty said, smiling against Wade's mouth. "Man, I am so glad I had a creepy teenage crush on you and decided I didn't care about looking like a stalker when I moved to Portland."

"Me, too."

It was almost dinner time, and Wade was nervous about meeting Carol. She was very sweet, but it was obvious Monty was her baby and that would put any partner on edge for a first-time meeting. The additional drama that came from his brief relationship with her son made him even more anxious, though Monty assured him she wouldn't hold a grudge.

"Are you really sure this is where you want to meet your mom for dinner? We have to wear bibs. And gloves," Wade whined as they got in the car. Monty won the coin toss and they were going to have dinner at the crab by the pound restaurant he'd been desperate to try for months.

"I mean, you don't have to. You can go rogue. But that shirt is so cute, I don't want you to mess it up," Monty said, referring to the Romeo shirt Wade was wearing.

Wade lost a bet about whether or not Jojo could eat five blood-worms (Monty said yes, because *that's my big guy*, and Wade said no, because *he is very small*) and Monty requested Wade wear the shirt to dinner as his reward.

"You know, this is more embarrassing for you than it is for me. You're the one hanging out with a guy wearing a shirt with your face on it."

Monty looked chagrined and Wade laughed.

"You can change if you want," Monty said.

"No way! It's too late now. I love this shirt. I am going to wear it to bed tonight, too."

Monty rolled his eyes and pulled out of the parking garage at Wade's apartment. They arrived at the restaurant at the same time as Carol, and she ran towards Monty with her arms in the air. When she reached them, she snaked her arms around his torso.

"Hi, mom!" Monty squeaked. She was really squeezing.

"Hi, Carol," Wade said. He put his hand out, and she slapped it away and pulled him in for a hug.

"It is so nice to meet you, Wade. I've been hearing this guy talk about you for ages," she said. "You'd think I'd never heard of you every single time he got me on the phone. I've been hearing about you for almost ten years now, you know. You should have seen his room when he was a teen—"

"Mom!"

"I'm not kidding! I mean, he had crushes on other wrestlers too, don't get me wrong. But you were always special. And look, I brought you some presents." Carol pulled a stack of wrestling magazines out of her purse, all of which featured photos or articles about Viper. She also had a stack of childhood photos. "Here's little Monty dressed as you for Halloween when he was seventeen. His friend dressed as Limpet and they spent the evening tagging each other out for candy duty."

"Mom! Please put those away. Oh, my God. I was seventeen, not little. And honestly, being seventeen makes it so much worse. I am begging you to stop."

Monty looked miserable, but Wade was loving every moment of it, so he took Carol by the elbow to lead her into the restaurant. Monty trailed behind, hiding his face.

"I'd like to sit next to you so you can share more stories about little Monty," he said, smiling at Carol.

"Oh, I have so many stories, Wade. Did he ever tell you about the time he got his foot stuck in his sheet when he was sleeping on the top bunk? He fell out of bed, but the sheet saved him. He hurt his ankle something awful, though."

"Really?" Wade said, feigning surprise. "Please, go on."

EPILOGUE

FIVE YEARS LATER
Monty

ROMEO HAD Limpet pinned beneath him, Limpet resigned to his fate. The audience erupted at Romeo's victory, and Limpet rolled out of the ring, cursing and screaming at Romeo's smug face. The two wrestlers' story arcs had intersected often over the last few years, their rivalry building but never becoming either wrestler's main angle.

It had been weird, at first, and Monty's anger towards Larry was difficult to ignore. As a new wrestler with CWA, he chose to ignore Larry for the most part. He didn't want to cause problems with the other guys, but he always enjoyed it when they were in the ring together and he was paid to take his anger out on Larry.

The ref held one of Monty's hands above his head, the title belt he'd just won held aloft with the other. He was thrilled to have won the title, even though he knew that going in, but it was still quite a feat. He was more excited to get out of the ring than he was about winning the title, though, because after tonight he had three months off.

Romeo's rise to fame and popularity continued after his debut and he had become one of the biggest names in CWA's current era.

Impostor syndrome had never left, but it was less intense and frequent. It still seemed unbelievable to him that his career had launched as quickly as it had, but Wade reminded him often that he was everything CWA loved: talented, malleable, charismatic, sexy.

Limpet, on the other hand, was nearing forty and set to retire soon. He'd done a heel turn the last two years of his career, and Monty didn't think it had anything to do with him, but Wade liked to say it did. *They need a new hero, and that's you, baby.*

The truth was, Limpet was still popular. If anything, his new evil character arc renewed the fans' appreciation of him and it seemed downright fun to Monty. He imagined his own inevitable turn, hoping it would be like Larry's.

Larry was tired and ready to be done, so Monty used this opportunity to give him the ass kicking of a lifetime since they may not wrestle each other again.

Monty got to the locker room and checked his phone, just in case, and saw four missed calls. His heart leapt. He scrolled to his texts with shaky fingers and saw one from Wade: *It's happening! Hurry home!*

Madeline had been experiencing early labor symptoms for twenty-four hours but promised she'd do her best to "hold her in," which Monty appreciated. He was pretty sure that wasn't possible, but Madeline had given birth to way more babies than him, so he went with it. She had offered to be a surrogate out of the blue for Wade and Monty the previous year, and after discussing for months and consulting lawyers, she got pregnant about nine months ago.

Monty knew the timing of this match would be difficult, but that was the reality of his career. Wade understood that better than anyone, so he'd promised he'd film the birth if Monty didn't make it in time. Carol was there for backup just in case Wade needed a mom around.

"Romeo!" Dom yelled across the locker room. "You in tonight? Vegas, baby!"

"No can do, buddy." He shook his phone in Dom's direction, smiling. "It's time."

"Holy shit! Yes! Tell her to hold on until tomorrow. I'll win two hundred dollars if she's born then."

"I'll give it a shot," Monty said. He watched several other guys file into the locker room. The headlining match between Romeo and Limpet signaled the end of the evening's events, and they usually went out afterward. Monty couldn't imagine wanting to go less. He had a baby to meet.

HE CAUGHT a cab to the airport and hoped there would be a flight he could take that would arrive in Portland before morning. Monty and Wade had moved back to the Portland area after two years in Boston, which was one perk to becoming top talent with CWA. He could kind of do whatever he wanted as long as he was willing to fly back to Boston and Vegas pretty regularly.

Monty loved that Wade was happy wherever they were as long as they were together, but he also knew Wade was happy to be back home. Mike was thrilled to have them back, and Monty knew that was mostly because of Wade. He'd taken over as Titan's head trainer and coach, and he even did some occasional remote writing for CWA. They bought a small farmhouse in rural Hillsboro where Monty had his cows, and Wade had enough room to run a small wildlife rehabilitation operation in one of the barns that came with the property. It was a good life, and on his way to the airport, he reminisced over the last few years, knowing once he got home, nothing would ever be the same again.

SEVERAL HOURS LATER, Monty ran through the hospital doors and found the elevator to the maternity ward. He ran to the front desk, passing Carol, Jack, Ramona, and Gavin in the waiting room. He gave them all hugs and kisses, then told the triage nurse who he was there to see.

They ushered him back to Madeline's room and found Kenny standing by Madeline's bed. He was stroking her hair and dabbing her forehead with a cool washcloth. Wade was sitting shirtless in what he assumed was the "dad's chair," with a tiny, pink blob resting on his chest. Monty walked up to the bedside and hugged Madeline so hard she squeaked. Then he turned to look at his husband and brand new daughter. He walked over to them, then stroked her palm as she grabbed his finger.

"Welcome home, dad," Wade said.

"Thanks, papa. Wow, so strong," he whispered, as their daughter squeezed his finger. "Future CWA star."

Wade laughed quietly and pulled him down for a kiss.

ACKNOWLEDGMENTS

I'd like to start by thanking my husband, Kris, for listening to me talk about this book and its characters for months and months, never once making me feel like I was annoying (I definitely was). Thank you for introducing me to wrestling, entertaining my fixation on it, and supporting the many, ever-changing crushes I developed over the course of my (ongoing) fandom. I wonder who will be next? It doesn't matter, because you're my forever number one.

To my betas and editors, A, B, and J: Thank you for your guidance, suggestions, and encouragement, and thank you for sharing your ability to see through the fog to see what you knew could be a fun book (with some editing). Any editing issues found are my own.

Jessica and Kay, you're the best, most supportive friends a gal could ask for, and your encouragement kept me going when I wanted to quit (which was usually during my luteal phase). Thank you for letting me send wrestling updates to you every evening and for responding to my way-too-long Marco Polos with interest.

Deb, my original cheerleader. Thank you for staying up with me way too late and telling me I wasn't an idiot for wanting to write this book, for your loyalty to the love interest in *the other book,* and for letting me send walls of text about the books I'm reading.

April, thank you for answering my texts and correcting me when I asked stuff like, "is this a thing that could happen in D&D?" and "what is it called when you get together to play D&D?" I'm sorry if I got anything wrong, and it's totally all my fault if I did. Thank you for sending me monster memes. If my next book is about a monster-fucker, I will be reaching out again.

And finally, to my parents, who are simply the best: thank you, and I love you. Sorry for naming one of the main characters after us. You can skip those parts.

ABOUT THE AUTHOR

Val is a romance enthusiast whose journey began with a broken ankle, eight weeks of bed rest, and a surprisingly prolific backlog of X-Files fan fiction (thank you, authors). Craving stories that didn't revolve around Mulder and Scully, she eventually turned to books. She spent years devouring stories that ended in happily-ever-afters before she decided to write the books she longed to read but couldn't find.

She was born and raised in Portland, Oregon, and just kept living there.

Made in United States
Troutdale, OR
11/19/2024

25079483R00162